AMBERLIGHT

For
Helen Merrick and Justine Larbalestier,
who first read this book in manuscript and
encouraged me to take it further,
with nostalgic memories of the TC hotline,
and many thanks.

AMBERLIGHT

SYLVIA KELSO

WILDSIDE PRESS

Amberlight
City & Houses

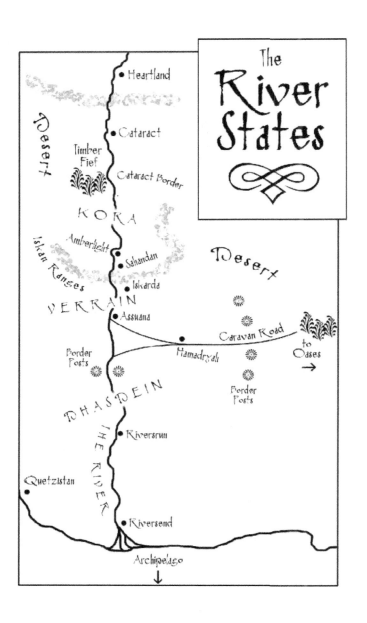

PART I

MOONSHINE

"... and nothing left remarkable,
beneath the visiting moon."
~ *Antony and Cleopatra*, IV.15.67-68

I

High moon over Amberlight, commanding the zenith, radiant, imperial, the city's fretted-ink porticoes and balconies gnawing that torrent of aerial snow. Domes shed it, men's towers drip with it. Under the vertical black rampart of the citadel wall, the qherrique outcrops glow to their depths with it: cabochon slabs girdling the hill's waist, broad as cathedral floors, zones of luminous milk slanted between ragged frames of earth and grass. Qherrique. Pearl-rock. Moon-stone. The core and crown of Amberlight.

Very little moon, though, and certainly no crown where Tellurith has haled her entourage from a wedding in neighborly Hafas House, leaving their guest-honor tarnished, their celebration scanted, by Khey's escape: apprentice shaper, House and cousin-kin; slid off in silk and silver festival gear to drink and dice, shiftless cow, down in River Quarter. Among the thieves and stevedores.

Tellurith fumes as House-heads must, oaths seething behind clamped lips. Her retinue thins to a straggle as moon-snow on fragrant Uphill vines becomes a mackerel stipple of cobbles under the effluvium of cat-piss, river-mud, dockers' sweat. A spot for hand-work, surely. Knives, at courtesy's best. And Khey, petted in the Craft-shops, sib to the qherrique, off here quick as a gutter-bred cat.

"Heugh!" At the fug in the first drinking-hutch Tellurith nearly chokes. "'Tender, fetch a light!"

Enough moon spills in that rabbit-door to catch her gold-worked leggings and frosted-pearl coat wings, the orb of a House-head's brooch, big as a baby's head, laid like intaglio snow on her breast. The dice-handler runs madly. In the weak tangle of oil-light comes a sudden hush.

"Hold it up."

Bare bronze arms and cropped bronze heads and drink-flushed bronze faces shrink like cockroaches from the revolving yellow shaft. Rickety tables awash, leather bottles careened, hardly a cup in sight, let alone crystal-cut Uphill glass. Dice on the throwing patch, a scatter of copper sequined round them, stevedores on their heels, shoulder to shoulder—sweat-acrid trousers and bare backs, men in with the rest. Only breastbands to show the difference. Tellurith shudders, delicately, and averts her eyes.

No sign, even among scuttlers jammed in the back alley-door, of a Crafter's brocaded wedding gear. Tellurith wheels before she can curse. "Out!"

On to another den, and yet another, alley after alley, down to the heart of the docks. The yowl of River Quarter night is all about them now, and Tellurith feels the procession close up, youngsters feeling for the first time less than invulnerable. Exposed, outside the bulwarks of their House.

Masts curtsy sleepwalker slow, black geometry on pearl-infused sky. From backlit alley ends, through smoky tavern glow punctuated by late-working prostitutes' heads, broad sheens of pearl and gold announce the river itself. As the last night-bird hurriedly clears their way of his hair-plumes and glossily oiled shoulders, Tellurith pulls up.

"Rot and gangrene her!"

Wisely, the rest keep quiet.

If Khey has not surfaced yet, Khey may never show. And they are clear across River Quarter, trailing a far more costly bait through the attentive dark. No single woman, not kin, not Crafter's blood, can justify risking half a House.

"Ahh!"

Spinning on a heel, Tellurith stalks off; away from the river, up toward the business quarter, dead as stone by night. And her folk close up in earnest now, watching the flicker and dart of shadows by every barred door and symbol-daubed entryway: for this is the riskiest part of River Quarter. This is the gangland zone.

Tellurith stiffens her back and sniffs. But she is not proud enough for stupidity. She twitches the brooch higher on her breast, and shouts into the street's moon-shoals, "Craft!"

And she has an entourage. With the brooch, it is protection enough.

Warehouse canyons broaden. A traffic divider, a couple of scraggy trees appear. In a breeze off distant water their shadows dance, delicate moon-theorems, on a symbol-spattered wall.

The graffiti subside. A moon sea spreads ahead of them, the polyhedron inaccurately termed Exchange Square. Below a rim of Uphill coffee houses, table umbrellas tilted like giant mushrooms to the moon, a sheet of flagstone slants up to the colonnade whose marble pillars stand pure as sugar-icing beneath its lustrous dome. The Guild-house of the Engravers' Craft.

Islanded in mid-square rise the worn marble seats and tall orange trees of the commerce grove. And halfway between grove and colonnade steps, a black pool marks the stones.

"Blight and blast!"

At Tellurith's heels, the entourage checks.

"Iatha. Your eyes are better than mine. Is that—"

Veteran cutter, impeccable House-steward, Iatha steps up beside her Head. Puckers her eyes into the flooding moon.

Sighs, and answers, "Yes."

The House-folk attend with deepened respect to the ripeness of their leader's oaths.

Not our House. Not our affair. Common ground here, the clan-patrols must pass sometime. Someone, somewhere, must be able to look after it.

Tellurith draws breath for, Let's go. And stops.

Leave Khey, somewhere in River Quarter, her abandonment a burr in the back of a House-head's neck? Perhaps. But then calmly dismiss a drunk or damaged stranger, here in the borderlands, to a passed-out sot's reward, or an innocent victim's further ruin?

Because even beneath the Guild-house walls, an unconscious woman is not safe at night.

"Rot her cutting ear—whoever she is!"

House-folk stream forward. Tellurith's long stride takes her quickly to the black puddle, so still upon the candescent stones. As the others press up she begins formally, "S'hur"—worker, fellow Crafter—"are you all ri—"

Nobody wonders at the check. Nobody has to ask. In the ripe moonglow every eye sees what she has seen. The so-still profile caught in the cloak's throat, whiter than the flags. Black cloak, black night-fall of hair. And the shadow of stubble, black, unmistakable, along the jaw.

This time, Iatha swears.

As profanity ebbs, her Head feels them shift behind her, already sure of her response. Not a woman in distress, were she just a Downhill stevedore. A man. An unknown man. If we would not wait for Khey, those movements say, and we would only salve a woman in this plight with reluctance and profanity, we will certainly not trouble for this.

Fifty paces to the colonnade, the Guild-house. Uphill. Sanctuary. A House retinue at risk. Tellurith gathers muscles for the stride. Looks back to the moon-cut profile, so still, so utterly helpless against that midnight span of cloak.

Grits teeth. Pauses. Works to make it sound cool, ironic, decisive.

"Well, s'hurre. Crafters' title. We stopped to play Save-her. Suppose we can't back off, just because it's a dangle instead."

The spurt of ribald laughter quickly checks. Iatha snaps names. Two muscled slab-shifters come forward, ready to heft the victim by shoulders and feet. Tellurith bends warily, sniffing for the reek of Sahandan rice wine or raw barley spirit that would say, Drunkard. Derelict. Expendable. But there is only the acrid, spine-chilling stink of fear and past brutality.

"Hmmh," she grumbles. "Must have been dirty business, who-ever he is. Did you ever see such a great black horse-blanket of a—"

And on a punched intake of air, stops.

At Iatha's gesture the porters check. Tellurith stands frozen. Then plumps suddenly on her knees, whispering, "Sweet Work-mother . . ." Her hand creeps out. One finger, reaching to the blackness on the cobbles, dares to touch.

Before she recoils half upright, snapping, "Desho, Zeana, run for a healer, quick! Thanno and Kyris, find something for litter poles—Iatha, come here!"

While the others twitch Iatha goes forward. Looks where Tel-lurith looks. Sucks in her own breath. But forewarned, she says almost at once, "Rith, hold the messengers—may be no need."

Tellurith grunts. Reaches a hand, quaking, so finely, the great cabochon on her middle finger palpitates like living pearl, under the stubbled jaw.

Feels the faint, faint throb of cold skin against her flesh, catch-es her breath again and snaps fit to catapult her messengers, "Go, go! He's alive!"

"Mother's love," mutters Iatha, and Tellurith all but slaps her hand from the cloak. "We mustn't try to move him. It could be anything—he could be disemboweled!"

Iatha mutters obscenities to drown Tellurith's. The square, the emptily rising streets resound to the messengers' flight, and more than one among the House-folk sits down with a bump as understanding spreads: that it is blood, dyeing whatever color the cloak had, saturating it, spreading far beyond the hump of body, which has laid that great black penumbra on the stones.

Tellurith does not try to conceive of its worse and worse ori-gins. While Iatha swears she edges closer. At what, she realizes, is the unconscious man's back. Looking down over his shoulder at an incisive profile, long nose, blade-sharp jaw, the shag of a black-avised man's stubble honing it, a surprisingly fine-cut mouth slack now against the back of a hand. Her own hand creeps out.

His flesh is chill. Not death yet, experience with cutting catastrophes tells her: wound-shock. Maybe—her fingers explore the black sheaf of hair—a bludgeon. Almost certainly a street gang, robbery and battery, if not worse. There is an oozing lump over his ear. There is a bruise, she realizes now, in his eye-socket. No River Quarter worker, to come up here. No decent house's man, to be out alone. No one from Amberlight, she speculates, re-assessing that black, black hair. But something, some impulse of Head-ship or simple human compassion, makes her ease a hand under his temple. Transfer his head, with infinite care though no little distaste, into her lap.

And if he bleeds on the brocaded wool under his cheek, she supposes she will find some recompense, if only in easing the closure of a life.

She is still crouched there when the pound and echo of feet announce her messengers, a stout physician panting, healer's satchel slung between her heralds, at their backs.

* * * *

"**D**on't move him!" are her first clear words.

Tellurith elevates her nose. Subtle snub, subtler reminder of rank. The physician ignores it, shouldering her aside to chase the pulse. Then a grunt as stubble grates her palm. "Mff . . ."

"We have a litter." Tellurith glances to Thanno and Kyris, poised with a pair of umbrella shafts threaded through someone's coat. "Shall we—"

"Not yet!"

With a flare of nostrils clear in the moonlight as with gingerly, fearful delicacy, she pries at the margin of the cloak.

"Ah!"—"Ugh!"—"Uh!"

"Gang-work." The physician awards their squeamishness a more forceful nostril flare. "Hereabouts, s'hurre, what'd you expect?"

Tellurith looks up at the Guild-house colonnade. Hands still busy, the physician snorts.

"They've hunted up here last year and more. Take more than a Craft-house to frighten them after dark." Slum-wise, she does not ask, And what is an Uphill House-head doing hereabouts? Tellurith watches those deft hands peel the cloak from a wiry, snow and bruise-mottled back, and does not ask either. Perhaps, still masked by the prone position, he really has been disemboweled.

"Stripped him, of course." The weariness of hated custom. "If it's good, they'll take the clothes—"

Not this time. Shirt, under-shirt, possible over-tunic are wadded under him, ripped margins of bloody rag. And the ruins of trousers, wound about two very expensive boots.

Tellurith's stomach is still rolling when the physician shifts place with an almost froggish hop. "Get water," she growls, slicing some blade between the hobbled ankles. "Take the cloak. Stop spewing, you. Haven't you ever seen a rape?"

"Mother's eyes—!"

It has been yanked out of Tellurith. Hunkered close over him, the physician shoots her one sour glance.

"They do it, yes, to a mark that's pretty. Or fights too much." Her steady hands ease the wrecked trousers clear. "Probably outland." A glance at the blood-patched but elegantly soft, buckled—gold-buckled—boots. Another glance up to the lake of darkness that has spread from under the bruised, black-caked thighs. "Maybe not just the men, either. I've known them use a mark's own sword."

Tellurith feels her shoulders sag. "If he's past help—"

"For the Mother's sake! He's alive!"

And, Tellurith deciphers that savagely outthrust jawline, I am a healer. While he lives, I will try to thwart their butchery. I will fight.

"What can we do?" Tellurith asks.

Hasty footfalls announce Zetho, self-appointed aide with a receptacle alarmingly like the sacred bronze beggar's bowl from the grove. The physician nods gratefully. Eyes her patient, and hesitates.

"The Mother's throw, whatever we try. If we wash him and he gets colder—if we try to move him without—if I try to work on him without seeing the damage—"

The household is quiet. The city lies silent round them, Amberlight couched like her gangs, aware and waiting, under the pearl flood of the moon.

The physician stiffens herself. "You, you, you, you. Take his feet—his knees—his shoulders—his arms." She settles her own hands at his hips. "When I give the word, we turn him. Gentler than you ever moved one of your poxed qherrique slabs. Onto his right side."

As those blunt fingers edge under his hip-bone, Tellurith remembers her own position. "What shall I . . ."

"Keep cushioning him. Don't let go!"

More delicately than any new-divided slab of pearl-rock, with infinitely small loosenings, supplings of caked blood and rigored muscle, they ease him over, the team working as at a mother-face to the physician's commands. As they steady him while half-a-dozen coats are hastily wadded at his back, the head in Tellurith's lap moves. Faintly, he groans.

"Careful, for Kearma's bloody love!"

The physician's god is invoked again, less frantically, as Iatha drapes her festival coat across his torso, while with oaths at the water's chill, at the flap of a wind-blown torch annexed from the Engraver's House, the physician begins to lave his groin.

"At least," she growls, "they didn't geld him too."

Tellurith shudders at the thought of mutilation atop the rest. The dark head in her lap shifts. Without thought she cups his face, murmuring, as to a daughter, "Keep quiet. Keep still."

* * * *

"**S**o."

Zetho withdraws the bowl. Tellurith reads, Trouble, from the syllable. One hand on a marble-white, marble-cold haunch, the physician glowers.

"Most of this is a stab. Right in the artery. Hadn't left him spread out, and on top of his clothes . . ." A graphic sickle-sweep of one hand. "I've tight-wrapped that. But there's a mess inside too, Kearma flay them." The hand flicks above that black-crusted haunch. "I need to look. It might . . ." Her lips set tight. "He can't stay here in any case. But if we move him, and that thigh artery opens—or he starts to bleed inside . . ."

Tellurith's mouth is dry. Ridiculous, for some stranger, some unknown, a man. More ridiculous to ask, in surety of an answer, "What can you do?"

The roll of eyes retorts, I can kill him out of hand. But the lips tighten. Before she says, dourly, "If the inner stuff is—mendable—I can plug him up."

One or two younger women cannot control the laugh. Iatha lashes at them. Undistracted from the silent proviso, Tellurith prods, "But?"

"But I may start a haemorrhage doing it. Or when we move him—that may happen anyway."

Tellurith holds those eyes, colorless in the brow-shadow. Looks away, amid her shadow-and-silver folk. Across the lake of moon-lacquered stone, up to the air-and-silver colonnade, higher. Where the great shields of the qherrique glow, luminous, alive, slabs of breathing moonstone, to the breathing of the moon.

She is House-head for more than inherited rank, more than fifteen years good decision-making, more than a superlative cutting ear. As she learnt in her very first rapport, as she fine-tuned the skill with polisher and shaping-tool, and tempered it in those draining moments at the mother-face, she listens for the oracle whence those decisions came.

And from the life and blood of Amberlight the qherrique's answer comes to her. Sure, inexplicable as the assent of a willing mother-face; the signal no Head, no cutter, no shaper, not the most novice polisher can mistake.

If we do nothing, he dies anyway. And it matters, if he dies.

She drops her eyes to the physician's face and says quietly, "In the Work-mother's hand."

It is the cutter's invocation. The physician's expression says she recognizes more than that. Before she lifts her own hands to re-invoke Kearma, and begins.

They have to ease him on his face again. To mound clothes under his hips. To hold, with profane and breath-held delicacy, his arms, his torso, his re-straddled legs. "If he jerks around he'll bleed for sure." Kneeling between his thighs, instruments in hand, she scowls up his back at Tellurith.

"Keep hold of his head. If he starts to move—talk to him. Just might keep him quiet."

Tellurith's own breath comes short. Not mere human concern now. Behind her quickened heart-beat she can feel the weight, the focused attention, almost the sentience of Amberlight.

She cups the drowned face lightly as a new-polished statuette. Trying for composure, says, as at the mother-face, "Yes."

Meaning, Go.

When the cold water starts to bite, he does move. Twitches. A gasp. Moans. Stronger flexure of the muscles as cold instruments replace cold water, probing deeper into his vital, his damaged and doubly sensitive parts. The physician mutters. Prayer. Endearment. Curse. The head in Tellurith's lap heaves before she can catch it, his body jerks as he cries out.

"Quiet, quiet, keep still now, it's all right, just hold on . . ." Ridiculous, crooning like a mother with a beloved baby to a complete stranger, a man who may not even use her words. But she catches his head, whispering in the drowned ear, smoothing the pain-tense cheek, wiping sudden sweat from the nameless brow. "Quiet, keep quiet . . ."

And though his body transmits shock, protest, pain atop older pain, though he lets out strangled noises and twists his head spasmodically, violently in her lap, whether of words or her cutter's ability, something must come through.

Because whatever the physician does to him, though he cries out, he does not move.

$$* * * *$$

Full dawn on Amberlight; Tellurith watches it in from Telluir House-head's apartment, hands propped wide on the balustrade.

The honey-tinged Iskan marble is icy under her palms; shoulders hunched in mahogany-brown double wool, she is grateful for her festival coat. Fifty miles south, snow bleaches the shaggy Iskan ranges' spine, a drizzle of winter sure as the qherrique dust frosting her lapels. But the sky is celestial blue, freighted with blushing hills of cloud.

"'Rith?"

Iatha comes to her side. Qherrique-tough, she has already bathed and changed for the day.

"He's out to it. Sleep-syrup should last till noon."

Tellurith's eyes lift slowly, sidelong. Across the House frontage, pine-cone finials topping the central block's four-storey attic roofs, over the green mushrooms of garden treetop, the snake of demesne wall. Native scrub beyond is branded by a line of stony steps. A hundred feet above them, the Telluir qherrique answers sunshine, a moat-wall of back-lit pearl.

Iatha breasts the balustrade. Goes on equably, "If he still won't take it for anyone else, you could always book a spot—"

"In my schedule! Blast and blind—!"

As she spins from the balustrade Iatha's eyes go wide. Then she bites off a laugh.

"I've noticed," demurely, "that Telluir carries the Thirteen's cutting-load . . ."

Tellurith spins again, thumping fist on stone. The men's tower is tucked behind House block and center court, with the garden as buffer beyond. She could not see the glare of sun on its shutters' lace-work if she did turn, but it burns her shoulder-blades.

"You block-cracker, you know quite well—!"

"Oh, ah, you've set up a week of it. Metal shippers, estate accounts. Moon-meet of the Thirteen. New cutter to try. Three statuettes—and one of 'em a king's—to tune. Bare compliments'll take a month. He's a bit of gangland flotsam. You're Head of Telluir House. Just tell me, 'Rith—did we pick him up, or not?"

Tellurith's jaw knots. She stares out over Amberlight.

Under the familiar frontage of distant House-blocks, Khuss and Jerish to the right, Hafas away left, the valley opens between High and Dragon Spurs, fifty-foot windmill vanes just beginning to swing along each crest. Turned on for the day-wind, they blur the squat stone towers. Already, downstairs, the visible veins of qherrique in the House-hall are glossy with new-fed light.

Sharply, Tellurith averts her mind. Stares lower, down past clan demesnes into the business zone. Warehouse, office, guild-house, coffee house. Inn. House of prostitutes.

From here the graffiti and the broken or boarded windows are invisible, leaving the city gem-clear and immaculate for dawn. And below the frontier's battle-zone sprawl the huddled humps and gaudy shrines and strangulated alleyways of River Quarter. Workers for the ships that come, upRiver, downRiver, trailing in like water-spiders on that glittering serpentine about the city's base. Hauling the silk and wool, the metal and timber, the multitudinous tribute to its one unique product that sustains, that recompenses Amberlight.

"Rith?"

She tightens her fists on the balustrade.

"No, we couldn't have left him there. Or taken him to a hire-worker's hostel. Or expected the physician to heave him home. So, yes, we do have obligations. Have accepted obligations." A deeper breath. "*I* have accepted obligations. Tell Hanni. Noon. Fit it in the book." And as Iatha turns, face lost but shoulders grinning, she yells, "And find what he is, you lump!"

* * * *

"**N**o, Ruand, troublecrew say, Nothing," eloqently, Caitha's nostrils wrinkle, "among the clothes. No money-pouch. No jewelry. Something torn out of his ear. Local clothes. Quite well-worn. Probably a lender's shop." River Quarter is full of them; pawned clothes are orthodox intelligencer's disguise. The senior House physician nods, underlining their own intelligencer's point. "Same for the cloak."

"The boots?"

Caitha inclines her head again, acknowledging her Head's wits.

"First-quality gazelle hide. Gold buckles. New. Cataract cut."

Tellurith's brows mark the double anomaly. Caitha drops her voice a tone. "No sign of—"

"No."

No weapon at the site. Not so much as a broken sword-belt, a table-knife. Which is only absence of confirming proof: Cataract is two hundred miles upriver, just beyond Amberlight's border.

Cataract is the River's most turbulent neighbor. And Cataract might pay a mercenary wages to merit those boots.

She and Tellurith eye the man in the bed.

The quietest bed in the infirmary, empty near a work-moon's tranquil end. In the center of the House-block. Women's ground. No call for Iatha's presence to point the consequence of his vehement refusal to take sleep-syrup from any other hand. Setting the cup down, she can see her steward's grin.

"Though I'm rotted," Tellurith mutters, "to know why."

The stubble is blacker now. Inclined on a snowy pillow, the hair lays a night-wing over the bloodless face. Sharp features burred by bruises, sharpened by loss of blood. Speaking anger. Decision. Arrogance. A very plausible face for a mercenary.

"Not Cataract coloring." Mistaking her silence, Caitha begins to state the obvious. "Any more than he's a Verrainer. And in Dhasdein, nowadays, it could be anything . . ."

With no way to tell, until he recovers consciousness, exactly what, or what provenance he will claim.

And, the physicians agree, he should stay drugged at least another day.

Tellurith lets out breath, an angry hiss. Caitha jumps.

"See Hanni. For sunset, fit him in the book. Midnight—I'll be home first. And," luxury, to pounce on someone, "see he's fed."

* * * *

"Ruand, I tried, we both did, but Caitha said don't upset him whatever you do and he keeps throwing his head—" the novice healer wrings her hands, her companion hovers with an arm-load of soiled sheets. "And you'll give him the sleep-syrup anyhow—"

"Yah." Tellurith sets her lips. Yanks the skirts of another ornate coat aside, threatens inwardly, If you wreck my evening shirt like those sheets . . . Dismisses thought of guests, an entire Uphill function waiting, the knives of long-term malice honing in Vannish House. Takes the soup cup. Works a hand under the tousled head. Murmurs, picking up cutter's intonation, "Come along, you need liquids, drink this."

And, repeated miracle, the pain-thinned lips relax. He mutters drowsily, a hand stirs under the sheets. Before the soup goes down, in small obedient sips.

"Now . . ."

Two sips of syrup. A demurring noise, a muzzy frown. More impulsion in her tone. Another shift of the head, a sigh. Concession, and slipping back then, into pain-blanked sleep.

"If he makes water from this, you know how to clean up without disturbing him? You know why?" Though they cringe, in truth the irritation is for herself. "I'll be back."

* * * *

"The Mother rot it, Iatha, I've broken an account meet and held up a Vannish dinner-party, and this girl's too good a family to insult—if he won't take it for Caitha, then let him hurt!"

In Tellurith's workroom the girl is already waiting. Sharp Amberlight nose and copper-gold eyes, squared shoulders that speak Navy louder than the grimly subdued crinkle of Amberlight hair. Bound in a tail, since she does not yet dare the Crafter's plait.

"Damis."

"Ruand."

Maiden. House-head. Inclining her head, Tellurith inclines a mental ear. Into the waltz of formalities, asking after mother and sisters' command chain on the *Wasp,* in whose seven-sister cluster is the heart of city defense. What man-powered galley can hope to out-strip, out-fight, or slip invaders past those small lethal stingers, driven and armed by the might of qherrique?

"But you feel there's more?"

"S'hur, the light-gun answers me better than anyone." She says it without pride. "But every time I power up—I feel—" she looks down suddenly. "S'hur, there's something in my hands . . ."

It is the proverbial cutter's phrase: *Something in the hands.*

Tellurith does not sing a jubilee. Just moves to the wall beyond Hanni's slate-strewn desk, where the deep polished glow of imported redwood yields to panels of apricot-colored stone. Skeined, patterned over with veins of pearl and silver-smoke, their flow knotted and woven like the root-falls of a banyan fig.

"This is House qherrique. Not dedicated to anyone." She smiles, her House-head, steady-the-panic smile. "Do you think you could reverse the feed?"

"It's cooler today," she adds, to the girl's dilated stare. "Soon be time to change in any case."

And therefore easier, as every Craft child knows, to wile qherrique toward its own approaching pattern shift. Less of a shock to Downhill folk, seeing the myth of House systems made real.

"Ruand . . . Uh. I'll try."

A deep breath. Centering the mind. In cutter's parlance, opening the ear. Tentative brush of finger-tips. If she can handle a big Navy light-gun, no surprise that the contact accepts. Touch, then. Awareness ebbing inward, to the secret, the inexplicable connection, flesh and rock-flesh, mind and matter, wits and light, bone and pearl.

The girl's lips move. The fingers caress. The qherrique glows, brilliant now as in the mother-face at the moment of assent, before the cutter steps forward and stakes her life.

The veins dim back into quiescence. Over Tellurith's waiting hand a hint, a touch, a steady spread of warmth instead of coolness breathes across the placid air.

Genuinely, Tellurith beams. "You've just made the winter change for Telluir House. Well done, damis!

"It was a pied block at worst, you know. House qherrique's patient. If you'd missed, there'd be no change at all."

She flexes her arms. The excitement of finding new potential is matched only by its relief. Crafters are the Houses' bone-marrow; Craft-blood comes down in families, but it can disappear as quickly, as mysteriously as it comes, and its vanishment is the nightmare of Amberlight.

"So I think we'll try an apprenticeship, next new moon, in the Telluir panel-shop. Good enough? Time enough?"

Straight into shaping, a Craft level higher than engraver or polisher; in the power-shops, the engineer's side of the House, at a rank only below shaper of statuettes. With half a moon's space to set her affairs in order. No wonder there is worship in the girl's eyes.

And in a moon or so, Tellurith tells her back, you'll be with me in the mine. If only, yet, to look.

* * * *

The next meeting is nowhere near so pleasurable. In the House-head's formal appointment room, down on second level, entombed amid state gifts and ceremonial furniture. Including the Dhasdein water-pipe, bane of Tellurith's lungs. As her visitor exhales a cloud of pungent skau-weed smoke, she grips her silver-worked leggings and tries desperately not to sneeze.

"Most honored, most highest . . ."

The compliments will go for hours here, working up between his aides, her Craft-heads, his private assistant, her secretary, her House-steward, his chamberlain, the phalanxes ranked out beside them on the velvet-covered stools. House-head's cohorts exactly facing those of Mel'eth's kinglet, ruler of Dhasdein's arid western province, prince under the king of kings who rules downstream in Riversend, who trades only by surrogates and only through the Thirteen concerted: Dhasdein's emperor.

Time was, perched stiff-backed on one of those lesser stools, she could be enchanted by Dhasdein garb, the ridiculous narrow trousers, the curled, pomaded hair; by Dhasdein ceremonial, so damnably long in the wind. When she could admire her mother, straight-backed yet graceful as a wind-pine, forbearing so much as a glance at the equally wonderful stew of color and shape amid the entourage. Today it is merely a wearisome ninth-year ritual. The kinglet knows, almost to a grain-weight, their asking price. As well send a shippers' slip upRiver and be done.

Except that statuettes do not come cash-on-delivery.

Nor does a state apartment door open in mid-interview. Her eyes stay fixed, the smile holds on her mouth. The kinglet's private aide—they have progressed that high—holds his own stride. But Tellurith's skin traces the message up from Craft-head to Craft-head, to Hanni, to Iatha—who rises, hiatus unthinkable, to whisper in her ear.

Tellurith does not swear. Go red. Grind her teeth. As the aide finds a pause she inclines her head. Makes obeisance, deep as a River Quarter whore before his phallus-god. "Most estimable. Most splendid. House Telluir is devastated. Obliterated. There is a matter—smaller than dust, but wretchedly, mine alone. A personal obligation. Honorable, convey to His Eminence that I am desolated. I must—momentarily—lose the brightness of his face. Deign to grace our house by tasting some meager refreshment." Her eye snags Iatha, whose grin vanishes in a punished bow. "But I will—I will within instants—return."

As she swirls in the infirmary door the young healers flee. Caitha bends under the blast, but can still cry, "The syrup's failed, he's coming round, we can't keep him quiet—!"

"The Mother blight—!"

He is conscious already, head off the pillows and struggling to heave himself up. Tellurith lunges, blind to all but images of black-caked thighs, blood's penumbra on lucent stone.

Caitha pounces too. Pinned, panting, he struggles more desperately, only weakness ceding them control.

"Rot it, lie down!"

Strength fails. He falls back with a gasp. The eyes skewer her, so black that iris and pupil are indistinguishable, the great bruise that lanterns one orbit powering an asymmetrical glare.

"Where am I? What am I doing here?"

Tellurith's hands drop. She does catch her jaw. And the initiative, demanding with equal cold ferocity, "Who are you?"

"I'm—"

The hauteur implodes.

"I—"

Some impossible sensation squeezes Tellurith's heart as he goes limp, a hand to the shocked, crumbling face.

"I—I—"

The great black eyes stare up at her, dazed, lost. More pitiable than physical wreck, that disintegration of the self.

"You were attacked." Tellurith's mouth speaks before she thinks, in a quiet, a Head's, almost a cutter's voice. "Knocked out. Robbed. Badly hurt. We found you. Brought you here. This is Telluir House."

And almost more appalling, after the look of stunned assimilation, is the pause. Then the equally dazed, "Telluir—House?"

Tellurith is House-head because, while her senior physician collapses into consternation, she can reach the sleep-syrup bottle, pour by guess-work, and say, "You need to rest. Drink this."

"No, it's sleep-syrup, it's addictive, I won't—" one feeble but determined hand fending the cup, the ruins of authority in every phrase.

"And you're in my debt and my House and you've interrupted a vital interview. I'll discuss this later. Now drink it and be quiet!"

The whip-crack is not wholly voluntary. But either that or "debt" shuts his mouth on a gasp and flush. And an equally instinctive hand-sign as Caitha re-presents the cup.

Leaving Tellurith to chew, all the way upstairs and through interminable extra apologies, on a patient who has lost his memory but kept the salute of the Dhasdein Imperial guard.

* * * *

"Cataract boots? Dhasdein *salute*?"

"And probably no memory." Tellurith jerks her coat into place. "Have Zuri scratch about River Quarter, Iatha. And they can keep him drugged today as well, because the Thirteen wait for no dangle, and neither do I."

The Moon-meets of Amberlight are held in the citadel, which, after two centuries of increasingly solid peace along the River's length, has almost no other use. Indeed, despite the thirteen carven high-backed seats, the clammy old walls veiled in heirloom Verrain tapestries, the wide modern windows open on highest morning air and hawk-inscribed sky, the train of underlings and business paraphernalia behind each Head's place, even the incense burners below the great boss of woken qherrique, from under the shimmering oak table there is an indubitable whiff of mouse.

Taking her place, Tellurith checks moods and faces in a glance. So long the thirteen Houses have held Amberlight, so solidly each is locked to its trove of qherrique, that their equilibrium, however testy, is impossible to shake. Vannish will bicker with Telluir, Jerish will try to snub Hezamin, Zanza and Iuras will ally against Diaman and Winsat and Keranshah. Hafas is president this month; Zhee's eyes glitter, ancient as a lizard's, as she eases her rheumaticky limbs into the chair.

The agenda is almost a rote matter too: up and downRiver intelligence reports, from Cataract, from Verrain, from Dhasdeini provinces as well as Riversend, a gesture, it appears, worn perfunctory as the citadel itself. And no whisper of untoward activity. No fresh news to settle a queasy House-head's stomach over the puzzle of a stray Outlander; not so much as a clearly emerging threat to affirm the jangle of recalled history down a less complacent set of nerves.

Nor is anything amiss in the estate and trade reports; from the quays, where the wealth lands even from the Heartlands upRiver beyond Cataract, and the Oases cross-desert where only Verrainers go. From the breadth of Amberlight's outer domain, the Kora, where House and city districts mingle with common land. Gifted too, most of it; much from Cataract, in default of other wealth. West of the city, the irrigated levels of the Sahandan that grow the city rice and the cotton that clothes River Quarter. North and east, the open sheep and cattle-lands that graze many a House's herds. Southward, the Iskan marble quarries, northward the newly gifted timber-fief. Cataract was bitterly hurt by that: the cedar-forest is coveted the River's length, Cataract's most valuable resource. With account tallies finished, the Houses bandy thoughts of that grudge between them, till it is lost in internal concerns.

Such as Downhill gangs who drop their flotsam in Telluir House.

"Blighted upstarts," opines Damas of Jerish House, fuming over tales of a warehouse robbed, another burnt. "Running the black-market, picking off travelers, right up under the Engravers' eye!"

"Of course they trade up there." Liony of Zanza smothers a yawn. "Uphill's the best price."

"In our rotted goods!"

"What does Telluir make of the—er—residue?"

Tellurith does not stiffen. But old warning tightens her ribs at the sound of Maeran's voice, Head—old balance, old bane, old sparring-partner—of Vannish House. She steadies her breath before she replies.

"Very badly hurt."

"Outlander?"

Friends can be more perilous than foes. It is Jura of Hezamin whose wit, usually so agreeable, probes the sensitive point.

"Outlander!" Damas sits up with a jerk. "Telluir, you don't think this is an agitator? Some trouble—paid or sent—over the borderline?"

Eye-whites show. Nobody has to say the name aloud.

"If Cataract were involved, I'm sure," Maeran's drawl has deepened, "Telluir would let us know."

The one nightmare that can still vex House sleep. And is it new caution or old animosity that makes Tellurith answer, levelly, holding that languid, copper-green stare?

"At present he's still drugged."

A pause. A lull. From Damas, a snort. From Jura, a growl. "There's enough trouble building in River Quarter. Dispossessed clan-folk. Docker brats. Outland jetsam. And the man-balance is out. It's been out for years . . ."

As many years as Jura's complaint. Tellurith could almost like Maeran for the raised brows, the silently recited, *I don't know why the Quarter can't expose boy babies like the Houses do. They know too many men make trouble. Why can't they ever learn?*

Zhee moves, folding her gnarled hands on the table. Speaks softly, slowly, as the glide of a passing hawk.

"Does Hezamin advocate that we—the Houses—Amberlight—set the balance right?"

A very awkward silence, growing appalled as the images fill various minds: man-hunts, Navy and House crews hurt, qherrique power unleashed. Lethally. On Amberlight folk.

Zhee re-folds her hands. Just possibly, within its folds, her nearly invisible mouth smiles.

"Is there other business?"

There is a freight-quibble between Prathax and Terraqa; an exchange on price for yet another Verrain Family, a discussion of river-heights. The autumn ebb is late. And finally Zhee sits back, intoning, "Praise to the Work-mother," and the meet is over for a month.

And Tellurith has not told her fellow-Houses assembled: I have a man in my infirmary who may be more trouble to Amberlight than all its qherrique is worth.

* * * *

But when she climbs to her apartments that evening, one blessed evening with nothing ahead but supper, and a glance over some Dhasdein colony offers, and, were she so inclined, a call to a musician—even a visit to the tower—Iatha is posted by her door.

"In," says Tellurith, walking past, and heaves the papers toward her workroom. "Shia! Set for two!"

Only over the wine, an imported Wave Island red that has already cost an Imperial ransom, does she groan and unlace her boots and demand, "What now?"

Iatha scowls. "Caitha wants to check that thigh-wound. Worried about a false clot or something. And the internal stuff. She wants the street-healer back. She wants you too."

"In the Work-mother's name! Can nobody in this House manage that pestiferous dangle without me?"

Albeit wryly, Iatha's grin revives. "Could you make it clearer to everyone in this House that you're the only one who can manage him at all?"

"But—"

In Iatha's silence the image recurs. Moonlight flooding black cloak, black blood, bruise-mottled back. The physician's taut face, the preliminary moment of prayer. The weakness of that hand against the cup.

"I suppose he's still at risk."

"Caitha's double twitchy."

Tellurith groans. "The Mother aid. Well, tomorrow I was doing accounts again. Tell Hanni—"

"I know. In the book."

* * * *

Next morning she walks in on medical chaos, and the eyes hit her, solid as night. Glowering over tight-clenched sheets, wide open in a rigid face.

"And who're you?"

"I am Head," startled into arrogance, "of Telluir House."

"And I'm the King of Zamba's daughter. Spin again!"

Then the eyes flick, absorbing local consternation, shouting in their turn: War-maker, agent, power. One too-brief instant off-guard, before he folds his lips. "What are you—"

"They want to change the dressing." Tellurith snatches control. Blight him, why couldn't this be a meek, ordinary man? "And check your—other wounds."

"*What* other wounds?"

"They'll explain—"

"Explain what? There's only one!"

The physicians erupt; are curbed by Tellurith's gesture. His eyes mark that, too.

"There's more," she says. Memory stressing it. "Believe me, there is."

"Then what is it?" There is panic gripped below the disbelief now. "Why don't I—" Did I, the glare cries, forget that as well?

Tellurith takes two long strides to the bed-side. Says, "You weren't just robbed. You were raped."

She has time to regret the baldness, the unlowered voice. Time for remorse, as his lips go white. Then the eyes glaze, the eye-socket's bruise comes out like thunder. The hands go slack. Before he drags himself over, burrowing face-down in the sheets.

Tellurith cuts off Caitha's forward surge. Out, says her hand sign. Quiet. And as novices tiptoe, there is time to signal Iatha, hovering half rueful, half amused. To consign accounts yet again to perdition, and know Hanni will get the message: until further notice, the Head is engaged.

A hand comes back round the door. The stout physician tenders a night-watcher's stool.

Blast him, seethes Tellurith, scrabbling for compunction, as the sand slides in the counting glass. And blast me for being a double fool. But to thoughts of intrusion, honor and guilt and instinct all give the same response.

The sheet rustles. A smothered intake of breath.

Very quietly Tellurith says, "It can happen to anyone."

A jerk. A gasp.

Then, low and vicious as a stab, "Get out."

Tellurith does not reply.

"Get out!"

"I can guess your feelings. But if you heave around like that, you could easily start another haemorrhage. And then they'd all be back."

The sheet storm checks.

A House-head's sense of timing makes Tellurith get off the stool. Sit on the edge of the bed. Pin the first furious lunge with a hand on a shoulder point, and say in her cutter's voice, "Quiet."

Coiled under her hand, savage but sapped, muscles plunge in more than revolt. In panic. Buried memory, stark burnt-in fright.

"It's all right, it's all right." Her inner voice has responded instantly, the real message in its tone. "It's only me. You're safe."

Another long, quaking breath. And his body is shaking now, harder and harder, uncontrollably, sobs choked, strangled in the ruck of it, bitten back between his teeth.

At some point in her low-voiced litany she has moved up the bed, and he has turned, and as on Exchange Square, as when they reached the infirmary, his head is in her lap, her hand smoothing the disheveled black hair, a freshly broken lip spotting blood on yet another shirt. Only this time his fist is clenched too, mindlessly, convlsively, in its appliqued linen front.

To be repudiated the instant the flood subsides.

You shouldn't have told him like that, says stinging reproach. For the Mother's sake, this is an outlander. You know their men's pride. At the very least, you could give him time to recover, learn to live with it . . .

No, retorts instinct, sure as in the mine. Not this one.

"Can you handle the rest now?"

He has curbed the head-jerk before she withholds her hand. More blood runs, generously, as he anchors teeth in his abused lip.

Tellurith lets the silence ask it: Have you nerve enough to face what happened to you? To face that others know? To withstand its aftermath?

If you do, I am here to uphold you, adds her fleeting touch on his cheek.

And after another two breaths he gets out, eyes clamped shut, voice choked but grim, "—handle it."

He handles it like a Kasterian martyr, the ignominy, the humiliation that undoubtedly burn deeper than the not inconsiderable pain, all without a murmur, without resistance, except the squeezed-shut eyes, the thoroughly bitten lip. And the sweat that Tellurith again wipes away, his head, without either's asking, back in her lap.

Until at last the interminable delicate operations are over, the physicians' faces eased, his humiliatingly splayed body refuged under the sheet. This time when Tellurith proffers the sleep-syrup, he does not demur.

But as he lies mutely shivering, shut eyes still denying reality as it removes itself from his outraged presence, she brushes fingers across his forehead. And says softly, "That was brave."

And though he does not move, a hint of easement softens that rigored jaw.

* * * *

Sunset on Amberlight, grey-veiled under a first winter shower. On the high hill's lap beyond Dragon Spur, wind-pines roar. Glowering through closed windows, Tellurith tries not to do the same.

"Zuri's intelligencers have combed the Quarter," Iatha says patiently. "Either he was cursed clever, or he'd just changed disguises. Or he'd just arrived."

"If the Mother were so kind!"

Rain hisses at the window; the veins of qherrique glow, rivers of moonlight on a marbled wall.

"We've found the gang." Iatha's intonation adds, Of course. "They scrap people all the time. He did fight. No weapons. No way to ask about the moves." Cataract's hand-to-hand school is as famous as its style is recognizable, but curiosity has a limit. Especially round gangs. "The money was forgettable. He had an ear-ring. Plain gold, the lead-girl was wearing that. Could be any sailor's. Or any Navy hand's." Viciously, Tellurith kicks at a priceless Verrain rug. "Seems the rape started because she fancied him."

"And he said, No? What taste!"

"He said, NO, from the way she talked." A perfunctory smile. "They got him in the alley by Demas' coffee-house. Coming up."

Across the rain-glittering balcony, a fresh onslaught rattles the panes. Glass freighted upRiver delicately as eggshell, its huge sheets only cast in the workshops of Dhasdein's capital. Riversend.

Iatha casts herself back in the broad brocaded velvet lounging cushion with a grunt.

"Cataract boots, Dhasdein salute—and an Uphill finger in the puddle? Damme, 'Rith!"

Tellurith glowers, pearl-lit, decided chin on thin-fingered fist. "There's no word?"

"Wish the roof up. What House would dare play with Cataract, but Vannish or, maybe, Keranshah? And you know what chance we have of knotting Huiza's lines." Maeran's trouble-Head is a consummate intelligencer. "Besides . . ."

Outland: trailing traces of upRiver, downRiver conspiracy. Hinting at the deadliest threat, a coalition between the two. With the encounter site pointing to connivance in the plot, if there is a plot, here in Uphill Amberlight. Whatever its present torpor, the city has not survived five hundred years of River greed, siege, sack, half-a-dozen wars, by waiting for dangers to reveal themselves. But if there is an apostate . . .

Then this is a menace without precedent. And among Houses grown touchiest over each other's threat, far more dangerous than ignorance will be the knowledge that you asked.

"So we're back to him."

Iatha sets her cup down. Hazards a grin. "Tell Hanni? Tomorrow?"

"Put it in the book."

* * * *

With the morning dose of syrup omitted, he is awake when they come in, and by his expression, in similar mood. From the bed-foot, flanked by steward and scriber, Tellurith asks moderately, "What do you remember today?"

"I remember a lot of misbegotten, impudent, so-called women doctors digging around in my—"

"That'll do." Tellurith bites back a smile. No amity in that fire to answer her. "Do you remember your name?"

"No."

Fire out. A flat, barely composed stare past them. At the door.

"Do you remember what happened to you?"

The blackened orbit comes into darker relief. With smooth speed Tellurith amends, "What do you remember?"

"I—" the eyes swerve back to her. With that midnight iris, impossible to tell if the pupils dilate. "Where am I? What is—Telluir House? Why did you—why are you doing this?"

House-head's, cutter's instinct spurs her to sit down by him, soothe that raw bewilderment, that belligerent distress. House-head's training retorts, Later. Interrogation first.

"You are here," Tellurith says precisely, "because we found you. Took on the obligation of your care." And feels a stab as the too-sharp cheekbones flush. "It would help us help you, if you could remember—your name. Your origin. What you do. Why you were here."

"Gods, if I *could* remember! *Where* is 'here'?"

Nothing for nothing; which nothing to trade is finally the interrogator's choice. "Amberlight."

"Amber . . ." Sharp alertness, search. Frustration. Aching bafflement. Rubbing his brows, he mutters, "If I could just . . ."

"Don't distress yourself." No mistaking the ragged foretaste of despair. No wasting it, either. "Tell me, were you ever in Dhasdein?"

The hand drops. "If you want to interrogate me, get the serif-juice!"

"Serif?"

And the ghost of knowledge and power is gone. "Oh, gods," slamming the bed, "if I could just *think!*"

Carefully, Iatha speaks.

"You had a pair of Cataract boots."

"I always wear Cataract boots, I like the cut . . ."

"Cataract?"

"Cataract . . . gods *damn!*"

He glares at the wall while they all regroup. Iatha and the scriber gather stools along the working side of the bed. Tellurith sits on it, with something like relief.

"The physicians say, with rest and patience, most things should come back." She cannot resist the hand on his, the shift to calming voice. "Don't try too hard. You're still very weak, and you need to rest."

The eyes pivot. Perennially startling, that live and living blackness in a human face. Patent, the struggle of defiance, of a formidable lost personality, in destruction's aftermath; and half-knowledgeable fear. "I don't need rest, I need—" Skill's caution cuts it off. She finds herself thinking, Thank the Mother we don't have to tangle with him whole. "I—"

The battered face becomes a mask. Melts again. Nothing for nothing; which nothing to offer is the interrogator's skill, but this price is from the bowels. "If you try me with—some more names?"

What you give away, I may double in return. And with the choice of offer, the vantage is yours. Palpable as confession of my need.

"Else I'll just lie here and fume!"

＊＊＊＊

"So far," snorts Iatha, "the scriber assays a Quetzistani 'a'"—the eastern province of Dhasdein—"a few Cataract 'r's, some common River idiom like, 'Spin again.' A good helping of Iskan burr, and he may well have been a child in Verrain."

"Bah!"

＊＊＊＊

"You had a pair of Cataract boots. Very expensive. Do you re-member Cataract?"

The accounts have been dismembered, the kinglet's negotia-tions extended, a new cutter's trial looms at moon-end, two days hence. Almost a relaxation to walk into the familiar room and watch the small changes to the sharp familiar face: the bruise's rainbow passage in his eye-socket, the softening of too-sharp cheekbones, the simultaneous calming and sharpening of that black, black stare.

"Cataract." Memories tug tide-wise. "Wooden walls. Side-set logs. Cedar—new cut. Catapults. Customs people in armor. A lot of grey—grey-black mud. Dinda—the tyrant—is crazy. I was—told . . ." The brows knot, struggle of need and caution, res-urrection of imperatives and secrets from another life. And then the demanding, pleading stare.

"You said you 'always' wear Cataract boots. So you were used to money. A lot of money." Analysis is how Tellurith pays. "And you've seen Cataract first-hand. Did Dinda pay you?"

"No." Too immediate and too decided for dissimulation. "I know about him. But not from him. I mean . . ."

"I understand." Briefed about him, under some other loyalty. "Cataract. Do you see anything else?"

And the eyes turn inward, the mind strains, for that moment that ends, over and over, in a clench-teethed snarl of, "No!"

* * * *

"**T**here are symptoms, Ruand, yes, for memory-loss. We get a couple most years." From, Caitha does not have to add, head injury in the mines. "Vomiting. Delirium. Light-stress. Often we have to bandage their eyes. But without deep brain damage, most of it passes in the first sun-cycle."

During which, she does not have to add, this patient was com-pletely drugged.

"Did he throw up at all?"

"Some retching." Caitha shrugs. "He might not have eaten much that day."

Tellurith glowers at the infirmary door, white-painted and bland as morning-lit qherrique.

"Nothing that would last longer?"

"Headaches. All over the skull. They can last a quarter moon."

"Does he . . ."

Caitha looks her Head unblinkingly in the eye.

"We gave him sleep-syrup—kept him completely under sleep-syrup—for three days. Headaches can ease well before that."

Tellurith takes a little breath.

"*Should* they have—with this one?"

A physician's loyalties are rarely in danger of division. Her patient is usually her House. Now it is Caitha who looks away.

"In my experience—I would think not. "

"And have you asked—has he asked . . .?"

Caitha looks back to her. Amberlight eyes, somber, darkened to unpolished bronze.

"Ruand, if there was head pain—he's said nothing to us."

* * * *

"**H**amadryah."

"Verrain. Caravan city. At the desert edge. Halfway to the capital."

"Caravan?"

"Caravan—I don't know!"

"What else could cause it? Mother's name, 'Rith! Caitha said there were no headaches. It can't be physical!"

Tellurith sets the decanter back, with care, on the gold-embossed stand that protects her dining table. Hearing, instead, that paroxysm of comprehension. Feeling the hand all but rip her shirt front; the tears, strangled in her lap.

"He's a man. He's Outland. Physical . . . may not be all there is to it."

Iatha slams her napkin across the silverware. "Bah!"

* * * *

"**Q**uetzistan."

"Dhasdein. Eastern province. Bandit country."

"Who do they raid?"

"Dhasdein, Verrain, whoever pays for them."

"Did you?"

"I—I—damn!"

* * * *

"**W**hat does Mother mean to you?"

"What does it mean to you?"

He has transgressed, and knows it, but the snap signals she has done the same. He stares stubbornly at the wall.

"Tomorrow, the physicians are due."

The head comes round in a hurry.

"To check your thigh again. And the rest. If everything looks all right, they may let you start on solid food."

"Looks . . ."

He says it on a breath. There is sweat on his forehead- bones.

Her tongue aches to say, I know how you dread it, more for the humiliation than the pain. I can make it easier . . . None of it can be spoken, lest it sting that vehement pride.

"I'll be here."

The eyes come round to her. Too black, too depthless, to read gratitude, but the loosening of their corners speaks relief.

* * * *

"Shirran."

"Ships. Oars."

"Who pulled them?"

"Black men. Chains."

"Was it in the Archipelago?"

"Archipelago?"

Tellurith sighs.

"Tomorrow, someone else will work at this. And," as well get it all over at once, "we'll be shifting you out of here."

It has been cleared by the physicians. And after tomorrow, they may need the infirmary.

The eyes are wide, all but wild. Arrogance is fragile in an invalid. Physically helpless, psychically shattered; and she has just rocked the foundations of his tiny world.

"What is . . .Why?"

She sits down on the bed-side, puts a hand on his shoulder. That he permits it is a measure of the shock.

"It's nothing to worry about. I—simply have some work I cannot put off."

No work, the wild look says what he is too proud to lay tongue to, should come ahead of *me*! Child's frailty, child's affront. Child's panic. "Where is this? Where am I going—"

"This is the House infirmary. You'll have your own room. In the tower."

"What tower?"

"The men's tower. We—men and women have separate quarters, in Amberlight."

The wildness has intensified. His face is slick with sweat.

"It won't be so different. A new nurse or two, perhaps, but Caitha will visit you."

It is panic now. Stark and white. And under it, the razed foundations of another man's, a redoubtable man's, perhaps a ruler's pride. Which is what clamps the lip in his teeth and the terror behind that harrowed black stare, the cry of a dependent betrayed, abandoned, which haunts her into sleep.

II

Moon's end over Amberlight, a sleek left-handed crescent in a bitterly cold, cloudless spectrum of blood-crimson-to-violet pre-dawn sky. *Red sky at light, sorrow's delight.* Shrugging on work-coat and bull's hide helmet and solid knee-high work-boots, Tellurith eyes it askance.

Mutter, shuffle, flicker of torchlight tells her most of the crew is already in the court. Helmeted heads, bulky silhouettes, merge amid huge marble vases of fern; a gift, doubtless ironic, from Shuya, president of Verrain. Slab-shifters cluster, well-known faces with the litter poles. Tunnel crew, a bristle of shovel and pick. Physicians' team. Stretcher-carriers.

And the one unfamiliar shape, edging up with an angle of instrument-case at her back. Darrya. Proven shaper, having made the device she bears, House-bred, from an old Craft family, now meeting the greatest test of all. Her first time at the face. First time approaching moon's dark has matched her womb's dark, the time of woman's greatest power, greatest receptivity, of hearing, as the Crafters say. The two or three days before her monthly flow begins.

They exchange salutes. Tellurith adds a couple of Head-like, reassuring words. It is never easy. Ever. But the moon presses. At her stance, more than anything, the crew begins to move.

Under the men's tower. Through the twelve feet high, padlocked, cross-barred garden gates. Up the steps.

The sun is still a long way behind. In the mouth of the mine-adit, screened by its clump of pines, Tellurith halts for the prayer.

"Work-mother, moon's lady . . ." Her tongue recites the phrases that her soul affirms. A light in the men's tower, a snail-track of torches further down the hill-flank, attract her brain. Jerish is cutting too. And sometime in the next week, before the new moon comes, they will be followed by the rest of the Thirteen.

The prayer ends. The crew mutter assent. The tunnelers pass out the shielded candle-lamps. In ritual order, tunnel crew, slab-shifters, House-head, cutter, physicians, stretcher-bearers, they file into the mine.

The way is short enough, up in a rough-walled, rag-roofed semicircle, by time-settled steps amid the carpet of debris. Rock fragments. Broken shoring timber. A roomy enough tunnel, but the hill is limestone, fractured, crumbling, and capricious in its falls. The lanterns pass in ritual quiet.

Until the tunnel widens and the mother-face confronts them, condensation glistening, a wall of frozen moonlight, grey and blank as some great, blind, living eye.

Silently, the crew group themselves. Slab-shifters in front. Physicians to the left, tunnellers behind, House-head to the right. Tellurith grips Darrya's shoulder. Then they all step back, and she is alone, one small human figure, facing the qherrique.

Silence prolongs itself. So quiet they all hear the breath, well-controlled, Tellurith notices, before the novice starts her song.

Never the same song, never the same as for anyone else, never sung for anyone else. Softer than a woman calling her own soul. Quieter than the closure of a lullaby.

Imperceptibly, infinitesimally, dimming, paling the yellow candle flame, the mother-face begins to glow.

Moonrise, pearl-light, too soft for frosting, too pure to call opalescent, too deep, too inward to say, illumination, filling, flooding the tunnel, a well of living light. As she watches, Tellurith's eyes fill. She feels, remembers the communion, Amberlight's greatest life at its greatest moment, the loss tearing her heart.

Darrya unslings her cutter. Clears it. Walks forward to the face. And the qherrique glows brighter, the full, pearl's heart luster of assent, under her caress.

Darrya sets her feet. Centers herself. The song closes as they always do.

"In the Work-mother's hand."

Then she wakes the blade. Slower, more delicately than with any scalpel, begins to cut the long upper face of the slab.

A good beginning, considers Tellurith, filing behind the slab-shifters with the litter, Darrya stumbling sweat-drenched and speechless in her arm. A clear assent, a steady cut. No fumbles in the loading, and Marghi's team can handle the padded leather sling in their sleep. The face hardly wept. By next moon, the scar, like so many before it, will be almost gone. It is not so often the Work-mother grants them such an auspicious pass.

Ten steps later, the ceiling comes down.

* * * *

"S'hurre." Tellurith clears her throat. "We have a problem to solve."

Not the posy of bruises, lacerations, broken ankle and strained shoulder in the infirmary. Not the setting of new timbers when the next tunnel crew has cleared the scree. Not the apportioning or working of the slab that came out without a scratch, protected by shifters' backs. In some puzzlement, the faces round the table turn to her. Craft-heads, Telluir House's decision-makers, several of them Head's cousin-kin.

"And I need a decision from the House."

On the fate of an enigmatic male picked up bleeding to death, a personal commitment assumed by the House's head, but also a dangerous mystery. An outlander whose purpose and origin are lost, even in his own mind, but whose rags of personality shout, Troubler of nations; King's emissary. With perilous hints of Amberlight, high Amberlight involvement, atop the smell of Dhasdein or Cataract.

"We know he isn't Dinda because he's the wrong color, or Shuya, because *she* has no extras, or his Imperial Majesty or his Illustrious Crown Prince," ironic cheers, "because there's been no to-do downstream. Otherwise, he could be any dangle under the Mother's moon. And short of some very expensive, very long-winded, very risky enquiries, there's no way of finding where he's missed.

"In two weeks, despite extensive work with me, his memory has not returned. He is now in the men's tower. Where he will not work with anyone else, and is now refusing to eat. That small—obstacle—we can circumvent." Some wry laughs. "The decision I need from you goes longer. Do we keep him? Or do we turn him out?"

* * * *

Some hurrying to work, some lingering to chat, the rest of the meeting has left Hanni and her two off-siders to shield Tellurith amid a mess of appointment diaries and voting slates. But though she has done all but hide in the big silver-grey conference chamber drapes, Iatha has dogged her Head up the two levels to her workroom, and seen Hanni herself dislodged.

"And now, my pretty vote-swinger, where's the twist?"

"It was a fair discussion—" Tellurith reaches for a slate-stack. Iatha snatches it away.

"Oh, they were three hours deciding if it was more honorable or safe or smart to waste food and risk murder keeping him, than to save time and lose secrets tossing him away. You knew how it would go, from the minute you said 'turn him out'."

"It's the only safe choice—"

"Of course it is. House honor, common charity, too Mother-blasted much to risk. So why—"

Iatha's eyes narrow. Tellurith waits.

"So why," says Iatha very softly, "didn't you twist the next one too?"

Tellurith scowls.

"Yes, 'Rith. If we keep him—just what do we do with him?"

Tellurith scowls harder. "I have to see Zeana—"

"She could cut that piece in her sleep. Where is this going, 'Rith?"

"I have a day's work—"

"Who's going to work with *him*? Or do we just lock him up in the tower and pretend he doesn't exist?"

"Rot it—!"

"Can it be—can it be that you don't know?"

"Rot and gangrene you, I do know!" And as Tellurith turns at bay, the qherrique, the oracle, whatever it is that speaks to House-heads makes good the lie. "We can't let it go, so *I'll* have to work with him—and I'm blasted if I'll waste more work-time or spend my life traipsing up the tower. Shift him over here—put him in a spare room—the Mother knows I have too many of them! Move in a couple of Zuri's troublecrew—let them peel parsnips and wash sheets for Shia if there's no other cover, I know you won't let me hazard my precious head with him alone. I'll work on him after dinner or at midnight or over the breakfast table. And *you* can figure how to make him eat!"

* * * *

"**W**hy did you refuse to go on with the words?"

"Why are you doing this?"

The gambits clash in midair. Visible as the best guest-silver with which Shia's eccentricity has laid the table, the embroidered cloth, the blood-tulips of wine, the costly furniture, the backdrop fresco of glowing qherrique, the prospect, beyond rain-gemmed glass, of city lights. The glare in those black eyes.

("In the Mother's blessed name, 'Rith!" After all the storms, Iatha imploring her, literally on the verge of tears. "Risk yourself, and the House, and for all I know, the City, but not this way! Have *some* sense!"

To which the only answer, irrational, inexplicable, compulsive as every signal from the qherrique, is, "It feels right.")

Iatha, naturally, has settled the hunger-strike with scurvy facility. Told him he will leave the physicians' hands as soon as he can walk.

And this same day he has negotiated his shaky way down the tower, up into the House-head's quarters, to the room nearest the servers', appointed fit for any Head's favorite. Down to the slippers he is wearing. At a price the barely-touched plate, the too-stiff stance and over-bright, black-ringed eyes announce.

"Do you find the clothes to your taste?"

The paled cheekbones flush; the glare becomes ice. All too easy, with this one, to make a gall of debt.

"Gods blast it, why?"

"Had you rather we put you on the street?"

"You . . ."

Too intelligent to hurl things, too furious for speech. Hefty troublecrew in earshot. But as he falls back in his chair, Tellurith's pulse-beat scores the fright.

Delicate as poison, he sets aside the glass.

"Just what *is* it you want?"

A King's emissary at the very least. From a multitude of responses, a House-head's intuition urges truth.

"We can't get rid of you. It isn't honor. It isn't safe. On what terms you stay—is your choice."

Were he not still so physically and mentally drained, no doubt there would be less signal than that bloodless face. Certainly he would not have to ask outright. Tensing, swallowing. "'Safe'?"

Tellurith sets aside her own glass. Beginning the real gamble, she is icy, self-oblivious, as if back in the mine.

"What do you know about Amberlight?"

Nothing. You know that. It is in the mute shake of the head.

"We are not a nation, even such a nation as Verrain. We are one city, with a limited number of folk, and a great deal of land. A great deal of wealth. It has been gifted to us over centuries. Do you know why?"

And at this hinge of destiny there is still time for triumph, at seeing the gamble work. When the huge black eyes blink, still riveted on her, and the fine-cut lips whisper, "Qherrique."

"What do you know of qherrique?"

And like a sleepwalker's, the lips speak.

"Pearl-rock. Origin unknown. Nature unknown. Value unlimited. The key to River-rule. Only found at Amberlight. Only worked by women, traditionally. Thirteen separate outcrops, each the property of a House. Traded, as statuettes of the city's Goddess, to any authority who can raise the price. For its ruling powers."

"Powers?"

"With pearl-rock, a ruler—down to a house or clan-head—can control his folk."

"Hardly 'control'." Whatever the cost of interruption, Tellurith cannot forego a frown. "A ruler with a statuette—which must be made and tuned specifically for her—can feel the folk's harmony. Can—influence it. Quiet trouble, reduce dissent."

"So it's a—peace-maker?"

No somnambulist now. All too much vinegar in the curl of the mouth.

"Yes."

"Oh, of *course* that's why Dinda's tax-collectors squeeze out blood for it! The worst tyrant that ever mangled Cataract! The most violent state in River's length! Of *course* that's why Mahash runs Shirran dry to raise slave caravans! And that's why Dhasdein's bankrupting itself for gold from the Oases—so they can conquer more of the Archipelago with pearl-rock to trade for more gold to pay for another statue to grab more colonies to—make *peace!*"

He has to sit and pant. Tellurith just manages not to gasp. To retort, "And Verrain?"

"Verrain too, where's the difference? They'll take over the Oases if they ever raise the men. Slave-broking with Dhasdein—flirting with Cataract—they use the things on their neighbors like everyone else!"

Then he freezes in mid-breath.

They stare at each other while rain splatters the windows, gagged by matched, comprehending shock. He at a world's betrayal. She at the answer to questions that Amberlight, secure in its vendor's monopoly, has never thought to ask.

She recovers first. At her shift in the chair that says, with winner's complacence, Value repaid, his hand jumps to his glass.

In the clear white qherrique light it lasts an eternity, she poised on her chair edge, his hand crushing the glass-stem, the black eyes, pools, lakes, midnight oceans, ravaging, massacring her.

Before he lets go. Sinks back, trembling with more than weakness. And whispers, "You bitch."

Carefully, Tellurith moves her own glass out of reach.

"How many days' keep was that?" His lips tremble as she knows they never would in health. "How many silk—Oh, no, bitch . . ."

"Sit down!"

"You offered the bargain," she goes on softly, into that moment's hiatus, precise and lethal as an entering sword.

"God's eyes—!"

The aborted lunge melts. Their eyes burn together like gold in king's acid, the echo of his words polluting the silent air.

Try me with some more names.

Very slowly, he sets both elbows on the table. Sinks his face into his hands.

Her own hands ache to work the pain out of his shoulders, smooth peace up into the rumpled hair. But he is no longer a bed-bound victim. And the interrogator's gamble, that has already repaid so richly, can only be carried on.

Not, says her own rebellion, at this cost.

"You're exhausted. You're nowhere near well. And today you've overtired yourself. I can call Caitha. Or you can let Verrith help you," the slight lift of voice brings her into sight, trained, hefty troublecrew masquerading as house-help, "take a dose of sleep-syrup and get into bed."

* * * *

"**L**ittle trouble with a razor."

Azo, Verrith's equally stolid partner, tamps her bloody nose. More phlegmatic than Tellurith, dragged home at midday from an extended freight-dispute. Far more phlegmatic than the culprit, all but foaming in his bed.

"Caitha said," Azo slides the reddened handkerchief away, "best."

Which comes to solid infirmary restraints over his chest, arms, legs. With matching efficiency, stripped. The disordered sheet bares naked torso, upturned, newly bandaged wrist. Face of a white fury, black-coal killer's eyes.

"So this is Telluir's, *Safe?*"

Inwardly, Tellurith swears. If he had to run crazy enough for wrist slashing, did the wardens need zeal to match?

"If you'll go this far, why not just let me take care of it?"

Foolish, foolish question. Her stare tells him that. The whitened mouth, the stricken look, is his involuntary reply.

Then the lips set. "I'll do it, you know." Ice-cold now. "There are ways. Even like this . . ."

Wrench on the restraints. A fresh view of wiry but muscular body that she remembers surprisingly well.

"I'll break something. Starve. Smother myself . . ."

"I thought," she says, low and keener than a knife-cut, "that you had more guts."

His body bucks, once. Before he lies back. Falls back, sweating, panting. Spits it through his teeth.

"*Bitch*."

The qherrique-tide moves her, as sure as it is inexplicable. She says, "Get these off," and starts undoing restraints.

Half a watch later he is still shaking, sweat printing the back of the pristine white shirt. Staring blindly across the balcony out to high noon on Amberlight, a pellucid, celadon-blue pre-rain day. Oblivious to Uphill food on the table, Telluir's House-head dancing attendance, a day's work gone begging, in listening, hearing quiet.

He moves at last. Says it, choked, to the table-top.

"Just tell me—Why?"

And Tellurith says, "Ask me what I know about qherrique."

It takes him a good minute to master the shock. The black eyes stare, all anchors, this time, lost.

"W-what—do—you know—ab-bout qherrique?"

"We mine it," says Tellurith precisely. "From the hill. From the inner walls of the qherrique. The mother-face. The only place it will tolerate us. It's dangerous. The rock's bad. The face—can object. There are accidents, nearly every moon. When it's cut, we make it into statuettes. That too is dangerous. We do other things. What do you remember of Amberlight?"

He can only shake his head.

"Can you get up?"

When he manages it, she holds his arm to lead him onto the balcony. He is too stunned to resist.

To left and right the blocks of Khuss and Jerish and Hafas Houses, close beneath their domes of qherrique, are familiar as her hand's shape. The mosaics glitter blue on Jerish's front. Downhill, smaller clan and client demesnes tangle garden-greens with glaucous roof-tile, the squared shapes of modest men's towers, and imported marble, granite, limestone among the wine-crystal red, as dark as drying blood, of local rock that gave Amberlight its first name.

Emberlight. Near seven hundred years since a nomad clan wintered on the hill and hewed permanent fireplaces below the place where a clanswoman first touched qherrique: Amanazar, legend says, equally legendary founder of Hafas House. Six hundred years since a ruler used that legacy to destroy bandits; and a decade less, since her daughter shaped the first statuette.

Below the clan grounds, in the business quarter, bright spots fill the streetways, busy Craftless folk at work. The tall, glossy grey-black power-panels of wheeled traffic thread the crowd. The press fills Exchange Square, suturing Uphill with the bitterly contested gangland-zone, where the jobless, shiftless youth of River Quarter skirmish over ground lost by day to be re-occupied at night. When she became House-head, that tide had barely risen above the slums.

And across those slums run the broad, uncumbered freight tracks where the big carriers move in procession, up and down to the quays.

"Do you see those vehicles?"

Maybe his pupils contract.

"Did they tell you about Amberlight's vehicles? The ones that use no horses? That are driven by the sun?"

His lips move. And suddenly, turning on her a stare he cannot hold from showing incredulity, he nods.

"Yes!" A different shock now, impossible to hide. The first thing recalled, however prompted, at his own will.

"Yes." Nor can she help the smile, the brief grasp of his arm. Whose muscle does not repulse her touch. "And they told you that no-one's ever understood how?"

His eyes open, black upon blackness, full into the noon light. At last he breathes, "Gods . . ."

Her stare tells him that she understands. Both understandings. We are getting, she thinks, too good at stares.

"And—gods—the ships as well?"

"You'd best come inside."

But though he wobbles in her grasp, she does not let him sit down. Instead she leads him to the wall.

"Have you looked at this?"

He looks now, over-bewildered, but with the resilience of those redoubtable native wits.

"Don't touch!"

The stare he turns on her is again growing wild.

"Yes. That's qherrique."

"You use it for—decoration?" Tripled disbelief.

"It makes decoration here." The glowing veins trace their arabesques, undisturbed, upon that apricot-marbled wall. "But it's all through the House."

"Through . . ." Absently, discarding pride, he removes her hand. "I have to sit down."

"The panels of the vehicles," says Tellurith, watching him across the table, "draw the sun. They're made of qherrique."

And waits, with complete faith in his wits. Vindicated when in less than another minute he puts one hand to his temple and says faintly, "And in the houses. It heats . . ."

"Only the Houses." Pronouncing the capital. "In winter, yes, it gives out heat. In summer, it takes it back."

"It cools the house?"

"More than that. Didn't you notice in the infirmary? No lamps?"

This time he is too stunned for speech.

She cannot control the smile. "I don't mean to put you back in bed." And is shocked when her mind adds, Not yet. "But you did ask."

In a moment, she goes on. "That takes a lot more power than sun. Did you see the windmills on the crests?" Still struggling, he nods. "They feed the mother-lodes, and the House-qherrique; all day, every day."

She reaches over to pour two glasses—the delicate, fine-blown Uphill glasses—of Shia's guest-choice, chilled white wine. Mutely, he sips.

And when she gives him breathing space, again it is vindicated. The head comes up, the black eyes waking to keen, intellectual life.

"You said—dangerous?"

"We shifted you from the infirmary because we mined a slab the next day. There were six patients that night. Half the mine roof fell on us."

There is respect in the indrawn breath. But the mind it does not deflect. "Dangerous . . . to make a statuette?"

Tellurith cuts a slice of the chicken in aspic, adds a helping of Shia's delicate sorrel and basil salad, a hunk of the crusty House-baked bread. Passes the plate.

"When you're fit, I'll show you what I mean."

* * * *

But already a Head's back-log is waiting, mandatory presence at first cut of the kinglet's statuette, two minutes' action, four hours ceremony. An equally mandatory birth-celebration for Jura's granddaughter, first girl-child to the eldest daughter of Hezamin House. A crisis in the polisher's shop, where some tyro has burred the face of a Verrain Family's piece, worse calamity than the girl's broken wrist. It is two evenings before she can sit down, still in her good day-clothes, to take a grateful sip of wine and meet that black stare across the dinner-plates.

"Can I ask," the Quetzistani "a" is broader than usual, "what you know about, Not safe?"

He has been impatient; Verrith and Azo have told her that. Iatha has belabored her ears for culpable, hideous breaches of City secrecy, while jubilating over the information's prize.

But he has waited till her main meal is eaten. And nothing he learnt in that last interview, down to a possible password, has been left to waste.

Tellurith kicks her chair back. Begins, one-handed, to unlace her boots. Quiets her breath before she speaks.

"May I ask you something first?"

The brows twitch. Straight black bars above the yellowing bruise, crossed by the black wing of falling hair. The eyes never shift.

"If, when I answer, you do the same."

"Good enough." She cannot restrain the smile. "Why wouldn't you work with anyone else?"

The frown comes in earnest, thunderous. "It's no use."

"Eh?"

"Nobody else knows the right words. Nobody else can—" the eyes deflect, are pulled grimly back—"follow them up."

"And why wouldn't you eat?"

Why would you think? Up from under the brows, a sullen, wordless scowl.

Because you would not come. Because there was no other leverage to bring you.

Because without you, without some hope of regaining my self, there was no point in life.

For a moment she savors it. Hostile, truest acknowledgment of a House-head's skills. Before she fulfils the pledge.

"When I asked what you knew about Amberlight, I was not looking for such a great secret as—as the things you said. I started to explain why it would not be safe for us to let you go—unless we knew why you were here."

A lesser man would exclaim, question. She reads the measure of recovery as he works it through, behind that unblinking stare.

"So you couldn't learn anything—except through me, myself."

Worked through, indeed.

"And when I wouldn't try for anyone else—you brought me here."

Terrifyingly far through. Far enough to leave unspoken, And you will go on trying. By whatever means available.

And because there is no surety my memory is truly lost, if I never remember, you will never let me go.

It is all there, perilously open, in those black-steel eyes. As open as what she has said about his value, his standing, what his menace must have been. She watches him think that through, and wonders if whatever she bought is worth the price.

He takes a long breath. Smiles faintly. The man he was has never been more clear.

"Nothing for nothing," he says, and jerks her heart halfway through her teeth. "You're a gambler too."

Throwing back the gauntlet of comprehension. If you cannot risk letting me go, neither, with information missing, can you risk my suicide. And if the only way you can get information is to give it, then you will give. You know that I have so little choice. Die in your hands, live in them as you so swiftly showed me, under total restraint. Resign myself. Or take the gamble, play your game, and try to re-win that self. And if I succeed, if I am what you think, the chance of losing me along with what you have already given is a gamble you are also prepared to take.

Neither has to mention the highest stake: That the threat posed by his presence, the vulnerability of Amberlight, is real.

Tellurith inclines her head. A duelist's salute to a fine pass. "I told you—the choice of terms is yours."

He sips his wine. Now, for the first time, comes a blade-thin, irony of a smile. "If there was a choice, would I be here?"

* * * *

Tellurith carries the caution of that subtle inanity to bed with her: Only a fool would make any other choice; therefore, no choice, for no fool would ever have the choice. When—she can almost see the black eyes slit—did you take me for a fool?

* * * *

But it draws a thunderous scowl when she has no time for him next morning, then reports of Shia badgered along with the troublecrew that night. And something perilously near a tantrum, after, with just margin to change for yet another vital Uphill dinner, where she must patch temporary alliance between Jerish and Keranshah over the burning question of freight-drivers' wages, she bawls through her bedroom door, "Mother blast, you're not the biggest thing in Amberlight! Wait your turn!"

Nor is there time for him next day. An untoward duty this time, whose harbinger catapults her upright in the bedclothes, staring into the lampless dark. Not, What? not, Why? Just the imperative, unmistakable: Wake!

Two hours before sunrise, the bitterest morning watch. Bitter as the word that meets her, stumbling night-robed to the apartment door, and returns her, for another pair of sleepless hours, to bed.

When she does reach the site, the evidence is all smoothed away. Noose gone from the ornamented lintel, body laid out, hands folded under the shroud. The mother to greet her in the doorway. Dry-eyed, amid the wreckage of a family's life.

A mainstay of the Power-shops, her skill has shaped light-gun, cutter, vehicle panels, and fitted their assemblies for over thirty years. But now her hands are knotted with arthritis. And her only daughter is dead.

Tellurith ignores the salute of hands clasped to forehead, stepping past to draw her straight into an embrace. To say into her neck, "Veristya. Oh, my dear."

The clutch tightens convulsively. Acknowledging a pain they both know is truly shared. It is a long minute before Veristya lifts her head.

"Well." The gesture, quiet and concise as are the best power-workers', takes in the apartment, its ground-floor windows open on the garden, among the choicest in the Power-shop wing. Inherited from her own mother, whose mother lifted them from the clan demesne when she first found "something in the hands."

From the inner room come the stifled lamentations of the family men. Around them the chattels of three lifetimes are being mustered; tallied, divided, packed or thrown away. Veristya meets her Head's eyes with composure, as she says, "We'll be out in three days."

No need to ask, will your kin receive you? They both know that Downhill there is no one left.

"I never blamed her." Veristya speaks abruptly, turning as abruptly from the too betraying light. "Right through her twenties, she kept saying, It'll come. It must. But I didn't worry. I'd have been happy to see her in any—any G-guild, I'd have gone along."

But, the silence adds, she would not believe it. She would not go. And now she is dead and I am crippled and it is all too late.

"She finally made Quira test her. Just yesterday."

Quira is behind Tellurith in the door. Power-shop Head, a frost of grey across her plaits, a frost of grief on her dour, broad, shrewd face.

And when the answer was, No, she had no heart to stay.

Tellurith says flatly, "See Hanni. I'll speak to Iatha. If we can't keep you, we'll remember you." What, says her glare, if it is charity? "It's the honor of the House."

And surety that a crippled woman will end her life in comfort, that her men need not go out to work, to break limbs or ruin backs as do River Quarter poor. That the illusion of House status will remain.

And it matters less than an illusion. What mattered was the work; the touch, the contact, the thing that makes Craft more than a trade, and qherrique far more than merchandise. The thing for which her daughter died, because she could not bear a second-best. What charity, Veristya's eyes ask, can recompense us that?

Out in the passageway, feeling the cold run down her backbone, Tellurith thinks, That could have been me. If my mother's blood had failed. If my father's line had not bred true. I could have been hanging from that lintel.

Or out in the Craftless street.

Right up to House-head, the custom holds. The limited room of a Craft-wing admits only active Crafters' kin.

Shoulder to shoulder in custom as automatic as it is comforting, Quira grumbles, "Mother's love."

Tellurith does not have to translate: The Mother witness how I hate my role in such deaths and banishments. Such cruel custom. Such stern necessity.

She does not have to utter such falsities as, They'll have funds, they'll be all right. She need only grip Quira's shoulder, solid as ever, if a little more bowed. And nod when Quira sighs and growls, "S'pose I'll have Kessa and Chreizo scrapping over the rooms now, like a pair of Korite dogs."

"Ah," says Tellurith. All-purpose agreement, acknowledgement. "Send them to me if it gets out of control."

"Harh!" Momentarily isolate in the corridor, Quira backs her snort with an insubordinate shoulder-slap. "You want to run a test on *me?*"

* * * *

There is nothing subordinate about the black-ice stare that beleaguers her coffee cup next morning. Hot, heart-starting necessity that she usually grabs one-handed on her way to choose a coat.

Tellurith sighs. Does up another shirt button. Says without looking behind, "Verrith, we'll survive five minutes without you.

In my workroom. Tell Hanni, noon-break today at home. In the book."

* * * *

"**Y**ou were going to show me what was dangerous."

"You were going to prove yourself fit."

"Prove?"

"By physicians' standards."

Biting his lip, he glares. Then, too swiftly for forestallment, "Talk to me, then! Explain this—if Amberlight's just a city, and such a limited city, why haven't Dhasdein or Verrain or Cataract tried to take the qherrique?"

Tellurith pushes aside her glass. Carefully averts her mind from an answer learned in infant's clothes. Takes breath as at the mother-face, and answers calmly, "They have."

Into that startled glare, she goes on, "Do you remember any thieves' tales?"

"Hey?"

"They still tell them, up and down the River." Garnered, she does not add, by our intelligencers. "Amberlight troublecrew are witches. At night they change shape. Then they sniff out thieves before they leave the quayside and run them down like dogs."

"Huh!"

She lets her own lip curl in response.

"Or the story of the Mel'ethi Master-thief, Bellissar? Who thought to seduce a House-head and get her swag an easier way?"

"Bellissar—Bellissar—something—about hands . . ."

"Hands, yes." Tellurith lets her own curl lightly about a piece of silverware. Fluidity of muscle and tendon, delicacy of knuckle and palm, instrument so vital, so lightly prized, until it is lost.

"Bellissar stole the password from the Head one night in her sleep. The guards," she does not curl her lip this time. All Amberlight know there are none. "The guards let her into the mine. They found her next morning, lying at the mother-face. The Houses said, From a Master-thief, the qherrique has taken its own toll. And they let her go."

"Go—" a hissing breath. "To beg her bread on a Deyiko street-corner. Because her hands were gone at the wrist. Burnt away."

"So you do remember that?"

Their eyes clinch. Before he tosses himself back in his chair. "Ballads! Old wives' tales."

"Then do you remember any history?"

"Of what?"

"Say—the first coalition of Verrain and Dhasdein."

The eyes slit. Concentration darkens to a frown. Becomes a baffled glare. Her pulse easing, before he can sink to fury, Tellurith speaks herself.

"The commander-in-chief, the imperial general Kassikas, captured Amberlight. His engineers tried to mine the qherrique. The shaft fell in on them. A fugitive House-head raised the City, massacred his army, and sent his head in a pickle-barrel to the emperor."

The eyes skewer her. Then the lip curls. He murmurs, with blacker irony, "Dangerous."

Tellurith nods. Steadies her breath, as for the second cut at the face. "Do you recall the first coalition of Cataract, Verrain and Dhasdein?"

The frown, the head-toss anticipate his, "Get to the point!"

"It was proclaimed at a winter's fall. By spring, a Quetzistani fanatic had assassinated the emperor. By next spring, Dhasdein had a civil war."

She waits, watching him as she would watch Maeran, across the table's space. There is fiercened intent now, effort to unearth memory. That ends in another infuriated breath.

"The second coalition," says Tellurith precisely, "was seventy years later. The Dhasdeini commander-in-chief cut his throat after a scandal that named him lover of the Empress. Raids out of Quetzistan overthrew Verrain's president, and when Cataract invaded Verrain territory, Amberlight refused the new president a statuette."

His knuckles are white on the table-edge. The eyes are all but burning her.

When she does not speak, he whispers it. "But Cataract had to withdraw."

Silently, Tellurith looks back at him. When he in turn is silent, she murmurs, "The third coalition of Verrain and Dhasdein—ended after an uprising in Quetzistan."

Very slowly, very carefully, he slides back in his chair. Lets the table go. Those eyes are still devouring her.

Presently he says, almost in a purr, "Amberlight's intelligencers must be very—dangerous."

No doubt that he has understood it all. No doubt that he has engineered such machinations himself. No doubt that she is playing with fire as dangerous as very qherrique. And no doubt that those eyes have never, for a moment, shown a flicker of remembrance, consciousness, recognition of anything but the past.

Tellurith answers as softly, "Oh, yes."

Their eyes hold, as duelists hold the balance of crossed blades. Then Hanni comes hurriedly out of the workroom, calling, "Ruand? Iatha says there's another fight on the quay . . ."

It is a relief to get up, indeed to spring to her feet. To call, "I'm coming!" and catch his explosion as a parting shot.

"Well, if you can't spare two minutes a day, give me someone who can! Let me talk to your blasted—minders! Give me some exercise! Let me out!"

* * * *

Out, Caitha cancels with one flat, No. *Exercise,* Iatha and Zuri take up with only less enthusiasm than Azo, granted leave to work out her charge, under Shia's strenuous protest, on the commandeered heirloom rugs. "Just don't bend him," is Tellurith's proviso.

Honors on the rugs prove equal. "He's a fine fighter," pronounces Azo with satisfaction. "Taught me two new throws. But he's not Cataract." Her opponent, favoring a shoulder, adds with a glittering smile, "Your security is up to expectations." And with a black frown, "Your godforsaken physician had a fit."

Beyond that, troublecrew conversation fails. So with malice aforethought Tellurith hands Iatha the job. "No one else," she smiles wickedly, "knows enough to ask without giving too much away."

Iatha's bout is even less use: "I don't blab," his black stare disdainful, "to intelligencers—"—"All he does is ask about you—rot it, give over, 'Rith!"

* * * *

"**Y**ou could always," sweetly, over the dinner-soup, "throw me out."

If, challenge unspoken, I'm more trouble than I'm worth.

Tellurith sets aside her glass.

"So we could. It costs three copper fiels a day for the cheapest shelter in River Quarter—shared straw in the tenements. It costs five silver darrin for passage to Quasharn," the nearest town over the Verrain border, "and thirty to Cataract. If you know where you're going. Just for the River Quarter, weapons would help. For eating—in Amberlight, you could always beg."

The silence is murder, holding its breath.

"And," she goes on gently, "we do own the clothes on your back."

She smiles more sweetly while he sits glaring, trembling, and her heart beats up in her throat.

Until with a great gasp he lets go his breath. The recoil of a catapult.

"So tell me, what's the going rate for whores?"

"Skilled ones, Uphill, can make fifty darrin a mark."

"Ah—! And you would know?"

Tellurith grins, marking the blow unworthy. "In Amberlight, whores are male."

"Gods damn you . . ."

Head in arms, fists clenched together over the table, shoulders flexing; then his wrists jerk and he thrusts both hands before him, palms smearing blood across the immaculate cloth.

"That's enough!"

Tellurith is up, all risk forgotten, catching at shoulders, gripping hands. He makes one savage attempt to wrest his fingers loose; then sinks back, spent and mute as Darrya when she left the qherrique. She holds him in the chair, part restraint, part embrace.

"You know," gentle as art and will can make it, "cutting at each other is pointless. People just get hurt."

He is still breathing like a winded rower. Probably unable to speak.

"If there was more time for you, I would make it. I don't delay for malice. Will you believe that?"

It is too familiar, the urge to comfort, the feel of that wiry, defiant, disabled physical presence in her grasp. That wing of hair is in his face again. There is a vulnerable look about the mouth. She takes her hands from his shoulders, and steps back.

Before she puts those hands somewhere else.

Finally he wipes his face on an arm, and lifts his eyes.

"I—when I'm cornered, I have to fight."

Where, Tellurith rages, do I find a matching gift?

She takes his hands again. Turns them palm up. With an also immaculate napkin, dabs clean abrasions taken on Exchange Square, opened back to the blood. "If you're careful, Caitha needn't ever know." From somewhere he manages a grin, stabbing her to the heart. "There are hundreds of things untried yet. If you could work with Iatha—if you could just wait . . ."

"Wait," he says, on a note that stabs deeper still. The eyes, somber now, stare into the blood-heart of his wine. "What is it—three weeks?"

"Mm." Like every craft-woman, Tellurith carries moon time at her fingertips. "That's not so long—"

He looks at her now without fire. Without hope. Her tongue goes on for her, "Will you wait until we round up the gang that attacked you? See if it brings back . . . anything?"

* * * *

Five boys, four girls. Twelve to eighteen, perhaps. Through the dirt, and the madly unkempt hair, and the bizarre layers of clothes, it is hard to tell. Sold for a pittance by their fellow gangs to the Telluir intelligencers, chained in a line in Telluir courtyard, for their first look at Uphill Amberlight.

"Watch them through the shutter when they turn." In the lower tower room, Tellurith takes her charge lightly by the arm. Far too fond, she is lately, of taking it. The one touch he does not protest.

Finely, through the hard-set muscle, she can feel him shaking. If no shred of first-hand memory remains, the pain must be indelible. The knowledge of what they did to him. That they have not only violated his body, but stolen his mind. Stripped away his life.

At a bark from someone, the line begins to move. Faces lift, turn toward the spectators' window. Sullenly closed. Expectant of nothing, except some mysterious Uphill cruelty. And most likely, death.

Seven, eight, nine. No need to ask, Do you recognize one? His body has not responded. Not by a single twitch.

* * * *

"Ruand! Ruand! Oh, Mother protect us, Moon-lady save and salvage us, Ruand, wake up—!"

Tellurith comes upright with a plunge, slaps the invading face away, just pulls her following fist. Shia babbles at her, full morning behind her in the hallway, calamity in her squawks.

"Verrith, Azo—they're sleeping, I can't wake them! And the door's undone—and him, he's gone!"

III

"Watched to find the sleep-syrup and dosed his minders along with you. Zuri's fit to burst. Anything last night he didn't eat? Didn't drink?" Tellurith shakes her head. Iatha grunts. "No matter. Shia remembers him fidgeting round the kitchen. Nothing new, he's in and out ten times a day."

And the rest hangs in the air: *Damned indecent, as well as disastrous. Into the tower with him, 'Rith.*

If, neither has to add, we ever get him back.

"How," Tellurith's voice is icy, "did he manage the rest?"

Apart from taking her own clothes, and a dozen small valuables, and basic dried food and the longest kitchen knife.

"The ground-patrol never saw him. Out a window on the uphill side. Down a sheet," Tellurith's own, she does not add, "straight into the road."

A very thorough plundering of the cuckoo's nest. And the thought of a straight-haired black-avised outlander man trying to traverse River Quarter in a House-head's leggings, coat and embroidered shirt would be funny as well as a sure trail.

Could they be sure he went that far.

"Jura would tell me. So would Zhee. Damas . . ."

The easiest, most terrifying, most untraceable ploy of all. He only has to knock and demand asylum. In the nearest House.

"And I told him—Mother blind me—the ones in sight."

Anguish has no place in Iatha's voice. Any more than abject guilt. Any more than the glimpse of Verrith in Desis' arms along the passageway. Lover's consolation, sought only for the most grievous grief.

Tellurith sits staring straight into the workroom wall; but she puts a hand out, briefly, to shut on her steward's bowed neck, under the crinkly, grizzled plait.

"Don't blame yourself, Yath." The old pet name is bizarre in that icy, direst-emergency voice. "It's not your fault."

* * * *

But when Iatha darts into the workroom at midnight her step is nearer a dance; she actually catches her Head's wrists and spins her about from the chalk-map on the wall.

"He went Downhill! Moon's turn, third morning hour! Quir clan's running a warehouse patrol at the Quarter edge, of course they noticed a man in women's gear—first ask-around, Zuri's people turned it up!"

Tellurith's eyes thaw. She shoves back crushed sleeves; even grabs her steward, a head shorter, in a bearish hug. "Mother bless—!"

Smiling. Crumpled skin, ice-topaz eyes alight. Before she adds, casually, "When we get him back, I'll have his tripes."

* * * *

Either he left the city, or he did not. If he stayed, he has to have found money. Traded that loot. Which could only be done, before daylight, in River Quarter. Which can be traced.

Likewise, the help, the hiding-place, must cost money.

Which can be traced.

Tellurith works down the decision tree, against the back of her eyelids, in faintest phosphorescent marbling of banked qherrique on her bedroom wall. In memory hang the fetid alleys, the filthy straw-beds of River Quarter, the flea-ridden winter clothes in the lenders' shops. In her nose is the scent of polished wood, under her, in the warmth, the touch of clean linen sheets.

If he didn't stay, then he left. Which also needed money. Which also can be traced. He has to have gone downstream. Or upstream. Which can be traced. How many ships left in that next day?

Or the one after. Or today.

Perhaps, having gone to ground, he doubled back.

The qherrique pulsates, faintest luminance. So deeply silent, the apartment, she can hear Azo's breathing, down the hall.

The intelligencers are at work. What if it's three days?

It would be quicker, with a reward.

And plain as blood in the water, to other intelligencers.

If he's in the Quarter, why in the Mother's name doesn't it show?

Tellurith gets out of bed. Catches up last evening's coat, the deep wine-red of Amberlight stone, goes silently, wrapping it round her, out to the balustrade.

In the colorless pre-dawn glow, River Quarter is studded with yellow seeds of light. Candles, lamp-lit windows. Waking stevedores, homing whores. Easy, terrifyingly easy, to beg a hiding-place down there. One woman with a good eye for a man, and exotic tastes.

Or perhaps, a whore.

Fifty darrin a mark.

"Rot and gangrene you," she says under her breath, stomach twisting at the memory of blood on moon-lit stone. "If you've come at that . . ."

The brothels are not choosy. Perhaps he has been enslaved. Instead of, as well as, being raped.

Perhaps he never reached them. Perhaps the gangs did their work, this time, once and for all.

* * * *

"**N**o, Ruand." Stolid, imperturbable, double-cured Zuri, troublecrew Head, whose eyelids are creased with sleeplessness and whose intelligencers are the best in Amberlight. "There were a couple of victims, but none outlander. And none dead."

Not, Tellurith does not have to retort, last night.

"No, 'Rith." Iatha, patient over the last evening wine. "No downstream passengers. I've sent *Wasp* after the upstream pair." As Tellurith opens her mouth, "Customs check."

One more danger, one more deceit, cozening the Navy atop all the rest. Only a matter of time until the Thirteen find out.

* * * *

"**M**other blast, 'Rith, you have to get some sleep. Take syrup, will you? What do we do if *you* fall apart?"

* * * *

What if a whore, a gang, a simple River Quarter brawl has killed him, and left the river to clean up? What if he has left Amberlight, but not alive?

"No, 'Rith. A very tidy survey, and no bodies in any of the usual places down the bank."

* * * *

If he never left the city, he must still be here. Tellurith sits at midnight by her dining table, staring out across Amberlight under a sinking moon. Wine decanter at her elbow. Stockinged feet on a chair.

Disguise?

But that was always understood. Money, again.

The same if he left. Her thoughts traverse the tired pathway. Up or down the River, without money, there is no escape.

Her jaw falls. Her blood stops. Then she slams her forehead, before she bounds off the chair.

Idiot. Imbecile. Bag-brained moron. Check the bridge! He's gone into the Kora! Tried to steal a horse—or walking out!

* * * *

Dead Dyke, the guard canal, cuts Amberlight's peninsula on the hill's western side. Its gates are opened to clear the stagnant water once a month, the center of its single span swing-bridge is cranked apart each night. Between gate-fall and dawn, nobody leaves Amberlight afoot.

"The gate-watch remember a strange woman that morning. Very good but muddy clothes. A cloth round her head. A vile hangover, she claimed. Cheated in River Quarter, and going to lie up till her House cooled. They even told her a hidey-hole along the bank."

Khey's story. Winkled from Iatha, no doubt, since he never met Khey herself, drawn out with casual questions like, How did you first find me? Silently, Tellurith fumes.

"No doubt the whore can act. And think. And charm." Iatha's forehead is rutted like a road. "But . . ."

We can trace him in the Kora, it is only a matter of space and time. Raise the countryside. Warn the borders. A matter of time.

But it comes at a price.

Tellurith gets up abruptly, and goes to the balustrade in her shirt-sleeves, heedless of the wind that razors Amberlight. Up the hillside, the pines surge and wheel like great dark sinuous windmills; half a day's feeding has put a glistening luster on the qherrique.

She turns on her heel. Striding back inside, says more abruptly, "Yes."

Raise the Kora. Pass the news and description of Telluir's escapee to the Thirteen's clans. To the Houses themselves.

* * * *

"The man has given us nothing—absolutely nothing—solid. He can't remember his name. He couldn't remember what the sea is! Oh, there's no doubt he's been an agent of the highest rank. Shall we write to the Emperor and ask, Excuse me, are you missing any top trouble-makers in Dhasdein?

"Or would you prefer to ask in Cataract?"

Eleven of the Thirteen flinch. Lounging on an unmoved elbow, Maeran drawls, "Isn't this, now, a City case?"

"First," Tellurith's purr is icy, "we have to get him back."

"We."

"You can sit on your hands if you choose, while we alert Telluir holdings. Whose problem is it, if he gets away?

"There is no certainty," the last throw, "that his memory will stay lost."

Damas scowls. The others squirm. Eyes turn to Jura, in the president's seat.

And Jura, faithful Jura, pulls her lips down. Lifts her shoulders. Braces them, and says, "First we get him back."

* * * *

"'Rith—'Rith! Dammit, are you listening? Zhera and Fathyar's lot are at it again—you'd better get down there, fast!"

A pair of rising families, first generation in the polisher's shops; uncertain in their House eminence, the two girls who put them there antagonistic as apprentices, clashing as Crafters, catalysts for a feud that has run to a score of irruptions over washing-space and procession-precedence and partners and apartment-rights, and bids fair to draw in the entire Craft. Tellurith curses under her breath and runs.

The combatants have disrupted the whole shop: apprentices, crafters, Sfina herself, Shapers' head, are surging and bawling in the bell of corridor before the Shapers' wing. Tellurith grunts under her breath. Then grabs the nearest arm, Desis, seasoned troublecrew, and snaps, "Shut 'em up!"

Desis does.

"I told you," though Tellurith barely whispers, it is clearly audible, "not to do this again."

Sfina rolls her eyes in seconding wrath, frank gratefulness. Apprentice eyes bug, Crafters suddenly recall business. The mass of leather aprons and irate faces melts away. To reveal Zhera's mother gasping against a wall where Desis' elbow has lofted her, and Fathyar's mother sitting foolishly on the floor, and the two principals gulping as if they had met a Heartland tiger face to face.

"Didn't I?"

Zhera's mouth opens. And shuts.

"You have disrupted the shop. Insulted your Shop-head. Upset your families." A pair of men's heads vanish down the quarters' passageway. "It's inefficient. It's also unseemly. You will each gift the Mother your work-fees for a month."

Zhera's copper-brown eyes bulge, Fathyar's jowls purple. The mass of current work is as well-known as the pair's avarice. An eye-corner gives Tellurith Sfina's gleeful beam.

"If it happens again, we will be able to proceed without you. Both of you."

Both faces change color. The ultimate threat. Not simply loss of status and wealth and position, but banishment.

Exile from the qherrique.

Tellurith swings on a heel, and tells Sfina, "In the Work-mother's hand."

Invocation. Work-prayer. House-Head's prerogative, sealing her decree as immutable.

Stamping off wet leaves at the inner House door, she wonders, Why was I so absolute? Why should my temper, usually longsuffering with House squabbles, fire like a mishandled block?

* * * *

"**R**uand?" Hanni this time, in some trepidation. "There's another problem on the docks."

Where, once again, the friction point of wages has ignited the stevedores; River Quarter overflows with Craftless, jobless, homeless folk, their numbers rising every year. The Houses have undercut each other, driving work-rates down, for the last thirty years, and against Crafts, or professions like weavers and engineers, the Longshore Guild is a laughing stock.

"Blight and blast it," Tellurith mutters as she clambers from her House vehicle amid a clot of troublecrew onto Telluir's sector of Main Quay. A familiar scene nowadays: carrier stopped, driver and power-handler vanished. As semi-Crafters, able to work with qherrique, they are all too often the focus of dockers' wrath. Warehouse staff barricade the door, light-guns drawn if not charged, confronting a tangle of ragged, raggedly gesturing men.

And stones litter the interval of empty street.

Tellurith steps forward. Stops, at the repulse of an unyielding troublecrew back. Silent message that they will not let her closer. It is not safe.

No women beyond the gap, to salt rebellion with sense. Women are preferred workers when there are jobs, women are more often kept on when jobs are lost. Inwardly, Tellurith sighs. Says over her shoulder, "Get Shiro." The warehouse controller. Then she raises her voice and shouts across the gap, "Do you have a speaker there?"

Shiro to summarize the episode; a speaker as the single voice with whom she can negotiate.

They are outside for three solid hours. A day's prime work-time, from mid-morning past noon. A bleak day, growing sharper as the clouds thicken and the wind gets up. Sliding back in the vehicle, gratefully loosening a fur collar that has hardly checked the gusts of southerly howling along open dock, Tellurith glances at the workmen, moving now toward the unprotected wharf-edge, and carefully does not think, No fur collars there.

* * * *

Winter in Amberlight. Warm inside the House, savage on the docks. And in the Kora beyond?

Rain, bitter winds, mud that chafes the very beasts. Flocks can die of exposure, if a bad wind blows from snow on the Iskans, on a truly rainy night. The inns take money. And farmers are wary, surly, whether eking a living on common ground, or warding some House demesne.

In the Sahandan, the rice district, there are paddies to soak unwary legs to the thigh, chills, fever, worsened by wet or cold lying, peril to a hardy woman. Let alone a physically fragile man.

Tellurith sets her glass down with a snap that fetches both Shia and Verrith. "No, nothing. I'm quite all right."

Just thinking like a blighted nursemaid about an outland dangle who took your House defenses on and beat them, who dared you to a gamble that, if he runs the Kora the way he did the City wards, he is horrendously sure to win.

And where is your City then?

In the meantime, thinking won't find him, or put a roof over him. Tellurith gets up. Goes with a steady step to the little dispensary. Pours a measure of sleep-syrup and puts herself to bed.

* * * *

Winter evening on Amberlight, drenched streets glistening, Arcis' summit walls cut black on sanguine cloud-sags between processional showers. In the Telluir House-head's vehicle, the driver peers, the handler mutters, stroking contacts, so stored sun-power throbs back into the wheels and the machine weaves, its lamps checkering streaks of shadow amid the homing feet.

While Tellurith, hunched behind them, bites her lips against a shriek of, Run them down and be damned!

"We have permission," Zuri beside her, cool as aged oak, "to hold the bridge."

Unanswered, she adds, "They'll be in Gatehead by the time we're through."

Gatehead, first village on the main Kora road, which runs all but arrow straight for thirty miles between a Diaman and a Telluir holding, its villages and inns dotting the boundary line.

Hill-foot Road opens, a yawning gap of dark warehouses, glittering wet stone. The vehicle surges forward. Tellurith stares blindly into the dusk.

At images from the report, sightings passed by mirror signal across the roused countryside, tracing a ragged zigzag, north-west into Diaman country and back. Clothes stolen at a farm-house, a beggar with a suspicious story, an attempt to lift a horse. Thwarted by a watchful farmwife and a pair of lively dogs. A ragged, tiring fugitive, her imagination constructs, hunted too hard for guile.

And a rowdy crowd of shepherds alerted for intruders, wandering back from an inn to their tents by a traveling flock. Startled to uproarious custody when the notorious invader walks out in front of them, showing empty hands.

Worse than accounts of the capture, superfluous beating, carting inn-ward slung like a hunting prize, from a pole, harder than the almost unbearable thought of renewed internal damage, that first picture niggles in her mind. Grim resistance, desperately subtle trickery, a struggle to the perhaps literal death. Any of that she has expected. But surrender?

Anything but that.

At long, long last, the wet dusk horizon rises, and a square door frames the lurid west: Dead Dyke wall. Gate-watch waving them past. Tellurith sits up and growls, "Can we get a move on now?"

The inn-keeper and unofficial posse, cloddish jubilation only partly cowed by sight of an actual House-head, escort her upstairs. One look at the trussed body, muddy rags still drenched, face worse battered than on Exchange Square, one touch on the frigid cheek and Korites go flying, impelled by a Headly roar.

"Get my people up!"

Iatha and Zuri help heave him down with their own hands. Say nothing when their Head climbs in the back compartment, degradation unthinkable, clutching a filthy outland prisoner's head in her lap, snapping, "Get us home! Go!"

He is still catatonic when they settle him on the infirmary table. A stupor balanced by Caitha's outcry as she cuts ropes and strips rags and descants on her work's undoing.

"Exposure—shock—battering—sweet Mother, look at that!—Did they have to use an ox-goad? . . . Rope-galls—blisters—did he run barefoot as well? Starvation—Mother's love, was there *anything* he missed?"

With an undertone of panic as stripped clothes and warm water reveal the damage; which surfaces, at the fresh blood on his thighs, on a moaning intake of breath.

Oh no, Tellurith's heart groans with her. Oh, no.

Caitha steadies herself. Snaps, "We have to look."

But when they pull his legs apart the stupor proves genuine. Not coma but withdrawn awareness that explodes in thrashing, struggling panic to the most harrowing wound-sounds of all. A full-grown man with every shred of control gone, screaming at the top of his lungs.

"Hold him!" Caitha bawls as five solid women fight to keep their grips. "Got to look. Get restraints!"

Panting, nursing stressed wrists, Tellurith eyes her fellow arm-holder's sprung thumb, Zuri's grazed cheek. Looks aside and loses composure. "Mother aid, can't you make him stop!"

"Take longer to get syrup down him." Caitha is wild-eyed too. "Get it over with!"

She does it, teeth clenched against struggles that even Tellurith's voice, touch, cannot calm. Examination; thankful notice of minor damage. Dressing. "And now . . ."

"We turn him over." At the timbre of their Head's voice, Zuri and Iatha roll their eyes. "Get some clothes on him. Into a bed!"

Easier said than done, with three other patients in the infirmary and a man whose terror is still running amok. By the time they wrestle him under sheets behind the makeshift screen, all Tellurith's feelings have transmuted to red, illogical rage.

"If he won't hold still, tie him down!"

When they buckle the restraints and he is still struggling, the fury bursts. "Rot you," she bawls, "wake up!" And slaps him across the mouth.

The sound reverberates through the infirmary. Nine women, suddenly quieter than mice. One man, staring with eyes whose space-black oceans obliterate his pinched, bloodless face.

"Do you know me now?"

The eyes get bigger. The fine-cut mouth, misshapen by blows, approximates a soundless, "Yes."

"Bring the sleep-syrup," orders Tellurith.

"No!"

He screams then. And keeps screaming, until fatigue and desperate worry and concern she does not want to consider go beyond rage to viciousness.

"Fetch," says Tellurith icily, "a gag."

Zuri and Iatha go more than quiet. Caitha, eyes larger than saucers, does what she is told.

And when the gag muffles but does not silence him, Tellurith says in a voice icier than the wind outside, "He's upsetting the patients. Take him where he belongs. The tower."

The noise stops as if cut. Zuri's troublecrew, already stooping to the bed ends, straighten up.

Terror, more than terror in those eyes now. But if ever eyes could speak, those do. Frantic, wordless lucidity. Imploring, beseeching, more eloquent than prayer.

Tellurith stands and stares. Stupid rage draining out of her. Time to remember now, the nightmares she envisaged. That her first emotion, at news of that capture, was stomach-turning relief.

That after all, he is not smashed. Not dead.

And not, now, insane.

And should not, that proud enemy, be reduced to this.

She says, more than roughly, "You rotted—idiot."

His body collapses. Tension breaking like a branch.

"I should beat you to a jelly."

His breath catches and goes out, a long, easing subsidence. The head rolls sidelong. Behind the gag, the bruises, his features relax.

"I ought to lock you in the tower. And feed you bread and water for the next six months."

The lashes flutter, settling, on his gaunt, stubbled cheek.

"If we take that gag off, are you going to keep quiet?"

Fervently, he nods.

Tellurith's fingers move. Undoing the tapes. Easing the cloth away. Blood and saliva splatters, a pang at the sight. Another at the stubble-blackened, battered mouth. "You *are* an idiot."

The head nods, eyes not opening. Yes.

"Zuri, what do we need with all these people?" Tellurith comes to reality with a jerk. "Leave me Azo. For everyone else—my thanks."

Zuri will see them made palpable. As the noise ebbs, Caitha mutters, "Hot liquids. Soup . . ." and vanishes to summon her own underlings. Only Iatha, quiet in the corner, remains.

Tellurith puts a finger on the webbing across his chest.

"If we undo these, there'll be no more nonsense? No fighting? No getting out of bed?"

A long sigh. Another nod.

"No more," her voice goes sterner, "running away?"

The eyes open, ink and ebony, alive now, too aware. Tellurith holds them, answering, Yes. You know exactly what I mean.

"I want to hear it. No more running away?"

The lids sink. The swollen mouth tightens. Resistance, awareness, surrender's last, painful relinquishment.

And then, barely audible, "No."

Tellurith feeds him the soup. Aware, too aware, of the weight of shoulders against her, his head on her arm. Heavier now in a different surrender. Knowing, feeling himself safe. A heavier weight than flesh ever had. Her commitment. Her obligation.

Her trust.

* * * *

"**Y**es," says Caitha, mildly puzzled, "he can stay in bed up there as easily—more easily than here. They can carry him up."

And with her prize ensconced in his former room, Azo on watch, a wary Shia preparing more soup, time till the midday break allotted, in the book, Tellurith sits down again on the bedside. And demands, "Why?"

The lifted eyelids, the reproachful expression answer, Must I spell it out? The mouth, lips scabbed and purple today, says painfully, "I just—couldn't stand—to be stuck here—"

"I can guess why you ran. Why did you stop?"

He averts his head. Shuts his eyes.

"I thought," Tellurith says very quietly, "we would have to hunt you down to the last step. Maybe shoot you, in the end. I thought you would—get through."

And this interrogator's commerce still functions. For his shoulders heave. He pulls his arm up. Speaks across it, finally, muffled, another, far harder surrender, only manageable from behind this barricade.

"There was— In the end . . . there was nowhere to go."

Shia brings the eternal soup and clears it away, while Tellurith chews on that. *Nowhere to go.* No restoration of memory. No way to re-thread the maze of whatever, whosoever intrigue brought him here. But enough remembrance to know it would be fatal, if his choice was a mistake.

Enough remembrance, and a high enough stake, for that proud, that fearfully resourceful, formidably subtle male personality to choose surrender instead.

Tellurith gets off the bed. As Azo comes, silent-footed, she says, "Let Caitha know. As soon as she judges her patient fit to reach the shaper's wing, tell Hanni, last morning appointment, and noon-break after. In the book."

* * * *

"**W**ere you born in this house?"

"Eh?"

The first evening he has been allowed up. Heavy snow on the Iskans yesterday, and a freight-carrier collision on frosted streets this morning that has given Tellurith leverage to postpone meeting the Thirteen. Dinner over, the convalescent chafing at more soup and salmon mousse, he has stretched himself on the rug. Conveniently distant for Tellurith to forget present reality, in brooding about its repercussions elsewhere.

"Were you born in this House?"

Laid out on his belly beside the heating vent like a drowsy boy. But no boy's idleness ever used those eyes.

Born here? "Yes." And the birth-cord never snapped.

Silence. Warily, Tellurith lets it stretch.

"How old are you?"

"How old are *you*?"

The parry is sheer reflex. But he frowns, considering.

"I've no idea. What comes to mind . . . is forty-three."

Tellurith adds quantities of body hair to weathered skin, subtracts boyish slightness, tops with that personality. Says with conviction, "Probably right."

Silence. Black eyes waiting, deep as lakes.

"By Amberlight count . . . I'm thirty-nine."

"Amberlight count?"

"Thirteen months and a dark to the year. We go by the moon."

Silence. Thought-chain destroyed, Tellurith is all too conscious of his presence. Impelled to take charge. "Do you remember family?"

A long pause. "I think . . . brothers. A feeling of soldiers—I think we moved a lot. I can see barracks . . . stone barracks. It feels like more than one."

"Our speech-assayer," she drops it, carefully casual, commerce returned, "thought you might have grown up in Verrain."

"Speech . . . !" Then, easing the startled breath into recovery. "You really did try everything. And *your* family?"

"I was an only girl."

"Are your parents . . ."

"My mother died—fifteen years ago." Seconding another novice cutter, when more than the ceiling came down. "My father . . . I see sometimes."

A slow, wary frown.

"In the tower?"

In Diaman tower. Glue for an old, a fading alliance. Tellurith nods. No point now in mentioning that.

The silence this time brings Shia in to clear away the after-dinner wine. Tellurith's chair pinches. She has tensed to move when it comes at last.

"Are you married?"

Carefully expressionless, Tellurith answers, "Yes."

He sits up, startled. Then the eyes widen. "You mean, he's in the tower too?"

Now it is her turn to stare. "Where else would he be?"

"Well, I thought—these are your apartments—"

It trails off in a frown. "When you said separate quarters, I never thought you meant husbands as well."

"It's only reasonable. His other wives want to see him sometimes."

His jaw drops. At the splutter, she cannot control her grin.

"Didn't they tell you that about Amberlight?"

"They—if they did, I lost it." He shoves hair back, grappling the shock. "God's eyes . . . how many does he—have?"

"We're a quincunx. Five. All in Telluir House."

He gulps. And thinks.

"So they aren't always in the one House."

"As often as possible." Especially for a House's head. "Otherwise, most often with a close-linked clan."

And don't ask how often I see him, or how often I've thought about him in the last three weeks.

"What about you?"

The silence is sinewed, abruptly, with old scars.

"I think—I was."

"Was?"

Too tightly, "Not now."

"Children?"

"No." Far too sharply. "You?"

"Not," says Tellurith bleakly, "now."

Silence. She is acutely conscious of his presence, the slight, lithe shape, the easy posture, one leg tucked under him, elbow on the lifted knee. Sharp-cut profile, against the pearl-flowers of the qherrique.

"Is 'Rith your name?"

"Eh?"

"The others call you Ruand. Is 'Rith your name?"

"Ruand means, House-head. My name," precisely, "is Tellurith."

Silence. Then, "Except to her."

"Except to Iatha. Yes."

Except to the House-steward, second-in-command, right-hand and alternate personality. Equal in experience as in Craft. Equal once, as partners, in love, in bed. Before the demands of family, of heirs and marriage-ties, drew them inexorably apart.

The silence deepens. Wind breathes beyond the frosted glass.

Very quietly, he says, "What's mine?"

Involuntarily Tellurith swings about. Stares into jet-black depths and pulls her vision back, to the thin marred face under its falling shadow-wing, to the expression that says he understands, understands the whole significance of what he has said.

And before she has time to hesitate, the qherrique, Amberlight, speaks through her. She says, "Alkhes."

Masculine version of Alkho, name and moon-phase and cutter's, House's, Amberlight's most sacred moment. The Dark. Moon-phase. The height of Crafter's hearing. High tide of woman's blood.

"Alkhes?"

"The Dark One."

The eyes are startled. Dryly, he says, "That's very good."

And Tellurith sits staring, her blood still roaring in its arteries, thinking, stunned, He doesn't feel it. He thinks it's just a pun, on his looks, on his forgetting. He doesn't understand what it means, to a woman, in Amberlight, around qherrique.

He doesn't know.

✳ ✳ ✳ ✳

"**I** assure the Thirteen, that when Telluir does find out, you will be the first to hear. In the meantime, there's nothing any of you can do that we can't improve. He was quite badly mauled in the Kora. It's more than bruises and wounds. There is absolutely no point in hauling him off, at the cost of superfluous distress and possibly a breakdown, to ask the same questions somewhere else."

"Except," Maeran's drawl is icy, "that the Thirteen speak for the City. And this is a threat to Amberlight."

"Is Telluir less a part of the City than Vannish?"

"Has Telluir behaved like a part of the City? Capture an outlander, a probably dangerous outlander, lose and reclaim him and now make wide and wonderful assertions when none of us have so much as laid eyes on the man?"

"If he was good enough to slip Telluir we must be careful!" Falla of Khuss weighs in, always quick to fright. "If he'd got away—if he'd reached Cataract—"

"He wasn't captured," Tellurith snaps. "He gave himself up."

"Because," she overrides the tumult, "he couldn't remember where he was supposed to go."

Slitted eyes. Then Zhee's slow, silvery tone. "You mean he knows it was too dangerous to mistake—going back?"

Time for the gamble again. Unavoidable, perilous. Tellurith meets Zhee's eyes. "That's what I believe."

Liony of Zanza and Sevitha of Iuras and several more burst into gabble. Tellurith's mind focuses on three. Zhee, immobile as a pile of sentient washing. Jura, scowling uncomfortably. Maeran's final-stab smile.

"If it is as serious as that, I suggest—I urge—he pass to the Thirteen's questioners. That we use serif—or any other persuasion needed—to restore this—his memory."

"No!"

"No?" The pause, the purr deepening. "Can Telluir House possibly have some stake—some other stake . . ."

"And can Vannish House possibly—possibly—want Dinda or the Emperor on their doorstep, asking how we came to torture, mutilate, perhaps murder a valued agent, a highly paid mercenary—maybe an Imperial officer?"

Liony of Zanza yelps, Diaman's Kuro lets out an aged, undignified squeak. Rolling a cool eye on them, Tellurith amplifies.

"Once, when he was drugged, he saluted—like an Imperial guard."

Consternation. Maeran's steel gaze overriding it. Into the first gap, she drawls, "The more reason to put the matter from the hands of one House into that of the Thirteen."

"The more reason," Tellurith lets her temper snap, "to leave a rotted fragile dangle where he just might recover enough to tell us something—before it's too late!"

And as always, when self-contained Telluir breaks, the earthquake is irresistible.

* * * *

"**Y**es, Ruand." She can feel Caitha's puzzlement. "He should be able to walk to the Shaper's wing. Tomorrow, or possibly today."

An easy walk for Tellurith, made every other day of her adult life: three floors down in the house, across the court, aswirl today with another ferocious southerly, the shapely flagstones strewn with leaves of fern. Athwart the shadow of the men's tower, coat gripped tight. Into the throat-catching scent of women's sweat and emery dust, countless cups of mint or cinnamon tea, long hours yarning. Or solitary contemplation. Or communion, in the heart's quiet, with the waiting piece. And the under-scent, ubiquitous, unforgettable. Worked qherrique.

The battered leather curtain swings behind them and she draws a long, easing breath. Remembers, and tallies with compunction the whitened lips and shaky limbs beside her, under wind-tangled hair the familiar beads of sweat.

"We always hurry when it's cold. Here . . ."

He resists a move against the wall. On his feet he is her height, which is not over-tall for Amberlight. Slighter, though, and whippy as a dueling sword. Or, a pang of imagination tells her, that was what he must have moved like once.

"I can stand up."

"So I see." She restrains tartness, with Verrith and Azo at their backs. "Get your breath before you try to walk."

The passage walls probably had color, before they were dusted by years, centuries of qherrique. Crafters' coats and cloaks festoon the pearl-grime, on age-blackened bronze hooks. The twilight ahead opens on a silver glow.

"The common-room." Unwashed cups, to-be-mended tools on the benches, their wood blackened by countless hands. A window on the garden, vista of pruned roses, a great green plunge of tree. A tunnel of striped, pearl-silver, pearl-grey light.

Short of the first door Tellurith checks. Raises her voice. "In the Work-mother's name."

A growl answers, "Come on."

As always, Ahio's back is to the door. Hunched over the bench, where the paraboloid mirrors focus their twin beams from the boss of qherrique glaring overhead. The paraphernalia of a work-shop fills the small square room whose heat grilles are the only vent. And the glow haloes her short, stocky body, throwing shadows from the tool-stands and worker's stool, flowing outward from the work-bench like the full of an earth-bound moon.

When he has had time to look but not to analyze, Tellurith says, "S'hur."

Ahio turns around.

Her left cheek, the left side of her head is seared by a broad white band of scar. A diamond stud, Crafter's defiance and honor and bravado, sparks in what is left of her ear.

In her low, grumbling voice, she says, "I ducked."

Do him justice, Tellurith decides. He must know what he is seeing. What no man of Amberlight, let be any Outlander, has ever seen. The workroom of an Amberlight House. The process nobody on the River has ever watched. But for all her probing intent, there is no sign of a flinch.

And he has the wit—the presence, the upbringing—not to move forward. Not to burst out in questions or sympathy. It is respect, as much as analysis, that informs the black, cool gaze.

Before he looks round to her. Raising a brow that asks, Closer? And when she nods to Ahio, her room, her work, he says, the perfect blend of respect and self-respect, "May I—"

Ahio's cheek muscles twitch. They all know he can, or he would not be here. But it is good manners, the respect.

"Stand here."

Tellurith comes to her other shoulder. The piece is just waning out of contact, brilliant pearl cooling to pre-dawn frost. The statuette is half roughed, the wide base and suggestion of skirt, the triangle of raised arms supporting the clumsy block that will provide the helical shafts of the thunderbolts. Ahio's shaper lies beside it, that no other soul will touch, until it goes with her to the pyre.

She can feel his body tense, read awareness of his fortune in every faint shift of jaw, cheek, flexing mouth. And follow the turn of his eyes.

"Is that what you use—"

Ahio palms the control-box, monumental, calm and knowing as her Head. "That's mine."

Protest is a swift, graceful swing of the head to Tellurith. Who says, "I said I would show you why qherrique is dangerous."

He knows quite well what a thin wire he walks. They are very long lashes, she notes, as well as sable-black. Politely, he turns his attention to the statuette.

Ahio surveys him, with an indulgence that says, Pretty, in her own turn. Glances at Tellurith. At her nod, says, "Touch it."

"Touch?"

"Carefully. One finger. Just touch."

He looks at Tellurith. At her blankness, extends a hand. A forefinger; thin, nail clipped and clean now, white skin that shows no manual labor's scar.

And kicked upward from the qherrique to one uncontrollable yelp, less of pain than surprise.

"You aren't House," says Ahio, calm without smugness or condescension. "Or blood. Or Craft."

His hand nurses its wringing fellow. The pain is obliterated in those black eyes' fire.

"It won't work for—it *repulses* strangers? Gods—!"

Ahio grins now, and lifts a hand to her scar. "Oh, it'll bite us as well."

This time, he gives her more than respect. "You didn't—you did it wrongly—what did—what *do* you do?"

Ahio flicks an eye at her Head. Sanctioned, says, "Can't just walk up and take a chisel to qherrique. It has to assent. You have to be in tune with it. And when you are—you have to ask."

"Ask—assent—Gods above." He must have stopped breathing. "You mean it *thinks*?"

Ahio grins. Slightly, warily. And makes the honor-sign before she replies. "The Work-mother knows what it does. We just know what works."

"Or if you don't get it exactly right—or if it regrets the assent," Tellurith murmurs, "what does not."

At amazement's leveled foundation, he can still raise his wits. "Can it—is that why the roof fell, in the mine?"

"Hah." Ahio applauds, the soft double-clap that is the accolade of Craft. "Got a bright one here."

"Mm," says Tellurith to both of them. "It can go that far."

"Gods' . . . eyes." Wonder beyond speech. And then the lance of intellect, quick as the lash of qherrique itself.

"Then how does any ruler get near the stuff?"

"It has to be tuned. I told you. To the person, in the flesh. Or to something they hold precious. There has to be—assent."

"They hold precious . . . So *that's* why Antastes parts up his beloved Prince!"

Black lightning, kingfisher-swift. A thunderbolt of mirth. As Ahio snorts Tellurith releases her own smile, ostensibly to the second point. "That," she agrees sweetly, "is why, every ninth year, the Emperor makes a hostage of his heir."

And as his teeth click in understanding of what he has just done, she takes his arm, inclines her head to Ahio and her piece alike, and wheels him neatly away.

✳ ✳ ✳ ✳

And having led upstairs at a pace that gags questions, she waits till he is settled across the table, before she says, "What do you know about Dhasdein?"

The eyes jerk up, ink-black. The white wine jerks, in the half-raised glass.

Before he sets it down. Shivers softly, the forgotten seals of trust and secrecy torn, if he cannot remember how. But all too aware that, for what he has been ceded, there will be—there must be—a sovereign price.

"Dhasdein."

Head bowed. Fingers clenched on the table rim. "Antastes . . . is the emperor."

"Can you see him?"

"Tall. Stooped. Except when he remembers, for ceremonies. Going grey."

"Do you see him close?"

"I—"

A deepened breath. Eyes pressed shut.

"I see him—close."

And for that, he knows the outrageous, the exorbitant cost.

"At a ceremony. In front of me. I must be—on the . . . dais."

"How are you dressed?"

A deeper breath. A look she has seen, when the physicians begin their work.

"Armor. Ceremonial. Breast-plate . . ."

"Trousers—or kilt?"

The clenched fingers tremble. She can barely hear the word.

"Kilt."

An officer, then. A cavalry officer, rather than a guardsman, even from the Imperial Guard.

So easy. So simple. So smoothly that she might, for less risk and a lesser gamble, have asked it weeks ago. The answer to all the questions. The heart of the dilemma. The summit of all problems.

Dhasdein.

His hands still grip the table-rim. What he has done, she knows, he understands perfectly well. And understands the raw courage that makes him lift his eyes.

But it is the qherrique that makes her go on, in the soft spell-voice, "How long ago?"

The lightless depths stir. The brows come up. Startled, the present man stares at her. "Gods, that was the

Flood-sacrifice"—autumn's end, Tellurith knows—"it must be eight years past!"

Then it is his turn to lie back in the chair, to breathe deep and wipe his face and savor mingled reprieve and infuriation. While Tellurith swallows disappointment. Dourly, prepares for the next gamble. "Do you remember the Imperial Guard?"

"I remember—guard-duty. I was new. Riversend. Gawpers outside the palace. Apricot marble. Very beautiful. But impractical. All those little perimeter towers. The palace quarter. So many high-class . . . trees and things. Expensive—very expensive wine-houses. I think—it's very new . . ."

"You were young ?"

"Very young—not my first post, of course. Not the Guard."

"Where was the first?"

The sweat is running, this time, glinting snail-tracks on the thin cheeks. She has no doubt that he is trying, with all his self, to meet the price.

"The first—I don't . . ."

"Where was the last?"

"Amberlight."

The eyes snap open. The body snaps tense. The hands clench, one on the table edge, one round the wine-glass. Verrith and Azo are in earshot. Tellurith sits quite still. Even at the face, she doubts she has been in greater danger in her life.

"Do you remember," almost in a whisper, "who gave it you?"

She is still holding her breath when the coal-black, steel-edged stare blurs. The body softens. And slowly, slowly, the hands undo. The head bends, that crow's-wing of hair hiding the expression as he whispers, "I don't know."

IV

Quarter moonrise on Amberlight, flooding up beyond the white and gold quilt of city lights. A silver-pearl and shadow hemisphere looks in Telluir House-head's window, under the great luminous window of the qherrique.

"What do you know about the provinces of Dhasdein?"

"Mel'eth. Riversrun. Shirran. Quetzistan. There's the colonies too, the Archipelago. Wave Island, Gray Island. Greenhill . . ."

"Wave Island?"

"A damned ship-breaking broker's tax, set by an Imperial governor and a pair of Imperial heptarchies!" Phalanx units, fifty men strong. "Imperial protection! Imperial blood-suckers! How many Wave Islanders ever taste their own wine?"

At Tellurith's raised eyebrow he growls and subsides. "Ah, you know how I feel . . ."

By now, she knows very well.

"Greenhill?"

"North of Gray. Ship-builders. The galleys are famous, but I don't think I've been . . ."

Inwardly, Tellurith sighs. Two sovereign states and an empire make a large haystack. Especially when she has begun to doubt that one needle will be clue enough.

"Shuya?"

"President of Verrain. A very—large—lady." Faintly, distractingly, now the black eyes smile. "With a reputation for, ah—intrigue." Shuya's list of lovers outdoes that of Dhasdein's Crown Prince.

"Do you see her?"

"A good Verrainer. Black as—Cataract mud. Likes a skau-weed pipe. Got a camel's roar of a laugh."

"Do you see her close?"

A very long pause. "Yes."

Tellurith suppresses the groan. But by now the process is routine. "How long ago?"

A deepening frown. "Recent . . . but not the first. I think—" he knuckles his eyes suddenly, "I think I served in Verrain. I remember desert. Those vile mud forts. Camels. Camels from here to the horizon, strings of them six deep . . ."

Guard-duty, border duty. Warding caravans.

"Tellurith, what can I do?"

"Eh?"

"It isn't going to come back. And if it did," the black stare is solid as a bar, "you said it yourself. You can't afford to let me go."

"Nothing's certain . . ."

"If you do, it can only be one way."

Her skin prickles. "That won't be necessary!"

"Not if I can do something—already am something—in Amberlight. What can I do?"

Tellurith's mouth opens to tell him and she yanks it shut.

"I think I was good with figures. I remember—organizing a campaign, once. Somewhere in Quetzistan. There must be something—in the House." He knows already that he may never be allowed outside. "Surely, you could give me a trial?"

Tellurith rubs the back of her head hard. Erases image of Iatha's, Maeran's, the Thirteen's faces. "Figures. A trial. Yes."

* * * *

"**T**hat's ten bolts silk and half an ingot copper, fifteen darrin minted coin, the discount's five percent. Take off three darrin for a chip Zeya made, shiftless cow . . . What's the running total, did you add that up?"

Hanni does not aim for cruelty. Told to take a raw off-sider, she has not flinched. Confronted with the Head's outlander, she does not so much as gulp. Ensconcing him with the counting-slate as she runs through yesterday's port-tallies, she is simply doing her job.

"I—uh—what was the conversion for silk?"

"Twelve darrin a bolt and you add a half if it's dyed. Did you—oh."

"Take a dose of sleep-syrup." Tellurith cannot help it. Coming round the dinner table, she begins to work her fingers into that hunched neck. "Don't expect to learn it all in a day."

His shoulders are wincing tight. At that, they droop. She feels him sigh.

"What is it?" Very quietly, her cutter's voice.

Silence. A struggle, she guesses, with masculine pride.

Then, bitterly, "No time may be enough."

Tellurith lets her fingers question, Why?

"I used to be quicker than that. I know—once, I could have picked this up in an hour—"

"Moon-mother's love, you're a week out of bed. For the second time, after a mess where you nearly died—"

Silence. Replying, too eloquently: *Where I lost more than blood.*

Tellurith says firmly, "Give it a few more days."

* * * *

"I'm sorry, Ruand." Hanni, quiet and competent as a Head's private aide has to be. And sure. "Maybe, one day he'll manage it. But it would be better if he learnt somewhere—less important."

"If I can take the risk—"

"It's not just his mistakes, Ruand." Hanni's eyes meet hers, the steady golden-brown of Amberlight. "I'm worried about mine."

Having a man around. Where no man should be, in the workplace of an Amberlight House.

Apprentice to some other number-head, no. Degrade to housework, even supply calculations, no. Yet what else is safe, demanding enough, possible, for an ex-soldier, high military agent, too intelligent mercenary who has already eluded the defenses of the House?

Defenses. Yes.

"Azo," says Tellurith as her minder pads past, "would Alkhes make troublecrew?"

Azo's jaw drops. They are used to the name, now. And it does, Azo confides in an unguarded moment, make it easier to avoid 'the dangle' at inopportune times.

"Mmm, if he was stronger." As she ponders it, a glint shows. "Tell you what, Ruand. Wouldn't take much."

* * * *

Waning moon on Amberlight, presiding over Tellurith's table, an over-ripe golden globe. A Tellurith distracted from House worries by that neat, new-washed presence across the plates, with its innocent black stare and its indubitably swollen nose.

"Rot and gangrene, Azo, I didn't say, Dent his face!"

A splutter from the kitchen. Opposite her a bubbling chuckle, the first spontaneous sound of joy she has ever heard him make.

"It *is* a trouble-school, Tel."

"*Tel?*"

The grin broadens. "I can't very well use 'Rith."

"Blighted impudence. Use 'Ruand.' You're nothing but a raw recruit!"

She scowls tremendously. As convincingly as the thunderous tone. The black eyes sparkle, a youthful imp's. As once by that bed-side, something clenches on her heart.

"I did think I was *half*-cooked . . ."

Azo and Tellurith chorus, "Ha!"

And he laughs outright, softly, unmistakably, and begins to describe the bout, with malicious awareness of his silenced audience. With a gaiety, a fulfillment that briefly obliterates her own skirmish for the day.

A special Thirteen-meet. Dinda has sent an embassy, direct from Cataract. A highly influential embassy, with presents to entice and military muscle to impress, for a tyrant whose subjects pour downRiver in search of work and life, who is in the stick-fork of desperately needing Amberlight and ardently desiring its ruin.

"His statue," Eutharie of Prathax complains superfluously, "doesn't wane until next summer."

"And now he wants the new one before spring." Quite as needlessly Denara of Winsat taps the blazoned parchment. "And bigger as well!"

Kuro goes to the heart of it. "What's he going to pay?"

"Thirty silver ingots—"—"Higher barter-rate—"—"Workers, that's ridiculous—!"—"He's got nothing else—!"

The voices form their usual melting pot. And suddenly, inexplicably but absolute as the qherrique's own, another voice fills Tellurith's ears.

"Does anyone," she finds herself demanding, "care what he does with it?"

Silence: eyes slanted, in polite embarrassment; disbelief.

At that expression part of her rises in incomprehensible rage. Part of her knows what to do next, part of her knows where the impulsion is coming from, even as some other, saner element howls, What are you *doing*?

"We know—now—they use them on each other. Do we ever ask," memory of the Dhasdein kinglet complacently tallying his salt-cakes, his copper ingots, his minted gold. Suppressed image of their price winding out across his province's western waste. Verrain's slave caravans. Irate outland voice detailing the Imperial military grip upon Wave Island, source of that luscious red wine. "Do we ever ask what they do to their lands?"

Silence again.

Until Denara in the president's chair averts her eyes as from some obscenity, and says, carefully blank, "Amberlight's work is to ease the work of ruling. To see our work is given in good faith."

"And what about the taker's faith?"

"If we interfere in the business of sovereign states—how long can we expect them to respect ours?"

* * * *

"**S**top her!"

Querya's response is pure reflex. A snatch, a twist, bringing a strangled yell in reply. But with the catch made, seasoned troublecrew turns and frankly stares. Her second and back-watch, Desis cannot look away from the alley-mouth, but her neck shouts, What in the pits!

"Bring her here."

Querya brings her, fighting like a maniac. Ten, twelve, fourteen? Who could guess, in River Quarter winter rags, with River Quarter starvation under the gapped teeth, the snarls of hair, the screaming face wizened with panic as much as famine and cold? The only certainty is that dart and cannon off a House-head foolish enough to sortie down an unscouted alleyway; and if she really thought to snatch a Head's brooch from her very lapel, was it madness that drove her?

Or what depth of need?

"What were you trying to do?"

River Quarter beggar. Uphill Head. What could she explain? What could Tellurith hear? The screams intensify, losing all coherency. The only thing she understands is her fate.

"Rot and gangrene . . ."

Tellurith grabs a shoulder, and through the ensuing convulsion, stares.

At her own hand, clean, manicured, brown against the gold-brocaded cuff of her double-wool, fur-lined winter coat. Her daytime winter coat. Against the sodden ruck of cotton, with some sort of wadding under it, over a shoulder thinner than a bird's. At the gold buckle of her boot, next to that filthy blue-tinged foot thrashing in the mud.

Tellurith opens her hand. Her mouth opens to say, "Iatha, give her—"

Ten fiels, fifty fiels, thirty silver darrin. A hundred? More?

"Let her go."

The child hurtles like a loosed wolf into the alley-mouth. Querya's eyebrows actually rise before she looks away.

Tellurith grunts and heads back to the vehicle by the warehouse door. Feeling the middle-winter southerly scythe about her ribs, the splatter of gathering rain. Hearing her own words, up in that exquisitely warm noonday workroom, how long ago?

We are one city, with a limited number of folk, and a great deal of land. A great deal of wealth.

Dispossessed clan-folk. Docker brats. Outland jetsam. Why can't the Quarter expose boy-babies like the Houses do? They *know* too many men make trouble. Why can't they ever learn?

She stares around her, at the bedaubed warehouse wall, the obdurately cleared and paven freight-way and the filthy alley behind her, the warehouse manager, snug in an outdoors coat to see her off, the scatter of unemployed stevedores beyond, hunched and crowded, shivering, in a wind that speaks to the marrow of snow.

A great deal of wealth.

Her brows come down and stay there in a slow, enduring frown.

* * * *

"**A**h—Ruand—where do we go from here?"

Verrith has waited to intercept her, in the main hall, behind the massive outer doors, first bulwark of the House. Swirled in on rain and snow-wind from another dock-side sortie, Tellurith is reluctant to stop. But Verrith would not be here without cause.

"He knows all the hand-to-hand stuff. He just had to remember street fighting . . . ambushes . . . tactics. What now?"

Tellurith stands between the inner door-wards and a very ugly presentation bust of some ancient Head, her retinue jammed at her heels. Knowing the lore-path of troublecrew as well as Verrith does: after hand-to-hand fighting, weapons. Blades, slings, bows. Hand-guns.

Guns firing light.

Powered by qherrique.

"And if he *could* use a weapon, Ruand," Verrith's eyes are anxious now, "what about the rest?"

The lore of House lay-out, weak spots, exits and entry-ways, passwords and guard-routines. Troublecrew's secrets. The heart of the House.

Tellurith swipes at mud on her leggings, silver-threaded leaf-brown, daubed with broad black spots. "Leave the guns out. Teach him," her tongue stumbles, her breath stops. She wrenches her will past. "Teach him the rest!"

"'Rith, I have borne with all the other idiocy, but this is too much."

Iatha's quirk, the House-steward's apartment has a long dormer window, with a garden view. Over the tower's shaft of fretworked light, Tellurith can just catch the glow, as of a pearl-fed fire. Qherrique, dreaming in the rain.

She takes another sip of wine-cut coffee and wriggles her stockinged toes. "Shall I tell him to count bullocks in the Kora, then? Give him a rice-planter's stick? Send him down to the wharf?"

"Put him in the tower!"

The snap speaks a demand long restrained. The silence adds, Where he belongs.

"'Rith, for the Mother's love. Zuri's having pups. An outland dangle, taught the passwords—knowing the House-ways—the troublecrew's ways—and this of all dangles, of all outlanders, oh, for the Mother's love, 'Rith, think!"

Open anguish. A plea from her oldest friend. From the conscience, the other heart of the House.

Black eyes glowing, smiling, a lithe wiry body losing its uncertainty, regaining command and skill and life.

"Iatha—he's not like our men. And he's not back to—usual— even yet. Rot it, he's got a mind that eats things like fire. If we keep him, we have to give it fuel.

"Or else," cold now, a rock's certainty, "he'll find it. And it'll be worse than running away."

"Then for the Mother's love, put him where we can control it! In the tower!"

"No!"

****

Zuri is more amenable. Alkhes is a fine brawler, an excellent street-fighter, with a leader's wits, she would be happy to have him on her crews any time.

"Except?"

Zuri files her nose again.

"Is it the guns?"

Zuri's eyebrows make one short tic. "With a sleeve-sling, with a throwing-knife, he could beat most of us to a shot." Tellurith's belly jerks. "We mostly use guns long-distance anyway. And if it comes to it, he need never go outside."

"If it comes to it?"

"Ruand—the problem is the crews."

Tellurith looks away. Across her work-table, to the piled records on Hanni's desk.

"They don't like," Zuri's voice is normal now. Quite expressionless. "An outlander," she picks words like a cat across puddles, "an—unproven—outlander . . . so far into the House."

An outlander whose loyalties are both unproven and unknown. And can never be wholly fixed.

Unless they are proven dangerous beyond all doubt.

"All my crews would be happy," Zuri's eyes affirm it, "to train, to work out with him. Tactics, unarmed combat, anything but guns. I couldn't ask better. But beyond that . . ." And now the House's warden, the troublecrew's Head, speaks at last. "Ruand, it isn't safe."

* * * *

"**T**rain for fighting. But not fight."

Her heart bleeds. To quench that joy, that anticipation, that quick, sure, renewed life. To watch the glow, like ebony qherrique, die in those black eyes.

"Alkhes . . ."

He stands up and goes to the door. Inadequate words to catch the fluid upward twist, the perfectly balanced transit into motion, the supple silent stride. Re-tempered. A dueling sword.

"It's an honorable place—"

He whips round. Against blue noon-sky he is a slight, shirt-haloed silhouette.

"I don't want honor, Tellurith. I want to do something!"

Biting her lip, she measures a breath.

"Can you be a freight-checker? A loading-master? A stevedore?"

She can sense the glower.

"You want a job in the Kora? Shearing sheep? Growing rice?"

"Damn it, Tel!"

"Or the quarries out at Iskan? Are you a stone-cutter? A carver? Do you know masonry?"

"Do I—by the gods, yes! Yes! Iskan! Quarry's up the ranges, right in among the snow! Eucalyptus smell—those big white helliens, always dropping bark. I was there for—anyway, I learnt stonework! Yes!"

He is practically dancing in the door. And before she can out-flank this he has caught her hands, pulling her from her chair. No time for alarm at that new strength, the latent danger that doubtless has Azo on her toes. "Tel, let me try the pearl-rock. The qherrique."

Tellurith does not gasp. Does not yell. When her breath comes back, just stares into those black eyes, so vividly alive now, urgent with all of a whole, redoubtable man's energy, palpable as an embrace.

"If I'm not fit to sculpt, I could do the rough stuff. Cut panels. Work in the mine . . ."

Nor does she scream and hide her eyes. Just says it, baldly, trying to make her lungs fill.

"Men don't work qherrique."

"I could do it—! Damn it, Tel, I could learn to make contact or whatever you do—at least let me try!"

"No."

"Gods *damn*, Tellurith! That's what's wrong with this whole blighted city. Ingrained, nailed-down, built-in, stone-weighted—prejudice!"

It comes like a qherrique blast. Harder than the hurling away of her hands, the charge across room to spin and skewer her, black eyes flinging their own thunderbolt.

"Men heave bales and carry ingots and pull oars and tally freights—men butcher cattle, men shear sheep, men weave wool and—and—I've seen them!" The voice is hissing now. "Men can do anything in the thrice-damned City—except in this House!"

Something is stifling within her. Struggling for breath. Yet she sounds perfectly calm. Even quiet.

"Or any other House. Men don't work qherrique."

They don't use it either, she wants to say. They don't cut the slabs or shape the statuettes or install the power panels, they don't drive the vehicles or fire the light-guns or sail Navy ships. But something, the qherrique or something wholly within herself, holds the words in her throat.

The tantrum has intensified. Become that soft, contained deadliness.

"So what *do* your men do?—whore?"

Some greater blockage in her throat now. Perhaps it is pain.

"Uphill men don't work. It's—indecent—for them to be seen outside the House."

His lips part. Even that black ice half-thaws, under the shock.

"Decent House-men," it comes out so calmly, so precisely, "stay in the tower. They have a gymnasium. A library. They spend a lot of time—training the boys. Preparing for—visitors. House-men are very particular about clothes. Body-oils. Scents. Their grooming. Their hair—"

"Hair!"

"A decent man doesn't *want* to work qherrique! He can hold a conversation, he can play a flute, he can please a wife! He's raised to honor his family and respect his wives—"

"And what happens when he gives them sons?"

There is a silence so deep Tellurith thinks it has sucked out the air. She hears Shia in the kitchen. She feels her blood pump. She knows, with awful certainty, that her face is turning white.

And his is answering, the tumbled hair grown blacker and blacker, the eyes hollowed into chalk-set pits.

"Is that what happened to yours?"

Fainter than breath. Yet it seems to sear her heart.

Her body and her awareness have parted company. Very far away, someone else has assembled the words.

"House women—must bear a daughter first."

He does not speak. Is not breathing. She confronts a seeing, thinking corpse.

Tellurith can only watch, in that remote, ringing quiet. As very carefully, very slowly, he lowers a half-raised hand. Turns away. Walks, with the conscious care and slow-motion gait of the critically wounded, out the apartment door.

* * * *

"'Rith?"

Sun-fall on Amberlight, winter-hastened, an ice-blade wind, an iciest lavender, peacock green and frost-burn vermilion sky. Across her balustrade, Tellurith regards it with vague surprise.

"Mother rot . . ." Mutter, lost obscenity. "'Rith," incongruously gentle, "come inside."

Her limbs are numb. Her face aches. Someone has amputated her ears. Stumbling over the threshold, she computes a House-head's lost afternoon, unscheduled, telescoped. And no one has said a word.

"Coffee, Shia."

It burns to her stomach's base. Laced with liquid fire.

"Rot and gangrene you, Iatha!" she splutters, when she stops coughing. "Kzensis would have done!"

Raw Korite barley spirit. Iatha's face swims into focus. Taut and hard, but now, unaccountably, smug.

Memory comes back. Blasting away speech.

"'Rith. It's all right."

Iatha is patting her. As Iatha patted her the day the mine fell, after they got her mother out. As Iatha has patted her, beside the birth bed, each time she bore a child.

"Soup."

And as in the birth-ward, she eats.

And wakes.

"Calm down, you needn't call the Navy. Your cockerel's still in the coop."

"What—how—"

"Came to roost in the garden, in an Imperial sulk. When it got late, Zuri and I put him in the tower—Sit down!"

"Iatha!"

This time the hiss cuts no ice. Iatha confronts her, with a glower she knows too sinkingly well.

"Iatha, what did you say?"

"I told him," the glower has become a jut-jawed glare, "a few things he needed to know. That you didn't build Amberlight. That the customs of the City are not your choice. That every mother who ever bore a baby dies when she loses a child. That you never asked to be House-bred, any more than you asked to throw three sons. That I'll tear his tripes out and feed them to him, in white sauce, on a plate, if he ever mentions it again."

"Oh, Yath." She is struggling, lungs blocked, throat choked, vision lost. Somewhere she hears Iatha's growl. Then they are locked in each other's arms, squeezing each other's breath out, catching each other's tears.

"Pox-rotten whore's-get dangle, Mother blight his—"

She surfaces. It is Iatha, still tear-choked, comfort beyond expression, rumbling in her ear. "Wipe your face, 'Rith. You look like jam on an alley-whore's plate. Want to wash?"

"No, I—"

"'Rith, wash your face."

And when she erupts from the bathroom, broken appointments howling on her heels, Iatha blocks her rush and says, blank-faced, "Not yet, 'Rith. Someone to see you, here."

Past her shoulder black hair, white shirt fill the doorway, and all the air leaves Tellurith's lungs.

The shirt is ripped. There is a blur, a definite scrape, running down his cheek. 'Zuri and I,' she would warrant, ran to five or six more. It is in the way he stands, too still, with Verrith and Azo close at his back. Too close.

"Tellurith?"

It takes all a House-head's composure to say, "Come in."

Carefully, too carefully, he obeys. Aware of those living restraints, so near. But out in full light, she sees the ashen face. The look in his eyes. Daze, darkness. As if he has been hit on the head.

"Tellurith, I—"

He swallows.

Then says quite simply, "I'm sorry," and turns on his heel.

"Where are you going?"

He stops dead.

When she waits, he turns about. In his shirt-sleeves, he looks about twenty years old. But what speaks is a grown, comprehending, accepting man.

"It would be better if I was . . . elsewhere."

In the tower. Iatha's work. Extreme, extravagant recompense. Literal sacrifice. Suddenly it is too much to unravel tonight. Tellurith flaps an arm at him, at them. "It would be better if you go where you belong. Azo, Verrith, see he gets there. In his room. In bed."

* * * *

It is a relief to miss him at breakfast. After a long mind-filling day, to have a dinner engagement as well. Something of a surprise to see nothing of him next day. At a fourth peaceful breakfast, she begins to feel concern.

When it appears that he has been dutifully if fiercely working out with the troublecrews, she dares to hope. Until, at dinner that week's end, she finally gets a look at his face.

A very subdued face. Her presence, no doubt. Yet watching him under her lashes, she feels another, painful certainty. That dulled look is more than fatigue, more than her proximity. If he is doing what he is supposed to, it is not by choice.

"Tellurith?"

She has looked too long. The black eyes are very big. Dangerously astute.

"Is something wrong?"

"Not," she says at last, "with me."

Imperceptibly his muscles relax. Iatha's scouring must have gone very deep. But then he goes tense all over. Sets down his knife.

"Tellurith . . . I am trying."

"Oh, rot it, I know you are." Her shirt collar has begun choking her, her plait drags at her head. I don't want you to try, she wants to bawl, I want you to be in love with it, I want you to be what you

were before, even what you were before Amberlight, who wants to
tame a hawk and watch it moult inside a cage?

He is on his feet. The eyes pin her, a black, aching uncertainty,
a physically painful hope.

"Tel." He is barely whispering. "Is there—something else?"

For a moment time crystallizes, as at the face. She is aware,
quite clearly, of her body, which has its own hungers, tidal, imperious; that she is a day into the Dark, and that body is saying, apolitical, amoral, heedless: I want. Of the backlash from the
previous hurt, the old wound that demands its own easement, an
equally torturing hope. And under these, that Amberlight, the
qherrique, that queer wordless certainty, is saying: Go on.

She is intensely aware of Azo, Verrith's surveillance, Shia in
the kitchen, a more public moment in a House-head's never more
than token privacy. And that this is one of the craziest risks to
House safety and personal pride she has taken in a gambler's life.

She gets out of her own chair. Walks round the table. Her heart
is hammering loud enough to time a galley's oars. He watches her,
not moving. Except the eyes get bigger and bigger, and as she
comes close she feels a wild creature's, a trained killer's reaction,
his whole body hair-trigger tense.

She is inside, right inside, his danger space. One wrong move,
every tiny shift of stance tells her, and she could be dead.

Tellurith reaches out, as she has wanted to do from that first
moment in Exchange Square, and draws her fingers through the
black wing of forward falling hair.

A tang of rosemary, a whiff of hard-worked, newly-washed
man. A slide of warm silk, outland fine, outland straight. Lightly,
slowly, her palm follows down the curve of his jaw.

His breath stops. Then he leaps as if cut with a whip. One
backward spring and grace lost with composure in frantic stumbling flight to an almost soundless, "No!"

* * * *

Awake and fuming two hours later, the noise makes Tellurith
plunge nearly as far.

Not a shout. Not a scream. A wildcat yowl so hideous it yanks
her athwart Azo's charge down the passageway and spins her off
the wall to find the door in Azo's wake.

Verrith's shoulder bounces her the other way. In time to clear
the rebound as Azo doubles over, clutching belly, Verrith hurdles
her fall and Tellurith bawls, "Alkhes!"

A black and white whirlwind flashes an unrecognizable un-recognizing face. A grabbed arm back-hands Verrith into the door. Azo lurches up. Tellurith is just in time to snatch before that scream and lunge reach the knife. As he hurls himself bodily the sheet wraps his waist, Verrith knees his down-crashing ribs, Azo lands full force on his back and Tellurith jumps for his head.

"Alkhes!"

He head-butts, he bites. She doubts intention now. Like that night in the infirmary, he is quite beside himself. Azo pins the earthquake, Verrith flings hobbling ropes of sheet. And in three or four endless minutes he is out of breath.

"Alkhes?"

The shuddering convulses him, violent as falling sickness and as involuntary. Panic turns to compunction as she changes her hold, patting his cheek, finding her cutter's voice. "It's all right, it's only me, you're all right."

The tremors ease. For one moment rigored muscles melt. Then he makes another sound of pure terror and tries to rip his head away.

"Alkhes, rot it!" More than compunction now. "I won't touch you." Blatant falsehood, panging guilt. But the tone should be clear enough. "It's all right. You're safe."

Finally they get him unwound. Azo's lip is staunched, Ver-rith's ribs checked, to nearly incoherent apologies. The bed is re-assembled, some verrian tea made, mild sedative. Azo and Ver-rith depart amid reassurances. Clutching the mug, he hunches on the bed. And Tellurith, unable to help herself, sinks down behind him, rubbing his shoulders, trying to convey comfort, reassurance, apology, through the newly-donned shirt.

It slides over muscle-shape, solid physical presence, human warmth. Whose inner flinch, whose willed acceptance of her touch, hurts worse than the blows.

"I'm sorry."

It is all she can find to say.

For a fearful moment she thinks the offer has been refused. But then he turns his head to her, and those eyes are vistas of the outer dark, haunted, hunted by ghosts.

"Tel . . ."

The cup starts to shake. She has just time to catch it before the wave catches up.

"I dreamt . . . I was back there. I thought . . ."

Exchange Square.

The gang. The rape.

"I *remember*, Tel."

She gets an arm around him before she loses the cup. Has time to thank the Mother that whatever else she has cost him, this refuge remains. And a far longer time to hold him, arms clinging for grim death round her waist, while she strokes hair and cheek and wipes sweat off as anonymously and impersonally as on those flagstones; before the aftermath finally ebbs away.

She coaxes him into the bed, then. In the qherrique's night-cycle glow he looks ridiculously young and defenseless, big black eyes against the pillow, reluctant to release her hand. But when she offers, "I could stay," he literally flinches; before he manages, with a semblance of composure, "No, no . . . I'll be all right."

* * * *

"**T**ellurith."

"What are you doing here!"

A grey winter morning on Amberlight, beyond the balustrade a leached prospect of soaked city and sweeping rain. Grey morning inside, where Tellurith has entered her workroom grimly bent on business. To find her trust, obligation, desire, embarrassment, ensconced in Hanni's place.

"I'm your first appointment. In the book."

"You—you—"

Wit and effrontery enough to circumvent her and suborn her secretary and coolly infiltrate her system as he needs. Tidy, shaven and somber as if he really were here to discuss freights.

"I just want to know, Tellurith—why?"

After a moment's thought she shuts the door. He rises. Comes to meet her, in the workroom's heart.

"I should have thought 'why' would be obvious."

"Maybe it would—with anyone else."

"Eh?"

"You're a House-head. I've started to learn what that means. And if just—that—is all there is to it . . . it wouldn't be you, Tellurith."

Distract him, before those wits work. The heart thumps over in her chest.

"You did want to be some use."

She has seen him pale but never blush. The red suffuses like a sunrise, up under the ebony forelock from the very base of the throat. It does not touch his wits.

"*Don't* try to off-side me! You do it far too often. What—else—was in it for you?"

She takes two steps, turns, and leans on her desk front. Cool now, as at the face.

"Do you remember, now, what you know about serif-juice?"

"Used for interrogation. You pour it into cuts. A half-inch nick can burn like—molten lead. And it goes on burning. After eight or ten . . ."

He rubs a hand sharply over his face. "What's this to do with . . ."

"The Thirteen want to question you. Telluir's unfriends are convinced they could revive your memories. They wanted you from the start. Ever since you ran away I have been fighting tooth and claw to keep you out of the City's hands; because they are convinced, now, that you are some vantage to the House. Every day without certainty of who and what you are increases the pressure. If they get you, the first thing they will use is serif-juice."

The sharp-cut face is ashen. But the wits remain.

"So if you—if I—"

"It would give me," says Tellurith gently, "a much more plausible excuse."

"More plausible! They'll think you've gone crazy—they'll push twice as hard!"

Tellurith shakes her head. "An infatuated Head is a known quantity. Much less dangerous than some secret gain to the House."

He opens his mouth and stops. His eyes narrow.

"Because a Head—would still put the House first?"

There is irony in her smile. More in his response.

"Nice to know my worth."

Tellurith lets her eyes repeat the night's offer. He stares at her; those wits, she is too sure, working through, deducing far too much.

Then he shivers suddenly, painfully, and almost involuntarily backs a step. "Once I would have—once I could have—but after—" his throat jerks. "No. Not even for serif-juice. No."

* * * *

Tellurith lets it go. Has to let it go, embroiled in a sudden fracas over Dinda's embassy. Where the Thirteen's special meet goes to old sores and profane insults, and finally, a vote.

All too clearly she reads the faces when at the end of her impassioned refusal, Denara demands, "How does Telluir House vote?" And when Tellurith shouts, "Telluir House votes, NO!" Denara ends the deadlock by casting the president's vote to supply the statuette.

And giving the contract to Vannish House.

"Not to worry, 'Rith." Iatha is not mystified, far less showing a sign of reproach. Much worse; she is unwontedly, all but hysterically flippant. "Next thing we'll have Shuya's people up here, and after throwing the balance that badly she'll have to give Verrain's piece to us."

Appalling them both, when, not three days later, an embassy rides in, winter traveling from Assuana, the Verrain capital, with that very demand.

Tellurith slams her fist into the window. Glass reverberates, Shia drops a liqueur decanter, Iatha almost leaps out of the lounging cushion.

"Blight and blast!"

Iatha glances over her shoulder. But Tellurith's outland aberration is off with Azo and Verrith. On quasi-patrol.

"If this is—what it looks—we can't let it pass."

A coalition. Preparing, with new resources, for another onslaught on their power's source.

"But if—"

Iatha stops. Tellurith spins around. The qherrique veins fluctuate, soft and customary and anomalous, in the warmly breathing wall.

"If the rest is what we think—what in the Mother's name can we say—out loud?"

About a possible House's treachery, still untraceable—before the hypothetical House?

Iatha looks down at her hands, clamped around the wine-glass, and lets silence answer for her: You are Ruand. The decision—and the words—are yours.

Tellurith draws breath. Sets her own glass down, delicately, on the abandoned table, and as she walks past, yanks Iatha's hair.

And says deliberately, "Well, Yath . . .. The risk is greater—here than there."

So Telluir House makes only a token objection when, after a positively rudimentary consultation, on her last day as president, Denara does exactly as Iatha has foreseen.

Which at the Moon-meet brings a vociferous demand from Vannish, backed by Khuss, Winsat and Zanza, that Telluir hand over its outland prisoner as proof that collusion and bribery have not corrupted the Thirteen.

* * * *

"**W**hat's the matter, Tel?"

She comes to with a start. One evening in five home from a whirl of politicking, she has been tired enough to fall in the lounging cushion after dinner, set the little glass of thick brown liqueur aside and forget his presence in tracing her problems on the entwined qherrique. Beyond the window, the moon rides out of cloud-mist, an icy silver scimitar, slicing, dismembering, gone. The last winter moon. Nine days past full.

She has meant to dissemble, minimize. Fatigue, perversity— nothing to do with the line of his jaw against the qherrique's half-light—makes her say baldly, "Trouble. With the Thirteen."

"About me."

Her nod brings a sharp quiet. Before he gets up, pacing to the outer door. Her eyes note the motion, almost clumsy, the tension that roughens his stride. Her mind, or something else, says maliciously, Let him suffer. I do.

"If you'd let me do something—in the House."

"I offered you something in the House."

"Dammit, Tel, let me work with Zuri's crew! That's one thing I can do! They know I can, else why ask for me to train with them? For the gods' sake, if I can train them, why can't I work with them for real?"

She looks up at him. Poised now, the slight lithe figure balanced and eager as a hawk. A weight settles on her heart.

"I would make you troublecrew, and be delighted." Each word feels heavy as a fistful of gold. "They refused. They don't want an outlander," she omits, man, "that nobody can be sure of, taken so far into the—trust of the House."

It is a measure of the hurt, she knows, that he says nothing at all.

"I may be sure of your faith. They may be sure of it. But of your memory—can even the Mother be sure?"

Silently, he turns away.

"Alkhes," suddenly she is angry, knowing, flowing with the fatigue, the pre-Dark testiness, "we could all be a blighted sight surer, if I had you in my bed."

She knows it a mistake before her lips close and can only silently curse. As he flinches physically and starts backing, his voice suddenly hoarse. "No—dammit, no!"

* * * *

It is Zuri who brings intelligencers' confirmation of Tellurith's own guess: that under the thrust of Vannish animosity and the unresolved threat of outland mystery, Telluir's coalition has begun to crack. Jerish is wavering. Diaman, never strong-minded, is fading with Kuro's age. Even Jura is dubious. And who can predict unquestioning, unreasoning loyalty from Zhee?

When Zuri has gone, Tellurith walks out on the balcony. She is still propping the balustrade, watching vehicles move through the sunlit afternoon streets, when Iatha arrives.

Having bent her elbows on the stone a while, she asks, "Cutter fixed?"

"Charras. Third day into Alkho."

Charras is an old, accomplished hand. For a slab like this, they will need it. Iatha nods.

And says, quietly, sliding the stiletto in, "'Rith, put him in the tower."

Tellurith turns round, very slowly. Trying not to burst into spontaneous flame.

"Zuri says so. Ahio says so. We've all read the intelligence reports. It's poisoning the Thirteen. It's starting to poison the House. Not just troublecrew. The shapers are nervous. They'll infect the power-shops, can't keep them apart. Once that happens—won't matter if you're right or wrong, 'Rith. They'll say it's bad judgment. And you can't head a House—with doubt."

Only Iatha could say this without going over the balustrade. She knows it. She stares, jaw out-thrust, into her Head's face.

The noise of the city rises like water round them, percolating from the busy streets.

"Thank you," says Tellurith, too softly, "for your advice."

Iatha shuts her eyes a moment. "I'm sorry, 'Rith." It is genuine pain. "I'm trying to do what's best."

* * * *

It is a long time before Tellurith goes inside. Down through the house, out, ignoring appointments, to the Shapers' wing.

Quira meets her just inside the door. An uncovenanted, unsolicited visit, but her aides and scribers are alert enough. As Quira rolls up with that old lazy stride, Tellurith nods, age-smoothed acknowledgement, to an ally who needs no other courtesy.

And catches that flicker before the smile comes, quick as a fish's passing in those chestnut eyes.

Down the corridor, then; familiar smells, sounds, faces. To the silence of communion, the closeted flicker that signals, Cutting, under a shut door. The familiar snatches of conversation, who is at work, who finished yesterday, who just had fingers nipped.

To the silences, the sudden, uncertain sentences, the effort with which they meet, or the involuntary aversions with which they dodge her eyes.

Tellurith farewells Quira and heads across the court.

When Sfina walks her out of the Power-shop, she nods in formal farewell, before she turns away.

No need to take it further. Not for one whose ear is attuned to the assent, or the refusal, of qherrique.

$$* * * *$$

It is a longer time before Tellurith goes back inside. Her feet have taken her to the garden first. Childhood sanctum, adolescent pleasure, adult refuge place. Pacing among the brown, pruned rose-beds, along paths littered with hellien debris or paved with the redolent waste of pines. The wind in their boughs is an airborne ocean, familiar as the rumble of wind-mills as each surge tops Dragon Spur. Familiar as the House around her, the buildings and functions and people she has worn so long they have become fitted to her like an old, malleable coat.

Presently she goes back upstairs. Tells Hanni to cancel her evening appointment. And sends a message to the troublecrew.

"Tellurith?"

He comes out to her on the balcony, above the glitter of city lights. A slight, dappled shadow in the zone between moonlight and qherrique, entering, warily as a predator, the one place in the apartment where a Head may be nominally alone.

"You wanted me?"

Without turning, Tellurith props both hands on the balustrade. Whatever she feels, it comes out quiet.

"Alkhes. Have you—could you—think again?"

She hears his indrawn breath. But the voice is quiet.

"More trouble?"

She nods. Gathers her voice. Turns about.

"I can fight the Thirteen and hope to win. I am still fighting. Even though we are losing support. But I can't fight my House as well."

The shadow goes tense.

"My Craft-heads, my s'hurre . . . if they won't back me, I have no choice."

He has grown very still. Now he lifts his head a little, with a curious suppling of bone and muscle that bizarrely suggests relief.

"So it's that one way?"

She is a moment understanding. Then she nearly slaps his face.

"Rot and gangrene you, do you think I'll see anyone—*anyone*—who has my protection, turned off like a—a—rice-cropper's pig?"

It does not soothe her to hear the little choke of laughter before the slightly breathless, "No. No, I don't. But if not that, Tel—then what?"

Tellurith gestures. When Azo and Verrith melt out into the dusk he starts like a frightened beast. But they are already between him and the balustrade.

"Alkhes, I can't keep you here any longer. I can't let you go. I won't have you—removed. So . . . it has to be the tower."

His limbs give one small, involuntary jerk. She does not need light to know what is in his eyes.

Iatha has threatened, Zuri has straitly forbidden it. In the flow of the moment, the qherrique says, Yes. Her own heart is almost impossible to deny.

"Alkhes." Close, too close, in striking range, so close she can feel his body heat, the touch of his breath. The sliding silk of that black hair under her fingers. Knowing herself wholly at the mercy of a killing strike, a ransom snatch, that her whole plan, her life, her House, her City can be destroyed. Here and now.

This time he does not pull away. His face is a collection of shadows and angles, centered round the unfathomable eyes. He lets her touch him, and drop her hand. And step away again. Before he says softly, "No, Tel. Please."

"Alkhes . . . it's too late."

"No." A little louder. She can feel the rigidity of his throat. "Not that . . . I can't . . ."

I know you can't, her heart cries. In that idleness, that frippery, you will be a clipped hawk, a smothered fire. Better if I cut your throat outright.

"I'll come and see you. There are visitors—"

"Tel, no." The finest vibration now, as fine as the tremor in his body. "I can't."

She looks at him across eighteen inches of moonlit air. The river, the gulf between nations has never seemed so wide.

"Then can you," it echoes in her ears, "change your mind?"

He puts both hands over his face. In the house shadow, a silent blur draws her eye. Zuri's silhouette, unmistakable. With Iatha behind her. Reinforcements enough.

"Alkhes?"

Though her voice is gentle, he seems to shrink before he drops his hands. And something in the posture tells her before he speaks. Quietly now. Without protest. Without hope.

"Can I—stay tonight?"

* * * *

Zuri and Iatha are equally suspicious, equally outraged. It takes all Tellurith's authority, and an oath from the prisoner, on the name of all his gods, that he will keep faith, not try to suicide, to escape, or some other nameless ruse, and even then, the surety that Azo or Verrith will be with him from that moment, before they consider consent. But Tellurith cannot find it in herself to deny him. If he has to go, then let it not be tonight.

If he has some ruse in mind, it is laid very deep. He does not argue. Does not attempt wild spectacles like a leap from the balcony or a dash for a kitchen knife. Just goes in that silence that pangs like a bruise on Tellurith's heart. Inside, to the lesser prison, under his warders' eyes.

Tellurith heads for her workroom. Where she stays till it is possible, with a measure of syrup, to imagine sleep.

The main rooms are deserted, twilit by darkened qherrique, the house sunk in midnight quiet. Shia too has gone. No lights show down the corridor, from guards' or prisoner's rooms. Stupefied with fatigue and misery, Tellurith gropes out of her clothes. Perhaps she will not need the syrup after all. Dreamily as a sleep-walker, she gets into a robe. Begins to undo her hair.

At the door, in her vision's edge, a shadow moves. She spins about, whipping up the hair-brush. And stops.

"Tel?"

Tiny as a whisper. Strangled by the noose of memory. Defeat. Coerced distress.

"I'm here."

V

He is a shadow on her threshold, a slight uncertain shape. His eyes swallow her. Enormous, condensed velvet night. Far more enormous than usual. Even when he is afraid.

Painted. Their darkness, their size accentuated by House men's skill, though rarely exercised on such raw material. And the cheekbones modeled with that subtle drama only expertly used cosmetics can achieve. Now she is closer, there is a tantalizing whiff of musk.

Mingled with henna. The black hair glistens, inviting, begging a touch. Neck-length, it is too short for the usual heavy, curled ringlets. The wing falls across his brow, but the rest is caught, a glint of jeweled combs, behind his ears.

And in House men's fashion he is bare to the waist, skin subtly oiled to give luster without grease. Highlighting the slight muscles to which the qherrique glow adds a fabulous tinge of gold.

It is gold. Tower extravagance. Dusted round his nipples, picking out his collar-bones, a faint but unmistakable mist. Deepening the contrast with the trousers, men's House trousers, loose and banded below the knee to bare the calves, black silk fluid as oil, molding the lines of narrow, elegant hips. Some disengaged part of her mind says flippantly, I never knew he could look so good.

Then he swallows. And all the tower's armor cannot mask the blankness of the huge eyes, the stiffness of the unconsciously parted lips.

"Oh, Mother . . . Come here."

He takes one step and balks. She holds out both hands.

He shivers. Swallows again. Then he is over the threshold and jammed against her, head buried between her neck and shoulder, clutching for dear life.

She hears his heart slam, heavy, plunging beats. The skin under her palms is gooseflesh, chill as ice. Instinctively her hands move, reassuring, calming, giving warmth. Saying, as her words so often have, I am here. I understand. It's all right.

At what point the tremors ease, who can tell? Any more than when reassurance becomes exploration, comfort a caress.

The skin texture under her fingers has smoothed. Her hands follow the flex of shoulders down the inward curve, shallower than a woman's, into the small of the back and out to loins rising, hard-ridged, under shifting silk. Against his neck, her lips taste salt and henna-wash and musk and separate, teasing strands of hair. Her arms measure the shape and size of him. Realizing, possessing the territory of desire.

Presently, very lightly, she runs her tongue around the inner whorl of his ear.

He jumps. Pulls his head up. She strokes the nape of his neck. Works her hand, as she has so often wanted, into his hair. Eases out the combs.

Rests her head, lightly, in the hollow of his throat.

When she does not move again, she feels his heartbeat pick up. The shake of his breath. And then the all-but-subdued tremor with which, slowly, delicately as a surgeon, he unlocks his hands from the small of her back.

And begins, strand by strand, to unravel, to ease and loosen and release, thick as a brandy-brown cloud over her shoulders, the rippling mazes of her hair.

Tellurith slides her hands to the trousers' waist-band. Finds the drawstring. He jumps again, as the silk telescopes softly round his feet.

The one moment when she might expect blind panic. But she keeps her hands lightly, either side his waist. And after a couple of quick breaths, feels him quiet.

When she waits, his hands come out, hesitant, tentative, to explore the fastening of her robe.

* * * *

Tellurith rouses slowly. To the unaccustomed sharing of her bed-space; to a weight on her shoulder, her throat fanned by sleeping breath. To a beard-rash in most unexpected places, gold-dust—a rueful tongue affirms it—silted round her lips.

To a posy of lover's memories, outland surprise that women could want more from love than intercourse, expect pleasure more surely, more frequently, and more inventively, than with a man in the usual outland place. Outland shock—Tellurith grins—that nipples are sensitive with or without breasts. Outland adaptability—she feels the smile grow smug—and invention, and once embarked, a skill and gentleness to match those wits. Her fingers shape the black, tangled head on her shoulder, and she feels the smile speak tenderness.

The rhythm of his breathing shifts. She knows it is a part of the old man that he does not wake, like most people, with unguarded movement, with smiles or yawns or protesting groans. That he lies quietly breathing till he knows where he is and with whom.

But is it the old man, she wonders, that, with reconnaissance done, with eyes still shut, he should reach the freer hand across her shoulder? And gather up, like soft gold wound about the fingers, a hank of her outspread hair?

On his cheek she feels the nascent smile.

"I suppose you've already made an appointment . . ." The eyes open, black and heart-shakingly soft. And then leaping with alarm.

"Gods, it's daylight—!" A plunge up, a wild stare around. The black trousers make a distant puddle. Tellurith bangs an elbow and brings him down just before the jump.

"Why the hurry?"

"I meant to be out before—" That fiery, boyish blush. "I didn't mean to—make a scandal, there's trouble enough—"

"Scandal." Tellurith lies back, into the luxury of a full-bellied laugh. "Who's going to see you? Except Azo and Verrith? Who," now she thinks, it is absolute certainty, "managed this anyhow?"

A startled look. A sheepish grin. Leaning on an elbow, he teases free a handful of her hair. His eyes stay on her face.

"When we came inside—they whipped me straight into their room. I didn't . . ." again the flush comes. "Azo said, 'Listen, man, if you want that woman you've got now to tell her. Mother knows, she wants you. Do you want or not?' I—Azo fetched her husband. And the things. Smuggled it all in." Sheepish, yet the eyes spark, a wicked, amazed grin. "'Just pray,' Verrith said, 'she don't want to pee while your head's dunked in the bath'." His hand goes, consciously, behind his ear. "They wouldn't miss out anything. And Herar—the husband—he was worst of all. Damn it, I never felt such a popinjay in my life."

The grin fades. "And," so very softly, "I've never been so scared."

Tellurith puts back the falling wing of hair. Ritual, pleasurable, possessive touch. Lets her hand say, But you were brave enough.

He turns his head to kiss her palm. Looks back into her face, in its nimbus of luxuriously out-spread hair. You, his eyes say. Candidly, reverently. You are unique. Without parallel in the world.

Aloud he says, more softly, "Tel . . . thanks."

For more, they both know, than the pleasure. Or the communion that is close to unity and self-oblivion as is possible for humankind. For exorcising the ghosts. For restoring his manhood, if not all the man.

Tellurith smiles. Then she heaves herself up in bed and he jerks in genuine alarm. "Tellurith, what do I—how do I—"

"Put on your pants. Walk out. To have it known is the whole point of this." Only troublecrew to see him, and troublecrew have already voted. Seen to their own. "Scandal? To a House-head's favorite, the word doesn't apply. If you want to swagger," she feels her own grin revive, "you can."

As Tellurith certainly does, taking a leisured breakfast under Shia's approving ministrations and her minders' bland stares, stroking her lover's knee and sharing coffee cups. Before she pats his backside and says, "Hurry up, caissyl." A proprietary, a lover's nickname; however incongruous, to call this one, Sweet. "Get dressed. Get a coat."

"What?"

Blandly as Azo, Tellurith meets the startled stare. "My first appointment's at the docks. I wouldn't want you getting cold."

"Cold—!"

"You've just been detailed," she can feel the smirk rise, "to my personal troublecrew." And as his jaw drops, "You did want to be some use."

* * * *

As they troop downstairs it does not surprise her to hear Azo and Verrith giving their protégé a low-voiced, rapid and comprehensive digest of outside procedures. When the vehicle starts she expects to find he has not merely regained composure but swallowed the instructions; and now, though the glow in those eyes speaks more excitement than surveillance, is using wits rather than tongue to process the avalanche of perceptions in the passing streets.

It does make her notice the mundanity of freight and passenger vehicles, the tall, tilted racks of sun-panels progressing above the crowd. The odd bright plume of scarf or garment amid the somberly billowing, clutched, buttoned, belted winter coats. The anomaly of coffee-drinkers ensconced on sidewalks behind sheets of Riversend glass, the wildly various occupations in River Quarter, from upRiver tumblers to artistically mangled beggars to the chromatic explosion of a Verrain Family's embassy. Downstream, her mind notes, the weather must already have improved.

She does more than notice when, having posted himself the obligatory two paces behind her shoulder, to the shock and then discreet blindness of the warehouse manager, he follows her back onto the open quay. And for a moment the lifted face, the little shift of shoulders, the deep, almost ecstatic breath make the raw Riverside end-of-winter air touch her own throat like wine.

Going back, he asks Azo or Verrith the rare, post-deductive question; where such a street goes; do House vehicles carry blazons. Then, "If the local stone's red, why's it called Amberlight?"

Azo and Verrith look aside. Their Head answers, working to be casual. "It was originally Emberlight. They didn't think it would bring good luck."

"Oh."

So why not Pearl-light? he gratefully does not ask.

But as they climb from squalid River to frenetic business quarter, then across the tacit boundary of Hill-foot road into the quiet of clan demesnes, she hears his silence stretch. And looking up, finds the anticipated frown.

"How old is the trouble back there?"

"In the—the working quarter," he expands, to Azo's lifted brow.

Azo tallies. Minimally, shrugs. "Five years or so."

"What sort of trouble?"

At Tellurith's intervention his eyes flick up. No lover's softness now.

"Wall-scribbles. Broken shutters. Burnt buildings. That's usually some sort of—battlefield. A border zone."

"Gang-country. Slum-folk, getting above themselves. Don't they have slums in Riversend?"

"Oh, yes." The eyes hold hers, somber as woken night. Before they flick to the clean, empty street sliding past outside, the luxury of a glass window, the immaculate walls, a cascade of flowering vine.

"But not so many. Not so—restive. Not for a city with—such a great deal of wealth."

Before Tellurith's eyes flash a cotton-wadded shoulder and a gold-brocaded cuff. But she lets her lip-curl acknowledge his quotation; and the tiny flame that flickers in those eyes, lover's willingness, lover's acknowledgement, wipes away unease under the warmth of memory, somewhere in her chest.

An almost sweeter revenge when Azo and Verrith fan across the sidewalk and he slides out behind her at the House door, the male shape, the lithe watchful walk, the wing of black hair unmistakable. Right under Iatha and Zuri's eyes.

It does not surprise Tellurith that Zuri should omissively approve, to the point of drilling him with in-House secrets herself. Her minions have usurped the House-head's judgment, after all. But she does not expect Iatha to walk into her workroom ten minutes later. Take her by the chin; stare into her eyes; growl, "Well, see he is some use." And stalk out without another word.

* * * *

Tellurith fully intends to have his use. As troublecrew, ostensibly, to escort her everywhere from docks to Uphill functions, with malicious pleasure in choosing clothes whose black or camouflage-green warn, Minder, but whose jacket and trousers contradict, Man. While the silk and brocaded wool and fur, not to mention the indiscreet jewels, proclaim arrogantly and yet more anomalously: Favorite.

It is the jewels that alarm him most. The night they are bound for a Prathax betrothal, she comes into his room, saying, "I remember they took yours." He is willing enough now to let her touch him, down to the raggedly healed scar in his ear. But when he looks at their mirrored faces, topaz and tawny, milk and coal, with the great ruby burning between them, it comes out as a gasp.

"Tel . . . Are you *trying* to upset people? This is too much—!"

"Pretty." She ruffles his hair, admiring the fitful red-wine star, and smiles. "Should I be ashamed of you? Why?"

"The way they look at me—at Vannish, the other night. Tel, are you sure you know what you're doing?"

"They wanted to see you. They're seeing you."

"And that meeting." For she has taken him to a Moon-meet, to stand with Azo and Verrith among the troublecrew who back every House-head's chair. "They see me there, and nobody says a word?"

"I told you. For a favorite, nobody will. You fit the patterns now. Not a very noble one, maybe, but one that's understood."

"Don't try to fool me, Tel." It holds no heat, but it is grim. "You don't make troublecrew of a favorite. Let alone take one up there. Tel—what are they going to do?"

"If they disapprove," says Tellurith coolly, "we will know when somebody tries an assassination." At the appalled face, she flicks his cheek, not all in jest. "I told you, you'll need to be of use."

Partly in case of that chance she takes him everywhere in-House as well: fulfilling the ancient promise of information with hours in her workroom, initiation willy-nilly into external and internal policy. Into Shaper's or Power-shops, learning, if only in theory, every Craft to do with qherrique; just as Azo and Verrith solemnly teach him light-guns' use and wards and dangers. Because he may find them in other troublecrew's hands.

And partly he is there for the other moments; the digression into the garden, yelps and smothered laughter in the bitter late-winter morning, hands freezing each other inside their opened coats. His stare from Arcis lookout, a hawk's scrutiny, while his hair flutters like a black silk flag and sun carves his profile, sharp as a cameo, on the clear blue air. The brushed hands, the arm that slides quietly round her in a corridor, a hall, a moment in some dark warehouse. Making love, swift obliterating passion in the maintenance attic of a windmill, with Azo and Verrith somewhere below them and the pound of vanes on a wild southerly to smother, to echo the blood's cry, careless, exultant, those black eyes blazing into hers.

"As if you don't wear me out here."

In the other times, the night times she has almost forgotten, when before or after or with love un-made they lie wound together, weaving the other union out of words.

"I don't notice signs of exhaustion." She works a knee between his thighs. Turns further to bring an arm across his chest. Lying back, exaggeratedly submissive, he produces a wicked smile.

"You." Tangling hands, luxuriating, in the wealth of her unbound hair. "With your crinkly curls." He plants a finger on her nose. "And your crow-beak. And your squinchy cheekbones. When it's this dark, even you look pretty. So what do you know?"

She bites a nipple, just hard enough to raise a yelp. "Tell me, then." Not about anomalous slums in Amberlight, not about coalitions or domestic traitors. "About Verrain. And statuettes."

The tangled hands still. In the black eyes' gravity she reads her reply. He too knows their love-play does not cancel intelligencers' commerce. That what he has learned about Amberlight will command an Imperial price.

"Verrain. Really, Shuya just heads a confederacy. One among—forty, fifty Families. Not inherited, tolerated. So she uses her statuette—quite a lot, at home."

"Is it just to feel the city's—country's—I don't know, currents, I suppose? Or can she—does she use it to coerce?"

Their eyes clinch, all play lost.

"Tel . . ."

Her eyes answer, implacable: You may have made oaths and understand secrecy and have served Shuya first. But to me you owe more than loyalty. Even if 'use' breaks the tenets, the foundations of your soul.

His hands move in her hair. Unconsciously, futilely tracing their bonds. He shuts his eyes.

"She can—influence people. I remember . . . incense. Midnight. Some sort of sacrifice. Blood. 'You see how I trust you? The fingers should know the power of the hand'."

"Sweet Work-mother!"

"Tel—!"

She grimaces at the involuntary jerk on her hair. On his face, the mirror of her appalled look remains. "To offer blood. To twist the qherrique—what was she doing?"

He winces too. To break trust and confidence so utterly is to be mentally crucified. "It was the Riversrun border war."

"But that was with Dhasdein!"

She bites the rest off. Having already given him too many clues to his past, when she resurrected his time in the Imperial guard.

"I don't—maybe I'd changed—maybe I didn't always—"

Maybe you were not simply a high Imperial officer but a high-flying mercenary. Before, after?

At the same time?

Tellurith speaks softly but firmly over the distress in that black stare. "What about the Families?"

"Oh . . . that's fairly simple. No—blood-things. Mostly they use theirs in the Oases. To keep the caravan-workers quiet."

"And?"

He knows she has heard the trailing intonation, but the rest comes reluctantly. "And of course, to help the trade."

Tellurith lies back, eyes on the ceiling, where the carven bosses of mahogany, imported clear from Cataract, acquire grotesque shadow-bulges in the night-cycle dusk. It is his turn to prop a hand under his head and wait, stifling knowledge, agitation, distress.

"And Dhasdein?"

She feels him steel himself.

"I told you—Dhasdein's in a loop. They have to pay you with gold that they can only get from Verrain, so they buy it with colonial loot—that they need qherrique to get. So the more colonies they take to raise gold to pay for pearl-rock, the more statuettes they need and the more colonies they have to conquer—every Archipelago governor has one, Tel, you know that." His voice is rough. Once he could scourge her city's supply of abuses with a clear conscience. "You know what a good trade it is."

For Telluir. For the Thirteen. For Amberlight.

Against the lace-edged pillow his profile is still and rigid as a blade. Until she turns her face. Absently, kisses him. And murmurs, "Caissyl . . . Go to sleep. I have to think."

****

"If the Thirteen feels no concern, I have looked into this. And I tell you now: Shuya has used the qherrique for bane-work. For blood-work. Beyond her sovereign state. If the means for that is to come from Amberlight, it will not be from Telluir House."

Amid the Thirteen's uproar she is most conscious of two sensations, both a prickling down the back. That black stare behind her. And the answer of the qherrique, strong as at the mother-face.

Affirmation. Assent.

For a single House to refuse service is unprecedented. In five hundred years of working qherrique, a gabbling Falla tells her, there has never been an act so iniquitous. The Thirteen have never seemed so hidebound. Outrage and imprecations embroil even Kuro, Maeran's rapier slashes are mere crests amid the waves. In the president's chair Sevitha of Iuras is reduced to cursing froth.

It is Zhee, humped in her usual lizard silence, who spikes a lull of exhaustion with a single, "Why?"

Oldest House. Oldest House-head. Old if not oldest mentor, when Tellurith was thrust into the whirlpool of House politics, a twenty-four-year-old, unexpected heir. Amid that whirlpool, Telluir House's oldest if not most reliable ally.

The one Head who may genuinely want to know.

"The trade," she says, as in response to their locked gazes, the others fall temporarily quiet. "It's being abused. It's draining the River as well. And it rebounds—it rebounds on Amberlight."

Liony and Damas bawl. Maeran adds an ironic slice or two. Tellurith ignores them all.

It is Zhee's way to answer rather than to ask ensuing questions. Tellurith understands the alienness of this entire vision, when Zhee says, "How?"

"The—River Quarter. They're getting poorer. The gangs are worse, we all know that. And the wages—"

The Houses move together, one concerted growl whose components she knows by heart. The poor are shiftless breeders who will not expose boy babies, who have no will to work and no aptitude for Craft. The pay is enough to drink and gamble, why not enough to eat? It is the city's grace that they are not all shipped off to Cataract. Sevitha herself breaks in with the exasperation of pure incomprehension, "Rebounds how?"

Tellurith opens her mouth and shuts it again. Locking away the image of gold-brocaded cuff and beggars' rags, the contrast's revelation she can take no further, even to herself. Only to the inarticulate uncertainty that this, this is not right.

As for saying, They are too poor, we are too rich. We are at the top of the city, and we are strangling Amberlight?

Just as Amberlight is strangling the River beyond.

Ask Maeran to give up her Heartland ivory collection, and Falla her six hundred heirloom tapestries, ask any of them to renounce their mere wardrobes, their jewels, their furniture, a House-head's accustomed luxury, a House's ordinary wealth?

To divide it with a River Quarter whore?

Tellurith bites her lower lip, hard. Lifts her nose and looks down it, Telluir signal of negotiation's end.

"Whatever it means to the city, we know what abuses go on beyond." Astonishing, how calm she actually sounds. When she is taking a stance that may mean the end, in one way or another, of her life. "Let the Thirteen vote as they wish. But Telluir House will not send Verrain a statuette."

The Thirteen erupt. Sevitha hurls her arms up, bereft of words.

Understanding the unspoken very well: that for the sake of the Thirteen's tacit equilibrium, to revoke Telluir's contract demands canceling the Cataract order to Vannish House.

So Tellurith can smile quite genially, if with teeth bared, at the ensuing fracas. Until Sevitha takes the only possible action, and the special meeting is adjourned.

* * * *

Sunset on Amberlight, crimson ribbons of wind-cloud dappled on a cerulean sky. In the garden, the first golden splashes of crocus star the needle-mats under the pines. In Tellurith's apartment, Iatha leans against the dining table and stares.

"'Rith—just tell me why?"

The hurt, the exhaustion, stab Tellurith in turn. She gives her troublecrew the signal that means, Privacy.

To them all.

"Yath . . . You know what I told them. We can prove it's true."

Iatha's hump-necked stare retorts, So?

"Yath, I—"

But what use to struggle through that impossible vision here? Easier to take the other, the bald, insane, yet to a House-woman, more comprehensible truth.

"I felt—the qherrique said, Yes."

Iatha rubs two fingers between her brows. Produces a look she cannot read. Then a sign she reads all too well. And then, softly, "I always wondered. 'Rith—is that how House-heads know?"

Over the honor-sign. As if she were, herself, a god. But she cannot shirk the answer. "I don't know about the rest. But for me . . . I think, yes."

Iatha stares a while at the huge, incarnadined sky. Then slowly straightens. Exhaustion metamorphosing to purpose, determination, strength. "Well, then, 'Rith—if that's what it is—whatever the Thirteen think, we know we're right."

* * * *

"**Y**ou said, assassinations, if they disapproved of me. So they'll try over this."

To deduce rather than question is the way of those redoubtable wits. Which have already convinced Azo and Verrith and Zuri herself.

"Blight and blast it, I can pee without taking a scout!"

He stares. Too quiet, the black eyes alarmingly still in a killer's face. 'Use', she has said. The old man, disconcertingly evident, avows that he will uphold his trust.

"And we don't need throwing-knives under the pillow!"

"I talked to Zuri."

And the knives, says the expression, stay.

But it is Kuro who dies.

* * * *

"**S**he was old, yes. Failing for years. Heart-stoppage, is the physicians' report."

Tellurith wraps arms about herself, in good wool coat and in-House warmth bitterly, bone-deep cold. Across the desk Iatha says it for her, the presence of troublecrew, a very outlander, all ignored.

"*Heart-stoppage* can cover anything. From aspnor root to a pillow over the head."

And of course there will be no proof. Impossible to query the official version of a Head's death. Not from another House.

Impossible to misread the message. Which is aimed at theirs.

* * * *

A House-head goes to death through water and fire, by the same road as the least pauper of Amberlight. But for a House-head it is no simple Gate Quay pyre and committal of ashes to the river; for a House-head it is a five day mourning dark, laid in state in the House's central court for all Uphill to honor with their parting gifts, their shorn locks, their ritual grief. And then the procession, all Uphill, even the men, with musicians and bells and burning incense, winding outward to Dead Dyke. Where amid final ceremonies the body is laid in its opulent death-clothes, with its gifts about it, on the Traveler's Ship. And when the pyre's ardent cennaphar wood is kindled, the Dead Dyke gates open, the River draws the ship to itself, and somewhere in the downRiver dusk, the great star of the conflagration takes a House-head's memory with it as it dies.

Impossible to shirk the funeral. House honor compels Tellurith's presence as much as an ally's respect. Or as enemies defied. "If we shirk, it says they've frightened us. They've won!"

"Then for the gods' love, Tel, take some care!"

Not Iatha this time, as sure of sanctity as all Zuri's crew. Murder a House-head in private, yes, but violence at an Uphill funeral? Tellurith's panicking outlander argues and curses and pleads in vain. The troublecrew will honor Kuro with their presence, yes. Alert for danger in the procession, yes. Crowding a House-head who should pace in proud and fearless isolation before her people, no. "I'm not Dinda, Alkhes!"

So she strides solemnly in the space behind Telluir House's banner, leaving a suitable hiatus after the scullions of Hafas: the Houses follow the bier in traditional founding order. The bitter-keen spring air swirls with fitful sparkling sun, with the patrol of distant showers, smoky over the threadbare green of sprouting rice, over the river's glittering back. Over the streets of Amberlight, business suspended, while stevedores, even whores silently line Hill-foot road above the River Quarter's sun-groomed shacks. To watch the passage of that tinkling, chanting stream of funeral splendor, from the black head-wrap of a garden-boy to the gold-brocaded, boot-length, silk-lined midnight swirl of a House-head's coat.

And amid the House-folk, the blacker cluster of troublecrew, whence she can feel the blackest stare arrow over Crafts and Craft-heads and even the shielded men's file, the smallest boy somberly demure behind his veil of jet-black silk. Aimed, with fury and fear to power its defiance, at her unprotected back.

Assembling at noon at the citadel gate, by mid-afternoon the procession has reached Dead Dyke. The Houses file to their traditional places for the eulogies, delivered by each Head from a rostrum beside the bier. Orchestrated to close by the turn of evening for the embarkation of the body and its gifts.

And finally, as the electrum arc of the new moon emerges above a splendidly purple sunset, the canal gates are opened. The Ship cast off. The torches fired.

By tradition, only family mourners watch the pyre's end. Also by tradition, House and Craft-heads offer the bereaved a last, personal condolence. And with it comes the afternoon's release into informality, House-folk mingling, House-heads too resuming their ballet of acknowledgement, support and threat.

Maeran is just leaving as Tellurith approaches the mourners: Kuro's daughter, her partner, her younger husband; the women frozen-faced, heads bare. The partner red-eyed, the husband little more than a tall black inclining shape that with House-man's skill manages to convey devastated grief. Tellurith bows to him, nods to her; clasps Ti'e's hands, offers ritual words. Turns away.

To a plunge and convulsion in the crowd-swirl, then a strangled yell as a thunderbolt knocks her flat on her back.

Cold. Dusk. A paralyzed hush. Tellurith is too winded to gasp. Cold stone mashes her shoulder-blades, weight pins her empty chest. Warm muscled human weight. Spread over her like living armor, straddled to shield her every inch.

Then her lungs wheeze as white blobs of overhead faces yell and shove and rush. A black spearhead slings them aside, drive of a body and grab at the mantling weight, Zuri's familiar whip-crack shout.

"Alkhes, don't move!"

A hand pins Tellurith's arm. Zuri rears up bellowing, "Caitha! Get over here!"

Tellurith gets her chin up. Surging masses of black cohere, Telluir troublecrew pinning back an appalled, babbling crowd. Cloud-inlaid purple sky, horizon lit with a wide golden ellipse from the pyre. Caitha coming at flat run, a frightful face. A body on top of her, black troublecrew jacket, familiar weight. Black head buried, familiarly, so familiarly, in her shoulder crook.

And the fletches of a blow-dart, a miniature six-inch mast, upright above the curvature of his back.

"Don't move, Ruand."

Don't shift his body. Don't disturb the dart. Don't distribute the poison. Well and truly seated, says that vicious haft, usually all of ten inches long. Barbed. Its three tines smeared with hatura, nerve poison. Inches from his spine.

Tellurith's belly dissolves. Somewhere inside her, beyond the body trying desperately not to twitch, not to breathe, someone is screaming, No, oh no, oh sweet Mother, no, no, no—

Another thud. Frantic gasps. Zuri again. "Got anything here?"—"Katsein, but I don't—"—"Give it to him. Never mind the dose—get it in him!"—"No cup—!"—"Use my hand . . . shick it, woman, move!"

Zuri, abusing Caitha. Zuri, using obscenity, who is never known to curse. Zuri's hand, gripping his shoulder, solid as rock, as Caitha pants and babbles by Tellurith's head. Zuri's galvanizing crisis voice.

"Alkhes. Lift your head. Very slowly. I'll keep your balance. Drink what Caitha gives you. Now."

The tone, and only the tone's ice, to urge what Tellurith's distant soul is screaming: Now, hurry, before the paralysis reaches your throat, for the Mother's love, quick!

She feels rather than hears his indrawn breath. Zuri's other hand steadying his head. Does feel the katsein drops, wet on skin through her shirt-sleeve, inside the opened coat. And close as in her own throat, the movement of chest and belly as he gulps.

"Not too fast." She has heard Zuri speak to troublecrew like that. After greatest, most perilous effort, for a triumph at most fearful price. Stern, without expression. The utmost tenderness.

"Got any more?"

"Not with me, there's tetsal in the infirmary—"

"Send someone—quick!"

Zuri's hand remains. Adding her own small best, to lie utterly still despite small tortures of crumpled coat, trapped muscles, bitterly chill, uneven stones, Tellurith is abjectly glad. Especially when his head shifts and she hears through her own lungs and bones' core the first checked, laboring breath.

"It's hatura." Zuri is all ice. "Don't tell me if you know. Don't fight it if you don't. It paralyzes. You probably can't feel along your back. Don't tell me! It will get your chest muscles. That's why you're out of breath. Caitha's given you katsein, but it has to come through your gut. It will work." *Mother help us,* Tellurith's brain screams, *Zuri, do you know!* "You have to give it time. Just don't panic. Don't fight."

All too familiar, such counsel in extreme injury. When she feels his mouth move against her shoulder, the image of the wry, agreeing smile fills her eyes with tears.

* * * *

Tetsal is administered straight into the blood. By the time Caitha slices shirt and jacket for an incision at a respectful six inches circle round the haft, his breathing is appreciably worse.

By the time the tetsal is administered, Tellurith has waited what seems eternal hours; hearing Iatha brusquely disperse all comers, shattering decorum and Diaman's funeral without a thought. And Zuri, still kneeling by her prostrate Head and outland troublecrew. Declaring war, clearer than Iatha's brusquerie, as she coolly, blankly declines every offer of tetsal from nearer infirmaries. Saying, *You are all enemies*, with every, "I prefer it from Telluir House."

When Caitha decrees he is within risk to move, it is long past dark. Iatha brings the Head's vehicle right to them. And when he has been lifted on a slab-litter and deposited inside like veritable qherrique by a multitude of troublecrew hands, Tellurith is finally free to breathe. To rise. To cosset tottery limbs among multitudinous other hands. To shove her wobbly way to the vehicle door and grunt, "Let me up!"

So she rides with him to the House, his head on her lap, her ribs strained by every wheezing breath. In the infirmary her flesh feels every deep, insufferably deep scalpel stroke as Caitha dredges for the dart. She experiences rather than watches the extrication of the triple layered barbs. And then literally sits with him, propped on the same pillows, helping the medical team who use tetsal, and more katsein, and at the worst shove his chest to work his lungs, even give him heart massage. Before his eyes open, and she hears him draw a clear breath, as the infirmary qherrique brightens to announce the end of that endless night.

The eyes are as ever, a single, drowning black. Their expression is vaguer than when he came round first. But when she puts a hand to that black-stubbled cheek, recognition comes.

And then remembrance. A quiet knowledge of success. A smile that makes her heart jump. When she puts both arms around him, she feels it widen to that wicked grin against her neck.

Before he whispers, "I told you so."

They have just finished making peace when Zuri arrives.

With a face that ignores love's frivolity along with patient's frailty or intruder's embarrassment. Just the question, and the hand full of triple-tined, blood-stained barbs.

"Seen one of these before?"

And he answers as dourly, "Cataract."

"Ah?" Zuri lifts her brows. At his recognition, not the news. "Heartland hunter-dart? The pipe's thick as your thumb, three feet long. Use it like a walking stick if you want. Any time inside twenty feet, stick the dart in, point and blow. What'd you see?"

He rubs his brows. Not absence, but re-creation. Head and troublecrew, after-action report.

"It was the first good chance. People moving, bad light. And leaving the mourners, they all turned toward the bier. It was cover. It was damn close. I followed—Tellurith. When she turned, I saw the pipe come round the bier. The Vannish mourners blocked me. It was too far to stop him. So I went for her."

Zuri measures him, a long, enigmatic stare. Then grunts and leans on the bed end. "If you dodged Vannish in time to reach her, s'hure, you must have flown."

S'hure. Fellow Crafter. The male version sounds more than strange. It may be the title, or the tone, but Tellurith sees the blood rise, a slow flush behind the stubble, before the wry little smile.

"I think I did. The last five feet, anyhow."

Literally throwing himself in the dart's path. Knowing what it was. That he might, literally, be shielding her with his life.

Tellurith's throat shuts, robbing words. She lays an arm across him as substitute. He leans his head against hers. Then raises a mock scowl for Zuri. "*Now* do you say I was right?"

Zuri grins.

A sight only less remarkable than the visiting moon. Before she stomps the bed's length and cuffs his shoulder. "*Next* time, dangle-wit, I'll give you an ear-spark," diamond ear-stud, Crafter's honor. "But only if you salute first!"

* * * *

The extraction wound needs ten stitches, but the hatura's effects wane fast. So fast that irate threats delay things till he can be up for next day's only slightly postponed council of war.

"It was rotted silly to do it at the funeral. When even the physicians would be there. Sounds like Cataract."

Iatha, supplying a Riverslength perspective. Belied by Zuri's glower.

"It would have been cursed clever to do it at the funeral if it worked. It would have told every-one: *We can get you. Even here.*"

"Amberlight, then?" Tellurith demands.

Zuri shrugs.

"Ruand, the pipe and the assassin may have come from Cataract. Or only the pipe. One or both could have been sent by Dinda. It could as easily have been cooked up here."

Iatha thumps the table. "There's no way to tell!"

"Then what matters now," Alkhes cuts straight through her, "is that it doesn't happen again."

Zuri adds flatly, "Yes."

Three pairs of eyes swivel. Confronting a narrower vista of confined living, cumbered movement, scanted privacy, Tellurith mentally groans.

"No more goddamn ceremonials." He is in deadly earnest now. "No more public access. Double checks, in here as well."

"No more dockyard trips," Iatha weighs in vengefully. "River Quarter's full of bullies for hire. One blocked street—one gang with picks—"

"No more House meets." Zuri sounds flatter than before. "Whether it came from Cataract or Amberlight, offering chances to another House is too much risk."

At which Tellurith regains her House-head's wits.

"No! *Call* a House-meet! Iatha, get Hanni to pass the summons the minute we're done. Take as much troublecrew as you want, but I'm going to see them. I want to see them all!"

Iatha yelps. Zuri stares. Alkhes' mouth opens. And shuts.

Tellurith feels the grin come, wild as a lunatic's. "It doesn't matter who did it. We have the witness, we have the proof. Cataract is implicated in an assassination attempt on a House-head of Amberlight. Telluir House will invoke the Thirteen. And the Thirteen will have to cancel Dinda's contract. They'll have no choice!"

* * * *

Thirty-six hours, an expedition in virtual war-mode to Arcis, an apocalyptic confrontation: Dinda's contract revoked, Vannish storming out of the meet. Climbing by dusk to the House-head's apartments, his arm about her shoulders, she can feel him laughing still. "Dinda snaffled, the assassin's lot checkmated, the Thirteen shut up in their own box! God's eyes, clythx, now I know what House-head means . . ."

Clythx. *Heart*. The first endearment he has ever used. Warmer than the pride, the breath of his laughter in her ear. Lost as Azo's step checks ahead of them and in a flash his left hand shoves her behind him while his right hand palms the throwing knife in his sleeve.

"Who's there?"

A cobra's hiss at Azo. Whose response is a more startling shuffle and grunt. And then, "Ah, Ruand—"

Utmost embarrassment. But Tellurith knows already. It is in the scent permeating down the stair. Light, achingly familiar. Flavor of hyacinths.

Tellurith shuts her eyes. Takes her troublecrew carefully by the arm. Puts him aside. Climbs the last five steps.

"So much caution, Tellurith."

Unforgettable, the lazy fall of that resonant, melodic voice.

"Or should I—nowadays—say, Ruand?"

Azo steps back. Tellurith is too aware that her other guard has not. That he is right behind her, knife ready, poised like a knife himself. She can picture the slight form, coiled. The killer's face, the unwinking, implacable black stare.

The man at the stair-head shifts weight, throwing a hip out, an exquisite, mannered curve. The qherrique-glow glistens on his torso, perfectly proportioned muscle, a statue in polished bronze. A ringlet cascades over one shoulder, the gold bead at the tip of its thick bronze-brown corkscrew just tapping his watered-silk bronze trousers' waist. Around one broad biceps is the two-inch gold band that was her betrothal gift. Gold glistens on the shapely, manicured hands, the elegantly posed wrist. Gold powders his collarbones, his nipples, the high smooth forehead above the silk square of House-veil, framed by glossy falls of hair. He is tall and perfect as a god, a god's presence, a god's physique.

Everything that a little dark outlander could never be.

The bronze-brown lashes drop. Gold-powdered too. The stare's aim is too certain. Tellurith forces her dry mouth to speak.

"Sarth."

"Enchanted." That exquisite bow, mannered and graceful as a sail's turn to the wind. "It's been forever." She can feel her ribs flinch, the dagger already in. "I hope—I do beg you to excuse my forwardness." Grace, acid only he can throw. "But you know, such stories. I simply had to see for myself."

Alkhes moves. With one hand she catches him. Feels, from his stifled flinch, what pressure she must have put on his wrist.

"And this is the paragon in the flesh."

"Azo." There is almost composure in her voice. "Open the door. You three wait here."

Soundless, breathless, Azo obeys. Edges past, to the safety of the stairs. The man at the top offers her a small, ironic courtesy. The man at Tellurith's back moves with her.

"I said—"

"I'm coming with you."

Argument? Worse display, worse humiliation. And nothing short of brute force, she can tell, will make him stop.

Tellurith gestures to the door.

Sarth turns, poetry in motion, upon her most precious rug. The backdrop glamorizes, the qherrique caresses him. Tellurith stands frozen. Hideously conscious of the human catapult at her back.

Accented topaz eyes smile. "I'm told he actually took a poison dart for you. Saved your life."

Easier to accept what is coming. Tellurith merely nods.

"I hear," the superbly shaped brows move, the slightest, most elegant curve, "that he shares the apartment. Too."

Her heart-beat has accelerated. Too much experience. She keeps her voice steady. "Politics."

"And what would I know of that?" Mellifluous dagger in the mourning cadence. "But to share everything?"

She does not feel the other's move. Is just in time to catch and jerk as the knife comes up on the soft, lethal hiss.

"Are you suggesting . . ."

"Dear Mother, is he threatening me, Tellurith?"

Grip, wrench and jerk. Use—misuse the fury, with anguish in the twist. "Stay out of this!"

"Gods damn it, Tel—!"

"Stay out!"

"Such violence."

Unbroken, Sarth's languid, deploring posture. That says, clear as burning acid, Such a barbarian. So uncouth. "But then, I'm sure he has some attractive points."

Tellurith looks at them both, and that something squeezes her heart. At Sarth, tall, splendid, elegant, perfectly tended and pro- portioned, all an Amberlight woman could ask. At her small un- tidy death-adder, outland, potential traitor, skilled only in death.

Brilliant teeth gleam. "For instance, I hear the strangest sto- ries from Herar—"

"Shut up!"

Sarth recoils, miming fear. "Oh, Tellurith, I do implore you. You know I'm not trained in—martial arts."

Alkhes all but spits. Under the House-veil, those lips shape a smile. Then face, hands, body modulate into grief.

"But perhaps, that is better. After all—I could only give you sons."

No, is all she can think, as the pain drowns her. For her wound, for his wound, for his damnable poisonous skills that can turn his hurt to a double stab in her defenseless heart.

"That's enough."

It comes over her shoulder, a single murderous hiss. Sarth recoils in earnest. Death stalks him across the rug, knife-blade glittering, circling, forcing him inexorably toward the door.

"Tellurith—"

"Shut up."

"Have you ceded even authority, Tellurith?"

At that his hunter stops. Poises, half-turned.

After all, the last blow must be hers. A House-head's authority—she feels the bubble of hysteria in her throat—even for a slighted husband, cannot be overthrown.

"I know what I am to you, Tellurith." How can such gentle, poignantly pronounced words give such a two-edged cut? "But I thought—I did think—you might have told me yourself."

"Get out!"

* * * *

New moon fine as a sickle's ghost over Amberlight, pure, remote in a black and lilac sky. Swimming, wavering, through the glass pane. Through the unstaunchable tears.

On her nape, the merest breath. Hands taking her arms, cupping her shoulders, delicately as fractured glass. The warmth of his body, its familiar shape against her, is a sentient wall. Against her neck, she feels his head bowed. The feather touch of lips.

And presently she can raise hands to her own face. Breath by breath, sob by sob, begin to cry.

When it finally eases, he folds his arms about her. With her hands resting over his, says it very quietly into her ear.

"I didn't mean to usurp—your choice."

Tellurith moves her head. It doesn't matter. Not now.

"Gods damn . . ."

A soft, passionless, lava river of obscenity. "Gods rot and strangle the bastard. Tel, if I'd known—if I'd only thought . . ."

Her throat is blocked, impassable. She moves her head again. Don't. There was nothing you could help.

"Just tell me, clythx. Is there anything—anything—I can do?"

New moon over Amberlight, pure and passionless and clean. A renewed world. A fresh beginning. If life were only like the moon.

She turns about in his hold. Takes his shoulders, stares into the wide, intent eyes.

"You want to do something for me?" It comes out choked but fierce. "Really do something? Then give me a daughter, Alkhes."

She hears his breath stop. Then he lifts his hands to hers. Draws her gently from the window, the night, the watching moon.

And speaks more huskily than she did. "I'll try, clythx. I give you my word, I'll try."

* * * *

But it is death he gives her first. Iatha's nightmare, a River Quarter ambush, half a warehouse wall dropped across the street in early dark, the vehicle immobilized by rolled-in rocks, a torrent of bludgeons and bodies and screaming alien faces flung on every door.

Behind which Zuri and her gadfly's providence have increased the escort to four, and before the return trip began his wary nerves have had the light-guns out and charged. So the first breached window brings the horizontal thunderbolts of their riposte.

Two hours later, detour made, House reached, bath and dinner over, Tellurith is still shaking. Mind replaying and replaying the appalled, the seared, melting, fleeing, falling figures, bodies, faces. Upturned in the gutter under her feet. Nose, face, center of the head burned clear away. A disconnected hand. A scarecrow dragging a hamstrung leg. The hideous, hideous screams. The more hideous stench. Excrement, incinerated meat. Amberlight's unique weapons. Turned, for the first time, upon Amberlight flesh.

A silent step. Silent presence, settling at her back. Over the cushion, a tentative, question of a caress.

Tellurith turns round. Takes him passionately, desperately about the neck.

When her shaking finally stops, he says, "I'm sorry, Tel."

"Sorry?" It makes no sense.

"It shouldn't have been so messy. There shouldn't have been so much . . . If I'd had a gun I could have dropped the first one who rolled a rock in, and that would have been it."

She is some time understanding. That for all his concern, all his tenderness, the killer has gone on thinking. The reasoning of death has never stopped.

Tellurith shuts her eyes. Tells the invading faces, You chose to reject the one with gentle arts. You can thank only yourself.

She opens her eyes and says, "It's not your fault."

"It is and it's not." Anger burns, deep in the quiet. "If I hadn't thought—the way I do—we wouldn't have had the extra guns. We wouldn't have been ready. They'd still be alive."

A pause.

"And we'd be dead."

Tellurith re-opens her eyes and stares past his shoulder, beyond the deserted table, to the walls' glowing labyrinth.

"It doesn't seem," she cannot hide the miserable laughter, "much of a choice."

"Well, damn it, there should have been! There would have been, if I could handle a light-gun . . ." A catching pause. A breath, and plunge. "Tel, let me try to use the qherrique."

Tellurith does not scream. Does not swear. Does not shout and throw things. In a moment, actually finds a haunted, turning-worm perversity that says, Very well. Let him see for himself.

"Put your hand on top of mine. Fingers loose." Slight, warm, hard fingers, calluses Sarth's hands never wore. "Now . . . I don't know how to describe it. Empty your mind. Be—receptive. The cutters call it opening the ear."

And to her startlement, he nods at once. "Like getting ready for unarmed combat. Yes."

The last thing she expected is that the skill should come from learning to fight.

Against her shoulder his breathing slows. The slight, hard, familiar body quiets. She can feel tranquility, palpable as at the face.

"Move with me."

Outstretch the hand, fingers bent loosely, his resting over it. Approach that moonrise tracery. Tellurith hears herself begin to hum. The verbal rapport no one ever plans. No one ever omits.

Assent is in her mind, light and palpable as a butterfly's landing. She lets her fingertips touch.

Warmth and expectation under them, tangible as a pulse. Sliding fingers sidelong, a brush that is also caress. Adjusting the angle, so his hand connects.

She feels the shudder go through him, strong as a lover's response. Sees the gooseflesh rise like incantation across the back of his wrist.

"Oh, merciful gods . . ."

Her mind incises his profile, sharp nose, ebony sweep of lashes, parted, fine-cut lips. A moment caught in amber as she eases away her hand.

His fingers slide. He has forgotten her. There is more than wonder in his face. There is acolyte's worship. Enchantment. Awe.

The qherrique glows brilliantly. His hand moves, as if he cannot help it, more in obedience than caress. Tracing the veins out as he does the blue pathways on her breast. Following the threads that turn and twine and part like the currents of the River itself.

Until at last, imperceptibly, the moonrise dulls. Fades, irrevocably, inexorably, away.

His lashes flutter. Against her, she feels the first easing as his muscles begin to relax. Before he can move, breathe, come fully awake, she slides a hand, more roughly than she intends, inside his shirt.

The nipple flicks, erect under her touch. He gasps.

"Tel, what are you—what . . . ?"

"You're in tune with me." Her own nipples tingle, she is short of breath. "It's in tune with us both. It joins us," her hands slide down. He moans, arching his body into hers. "So it wants . . ."

His hands come over hers, closing them on his body that is now quickened to full arousal. "Oh, gods, Tel." His heart is thundering against her ear. "I know what it wants."

* * * *

Tellurith rouses slowly, to an unfamiliar touch. Velvety but hard nap, rasping her ear. No sheets, but a familiar scent and weight over her. Puzzlingly identified as that day's outdoor coat.

And no sleeping human shape against her, warm and close.

She is naked on the heirloom Verrain rug. Curled like a child, under the protection of that mysterious coat. In the dimmed qherrique light, blurred islands mark her clothes.

And nothing more.

A hammer starts under her throat. Hauling the coat round her, she clambers up.

No one in the bathroom, the corridor. No one in his old room, where he still keeps possessions, unused gear.

No one in her own room. The bed is intact. No sign of a slight, sleeping shape.

The hammer is beating fast enough to block her throat. Below it, ice is creeping through her chest.

No one in the kitchen, the scullery, the washing and store-rooms. No one in the hall. No one in the workroom, its piled desks deserted, desolate.

With one slate, isolate and conspicuous, on her empty chair.

The hammer stops. The ice is already a dagger, a knife opening her belly, before she picks the message up.

So short, so simple. Unmistakable, the angular outland script. Clear as a sentence of death.

Tel,
I'm sorry.
A.

PART II

SUNLIGHT

. . . the hidden paths that run
East of the Moon, West of the Sun.
~ J.R.R. Tolkien, adapted

VI

High noon on Amberlight, glaring, quivering unhindered from the zenith of a leached turquoise sky. Color, coolness, shadows erased. Head foolhardily bare, Tellurith squints out from her balustrade into the mid-summer day.

Windmills swing fitfully in oven-hot westerly breaths. Vertical leaves tremble in the valley beneath, changing the familiar vistas of tower and garden, whose colors pale and deliquesce in the glare. The streets are deserted, heat-haze and sun-stare, all Amberlight panting under the weight of noon.

And beyond the mirror-glitter that loops the city's perimeter runs another loop. Braided with overlaps and entrances, beaded with standards and sentries' heads, stapled with palisade stakes, its bare-trampled dykes and massive interleaving earth-banks dirt-brown as the huge scrapes whence they have been torn. Hauled up on a multitude of carts and wheelbarrows and forced-laborers' baskets, tamped and stamped into this new perimeter loop. This noose. Which cuts off the emerald rice-plots, the golden wheat-harvest, the silver-beige of hayed-off grazing land that recedes into the Kora's blurry summer heat.

Amberlight is under siege.

* * * *

I'm sorry. A.

Sorry for what? she wonders, as she has wondered endlessly. For running away? With no slip-ups this time, out the main doors on a word to the watch-crew, commandeering a vehicle to the waterfront, a dinghy to reach the Kora, a horse from the first inn. And then? Upstream, downstream, to whichever intriguer's nest he has flown so unerringly, none of their intelligencers knows.

For her hurt? For the sheer physical pain of losing him, lover and protector-killer, for two months the closest human presence in her life? Shield and sweetness lost, sharing and loving lost, smashed along with her pride, her self-respect.

Her trust.

For the repercussions? For the uproar and recrimination and bitter, bitter in-House, "I told you so's." Iatha's rage and outrage, Shia's disbelief. Zuri's humiliation. Did he feel, she wonders, for her and her troublecrews? Who no less, if not so deeply as their House-head, have trusted and been betrayed.

Or was it for the external outrage, yet more acrimonious, Telluir House left to face a Thirteen whose wrath can barely be contained? Censure and revocation of contracts, insult and abuse; and worst of all, from Maeran's rapier stabs downward, the knowledge that there is no counter. That they are right. That whatever calamity Telluir House has brought on Amberlight is their fault. Her fault.

Or the wider political results? Demands from Verrain. An ultimatum from Cataract. Increasingly undiplomatic correspondence, which within a month issues in an outright threat of war.

Since Telluir House resolutely continues to trumpet the assassination attempt, and enough of the Thirteen have been frightened, bullied or badgered into backing her to hang a deciding vote. No decision being made, the statuette is withheld. If Vannish was behind that blow-dart, Tellurith reflects, they must have long rued the failure of their bluff.

As she and all Amberlight look to rue the recoil. Since Dinda has not been content with threats.

For the war, then? A war pressed with alarming alacrity, barely a fortnight from the ultimatum before frantic reports from upRiver intelligencers that Dinda's forces are on the march. Not merely summoned, not merely mustering. Marshaled, provisioned, and on their way downstream.

Far too swiftly, Tellurith thinks yet again, for this not to have been already planned. And its intent far more than threat, or Dinda would not have raised such a force, would have yielded to the pleas and appeasements from a panic-stricken Thirteen. Which he has brushed aside on his way downRiver as so many flies.

As the pleas for help, or at the least neutrality, have been ignored by Verrain.

Sorry, then, for remembering what he already knew? For running when he knew quite well what a wasps' nest he left behind?

Or sorry—and for five months this has been the ulcer's core— that he had remembered long before? That he deceived her in everything? Deliberately influenced her to resist the Thirteen? To provoke Dinda, and trigger the prepared avalanche of her City's ruin?

No, she tells herself, as she has also done endlessly. It wasn't just him. When I refused, it backed me.

The qherrique said, No.

Or did I simply not read it aright?

Over the House-roofs the qherrique burns back at her, a color-less quaking refractive lake. Eyes quailing, she wipes the tears, turning outward once again.

Sorry, then, for playing some role in this great onslaught? The thing she and Iatha feared all along? Sorry because he remembered that his intent, his information, action, was the lynch-pin of the attack?

Because he went to re-assume that role?

Because that return completed the alliance as the alliance did the siege-wall? So that Dinda's tribesmen, officered by a core of Cataract mercenaries, are supplemented by Verrain desert-scouts and camel-corps. And both by the massive contributions of Dhasdein.

Sorriest of all that his artfully broken memory concealed that truth? That Dhasdein was the instigator all along? Dhasdein whose drilled, heavy-armed troops man the greater part of the siege-wall? Dhasdein who has supplied the high command, and the commanding officer?

Dhasdein, above all, who has supplied the ships.

"You trying to get sunstroke, 'Rith?"

She starts. Obediently, leaves the balustrade.

"Dhasdein dangle's smarter than you are. He won't stand to talk in the heat."

Tellurith shrugs. Wanders across the main room, in the shadows where the qherrique, feeding—forget how it woke that night—sucks heat up like a sponge. Surprising how little there is, now, for a Head to do. All the shapers' orders are stalled. All the tribute trade is stopped. The food . . .

Better to remember the crowded refugees. Amberlight is crammed with House dependents from the Kora, who have fled before Dinda's, Verrain's, Dhasdein's advance.

"Did we sort out the laundry queue?"

"Yesterday. Sending out."

"I should go down to the Power-shop—"

"You've lived in the blighted Power-shop. It's in hand. There's nothing more for you to do."

Nothing, having planned it, except to avert the mind from that as well. Amberlight's weapons, prepared for its greatest war.

"I ought to see Zuri. Check the guard—"

A hand on the shoulder all but slams her into a chair.

"You think Zuri don't know how to do it by now? You sit down here and put something in your belly, so you'll have fed your brain when you go out there."

* * * *

Silencing Tellurith. Since in the five months after his flight Zuri's troublecrew have had all too much practice in deflecting attacks, ambushes and attempted assassinations, whether from Cataract or the Thirteen. Have, ironically, re-applied the principles their traitor taught them, with considerable success.

Since the most hunted woman in Amberlight is still alive.

Not only alive, but summoned by name to the parley the Dhasdein commander has requested for this afternoon.

* * * *

In the beginning, she recalls, they were a good deal more sanguine. That is, after that initial explosion, when word came that Cataract was on the march. When she faced death a good deal closer than a blocked street or an escalade of knife-handlers across the garden wall or an archer trying to establish a long draw on the House front; Maeran's eyes slitted, for once without languor, Maeran's filed-steel voice echoing in the Council-chamber roof.

"Precisely what connection there may be between Cataract's march and Telluir House's outlander, Telluir appears determined we shall never know. What is clear is that the City is under attack, with its secrets bared as never before. And the traitor remains in our midst. I propose execution of Telluir House-head for treachery. And the abolition of Telluir House."

Maeran's first, or perhaps second crucial blunder. Had she aimed for the Head alone, Tellurith is sure the Thirteen would have agreed. But to destroy a House . . . Her yet unthawed backbone recalls the hiatus, the dropping of eyes; the leap of her heart from terror—and was it despair that retorted, What is there to live for, why not?—to more terrifying hope as her politician's experience pre-recorded the vote: it's too close to the bone. They see their own fall. They're afraid.

But it is Zhee's passionless voice that fills the gap.

"How will this stop Cataract?"

Tipping the balance so faithful Jura can swing the waverers with acrid reminders that Telluir House may have brought calamity, but Telluir House therefore owes a double load of help and resources to set it right. A fine in time and money and personnel that Tellurith is only too glad to pay.

Especially when all her attempts to sway the view of Dinda's assault fail.

"How often have we seen it?" Liony of Zanza leans back, sweeping an impatient hand. "Ten years Dinda's run Cataract. And how many before him? How often have they thrown a tantrum and marched downRiver? What good does it do them? Shift the Riverside people and stock. We may lose some crops, but we have supplies. With the people safe he can sit and fume on the canal-bank until he's ready to go home."

"Or until," Damas shows her teeth in a very un-Headly leer, "he wakes up that his statuette's failing. And he may very well lose Cataract as well as his—army—if he sits around."

Since only the statuette ensures control of the wild Heartland tribesmen and landless poor of Cataract who form the majority of Dinda's troops.

And only a brilliantly clever military leader, she reflects, staring out into the haze, Shia's valiant work on a stringy old fowl forgotten in her mouth, only a military master could have kept those troops here, let alone used them effectively in a siege.

But seeing only the past, the Thirteen vote Telluir House a double share of defense work while ignoring her arguments, her assertions, her shouts that Dinda means more than a punitive tantrum. That—desperately double-edged weapon—the very riddle of her lost outlander argues there may be other, far more dangerous fingers in the puddle, that they should prepare for more than a simple Riverside raid.

To which, growing exasperated, Maeran votes yet another censure motion, silencing Telluir till the meeting's close.

* * * *

"**Y**ou think it's real."

It had been Ti'e's voice. Ti'e's presence at her elbow, too quiet to be abrupt, her partner Dyra as always a shadow beside her, as Tellurith leans both arms upon the archer's parapet. Staring, despair and fury mingled, into the green spring blur upstream. Ti'e, quiet young daughter thrown into Kuro's position, the new, all but cypher-mysterious head of Diaman.

But no scorn or combat in the tone. So Tellurith turns about, feeling a tiny hope rekindle. And prepares to go through it all again.

"He marched too fast for it to be just an answer to the ultimatum. You don't assemble a Cataract army in a fortnight. He was ready. It has to have been planned."

"They've always done it. Why should this be worse?"

"Because . . ." She stares into the grave young eyes. Stiffens her back, and thinks, Too new to be a traitor. Even if Kuro of all people was . . . In the Work-mother's hand, then.

"Because we don't know why Alk—my outlander—was here. But a Dhasdein background argues collusion. And if Cataract has backing from Dhasdein . . ." She reads that jaw's tightening and her pulse quickens. No need to exhume the nightmare. Ti'e has it too. "And . . ." the last pause, the most dangerous, "because I feel it. The—I know."

The eyes assess her. A true House-head. Impossible, even so early, even for Tellurith to tell what she is thinking. Until the eye corners relax. And Ti'e says, casual as if settling ship-turns at a quay.

"What do you want to do?"

Wherefore, while nine of the Thirteen vainly try to negotiate, Telluir, and Diaman, and to Tellurith's wonder, Hafas, have scoured their Kora holdings, shifting people and stock and supplies into the city, cramming clan and House lodgings, setting up makeshift pens and byres, filling warehouses with fodder and seed-grain and any other moveable possession.

Especially those that would help repulse a siege.

With the other unexpected ally, Tellurith thinks, chewing at last. That day down at the Dead Dyke, dispatching yet another crowd of Telluir villagers to their temporary lodgings, to be astonished by the appearance of a second House-head's guard.

And among her spic-and-span troublecrew, leaning lightly on the mahogany stick that is pure idiosyncrasy, the languid, elegant form of Averion. Head of Keranshah.

Who, having exchanged greetings and watched the villagers' file depart, stares upRiver a long time before she wonders, "What—precisely—are you expecting, Telluir?"

And to Tellurith's somewhat confounded, "I don't know," slits her eyes into the distance. And goes on, at last.

"I rather think—if he's not just here for the tantrum—that his only tactic is a siege."

Averion's taste for military theory is exceeded only by her strategist's talent. Tellurith has found more than an ally. She has found, she discovers with dazzled gratitude, a general.

It is Averion who decrees they will form forage parties to use the Kora as long as possible, who urges them to pull in supplies from farthest upstream first, who demands makeshift bridges to move materiel faster, who forms auxiliary naval units from commandeered ships and Downhill or River Quarter volunteers. To be paid three fiels a day, if war actually comes, from Telluir's treasury.

And Averion who grimly backs Tellurith's other visions, who plans for the worst and sketches the barricades, the new wall along Dead Dyke, and the means for manning them. Whose urging opens Diaman's workshop along with Keranshah's to see those plans made real.

* * * *

Tellurith averts eyes and mind. The delicately sauced fowl is ashes in her mouth.

Ashes. She gets up again, drawn to the window despite herself. Averion's other fall-back was truly drastic. "We'll lose this harvest," Tellurith hears her saying coolly. "They'll be here first"—somewhere it has become tacit among the allies that Dinda will not be alone—"but we'll deny them what we can." So foragers are made ready to ride out at first sign of the worst scenario, and fire the ripening fields.

"We don't do it till we're sure it's serious." Averion's worst-case scenario is the arrival, in force, of Dhasdein. "Have to skip the Sahandan anyway. Those paddies will never burn. But we can take out the fodder. And the grain."

Tellurith's scalp shrinks at the recollected image. Dust and skirmish swirls spread across the Kora as on some miniature, general's world. Averion growling softly beside her at the balustrade. Response to the warning mirror-signals, scouts springing from a dozen picket posts. Gallop of small black ants. First plumes of black-bronze smoke. Burning grass. Burning wheat. Averion's indrawn breath, strong as at a wound.

As from the western horizon a furious spray of faster more ferocious ants swarms upon the fire-setters like a four-legged mist whose action is less frightening than its speed. Half an army thrown lawless as a flood-head across a plain.

And as smothering. Amberlight scouts taken or dispatched. Fires out.

Averion beside her, cursing fastidiously, a bouquet of archaic military oaths. "Now by the two-edged sword of Koriess. Skirmish cavalry. He's made skirmish cavalry, out of those blight-bitten desert nomads. How did the bastard get Verrainers to do *that*?"

While with ice down the backbone, Tellurith wonders: How did the bastard know?

Amberlight's first casualties. Amberlight's first taste of the mind directing this campaign.

****

Shia is inside, fussing with her Head's chosen clothes. Fine enough to impress an enemy, not so fine as to invite covetousness. To impress an impressive enemy, whose anticipation of their anticipation of his reaction to their action in anticipation of his action has made a mental nightmare, a constant high-wire dance, of these last three months.

Which began in the first minutes' shock at seeing that charge of Verrain light cavalry, the bridleless pony riders who escort caravans. Augmented with almost hysterical astonishment when the vanguard behind them proves to be Verrain cameleers.

****

"**V**errain don't attack us! They've *never* done it! They never do it! This is ridiculous—impossible!" Falla and Sevitha and Eutharie, the least forward-looking, most timid of the House-heads, a panicked chorus whose descant takes half a glass to die. Before Maeran's furious onslaught on Telluir, whose intransigency has brought this plague. Cut off by Averion's ice-edged drawl.

"That's fine, Maeran, and we respect your care for your House interests." At a time, says the slicing inflection, when nothing matters less. "But meanwhile, the rest of us have a war to fight."

"And the one person who may know more than anyone about the rationale for the attack," Ti'e's quiet, rare intervention is almost a greater shock, "is the Head of Telluir House."

****

"**W**hatever they want, they can't get at us without a siege," Averion re-summarizes the situation. "And even if they now have the supplies for it, you can't maintain a siege with a rabble of spear-throwing tribesmen and a horde of cameleers."

But you can do it, Tellurith thinks, leaning her forehead on her window frame in sudden weariness, with heavy-armed, disciplined, Imperial infantry.

Beyond the river, the sun gleams fang-bright on massed, tempered steel. Helmets. Spear and sentry heads. The broad circular shields of the Dhasdein regular army. Blazoned with the too-familiar badge that she has seen every nine years on the Imperial embassy: Dhasdein's snake and thunderbolt. Discard memory of the further confrontation, her mind tells her, when word came in from their waterborne scouts downstream: that the worst-case scenario was no longer scenario. That the two Dhasdein border brigades have marched into Verrain.

Averion's answer comes after a thirty-minute pace about the Arcis parapets.

"I've never been one to sit and wait."

So, since the enemy must already know about the light-guns, *Wasp* and two sisters are dispatched downstream. To bring long-distance confusion, horror and casualties on the marching columns, to force them, at the least, from the easy Riverside going, and at the most, to provoke desertions and ruin morale with a fearsome preview of the weapons of Amberlight. "Just think how you'd feel," Averion murmurs, "if you knew that was going to be used on you."

Remembering an ambush in River Quarter, Tellurith has no doubt of how she feels.

In the meantime, Averion and the Verrain commander play how-d'you-do with nuisance raids. Picket lines stampeded, camels hocked, first by desperately grudged troublecrew, then, Averion's genius, by gang-volunteers, set cross-River at night, by dinghy, and then by Navy ships. "I never thought," says Damas of Jerish in outright amazement, "that those scoundrels could be some use!"

More catch-as-catch-can then, as the Verrain camp is shifted and the guerillas bicker with irregularly moved guard-posts. A light, nagging, almost playful prelude, if there can be play in war. "He's teasing me," says Averion. "Learning my moves. But then, I'm learning his." Almost, faintly, tigerishly, amused.

Until Dhasdein arrives.

* * * *

"**W**e never expected to stop them." Averion in council, wearily tolerant of Falla's shrieks. "When you launch two brigades at something, you're not going to turn around for nuisance raids." And when the uproar dies at last, she adds the real blow.

"They know perfectly well the numbers are on their side."

Tellurith's stomach turns over again as it did that day, entirely, sickeningly the same. Against numbers, the most terrible weapons, the best defenses, the most brilliant strategist will not prevail.

"Which is why," Averion again, ice-calm, ice-cold, "we did not make major attacks downRiver. Which is why those of us who looked ahead," at the intonation half the Thirteen quail, "have hauled in supplies and prepared weapons for those who would not. Our only hope is to maintain our defenses. To wait them out, while taking as few casualties as we can."

Which is why, Tellurith thinks, we could stop the first assault in its tracks. With *Wasp* and *Hornet* and *Mosquito* and the *Spider* trio, and above all, with the big new light-guns on *Horsefly*, Averion's sardonically renamed *Queenbee,* and the auxiliaries ploughing in their wake. A living, moving, burning, fighting-wall that seared the troops on the bank and rammed or ignited the assault flotilla, tearing back and forth like fire-armed juggernauts even when the assault commander threw his main forces in, trying to overcome them with sheer mass, when the paddle-wheels churned blood rather than water, at the height of the attack.

A very, very costly, perhaps humiliating defeat. A tactic they have never tried again.

Rubbing her squinted eyes, Tellurith wonders anew about that attack, as she has wondered for the last two months. So costly. So extravagant. So unimaginative. So out of character for the mind behind this campaign. Which otherwise has preferred to trap and slap and anticipate, never to stake pride and human lives in a situation where only brute force and massive losses can prevail.

Was it an aberration? A loss of patience? An unschooled arrogance?

Or something else?

* * * *

Shia has cleared the table. Only the delicate glasses, the chilled white wine, remain.

Tellurith pours a glass and takes it back to the window. Trains her eyes, watering still, but not now with sun-glare, down the river's curve.

That glittering serpentine is empty now. Empty as her heart, as she mourns yet again, in the hollowness of useless grief. For *Wasp,* and *Hornet* and all the rest of them, and the tough, brave, stubborn women who were the Navy's inner core: the love band, one in death as they were in life. The core whose spirit and expertise and experience they miss so bitterly, far more than the mere presence of another fighter at your shoulder, another hand for gun-pad or bowstring, another occupied space.

At first, when the enemy did not repeat their assault, they thought they were safe. "They can sit there till winter comes," Denara of Winsat proclaims triumphantly from the Arcis parapet, "and they'll get no nearer than they are."

But of course, as the morning shows them, the mind behind the campaign is not intending to come nearer.

Not yet.

The siege-wall's beginning alarms but does not frighten them. What is it, except a ratification of defeat? If the enemy is prepared to admit he cannot get in, Amberlight need only ward its defenses against surprise attack, keep its waterways open, and wait. "What good," wonders Denara scornfully, "is a siege-wall with a river on both ends?"

Denara's answer arrives a week later. When the forced laborers rounded up across the Kora, not to mention Dinda's protesting rabble, stop their basket-carting and barrowing and stare openmouthed downstream.

At a Dhasdein military fleet.

Ten galleys. Tellurith numbers them in memory, sipping on the bitterness of white, chilled wine. Little enough, we thought, with *Hornet* and *Mosquito* and *Wasp*. Especially after we sank two, with no losses, in the first fight.

Until the auxiliaries arrived. Until the galleys, with a wall of floating refuse—dinghies, ruined freighters, rafts—between them and us, began to haul out the chains.

Massive, double-strength harbor chains. Anchored to rock-piled moles, the most impressive bastions Amberlight watercrew have seen, and they remember the construction of their own flood-proof quays. Fixed across the river to points beyond Dead Dyke, where only costly, too costly assaults will let Amberlight cast them loose.

Not that Amberlight does not try, council of desperation before their Navy is trapped in its pond. One try. Before Averion decrees it is too high a price.

"They have the numbers. We don't."

* * * *

The glass has made a ring on the shining mahogany, unshielded, protected, usually, by Shia's utmost wrath. Tellurith shifts it, the word echoing in her head.

Numbers.

Numbers enough for extravagance even by that thrifty antagonist. Despite various attempts to cut the chains by light-beam, to portage Navy ships over their ends—Tellurith puts the glass down at the bitter, bitter taste of that, half *Black Widow*'s crew caught and slaughtered on the beach—to draw off the defenders by sham and ruse, to land desperately grudged guerillas to attack the siege wall, even, at wildest aphelion, an attempt to kidnap the enemy general—despite all this, numbers enough for the day when he fills that circumscribed pond with eight Imperial galleys and every other scrap of junk provided by an army's ingenuity, down to saboteurs sent to jam the Amberlight waterwheels, floating on inflated skins.

So those in Amberlight can only watch, watch helplessly, as the remaining six Navy ships and their auxiliaries are crowded, immobilized, fought over, the crews killed, or captured, drastically wounded. Finally, at least three times by their own folk's volition, sunk with their secrets still aboard.

Despite a slaughter with those light-guns that Tellurith's spine shrinks now to contemplate.

Far less vengeful, even now, than Averion, red-eyed at her balustrade next morning, when from the farther bank comes that searing flash, the thunder crack, and then the spouting pillar of black smoke. And Averion laughs, murderously as a widow avenged, and shouts, "Meddle with *that,* you whores!"

Both of them knowing that a captured light-gun, or a power-panel assembly, with or without its engine, has met outland meddling with its own revenge.

Except, of course, Tellurith thinks wearily, the numbers are still there.

And now they can reach Amberlight itself.

Which perhaps, and perhaps not, makes less astonishing this offer, a mere four days after the siege wall closed.

For the nine-hundredth time her brain asks, Treat for what?

For all we could do, he had too many hidden dice, and too much advantage, for us to overcome or anticipate. Why does he stop? With our ships gone and our supplies blocked, and no sign that he ever worried about losing men, why does he simply not attack? Pour men at those open quays, that dyke and defense wall, absorb the losses, and get what he wants?

Alternatively, why doesn't he sit and wait?

Shia comes down the corridor and stands, hesitating, at the inner door. Tellurith sends another glance through the balcony window. The sun's limb is just beneath the eave.

By the time she is dressed and down to the Dead Dyke, it will be middle afternoon-watch. The appointed time.

＊＊＊＊

In the torrid heat of the glacis behind Dead Dyke wall, the other entourage has already disembarked. Emerging from her vehicle,

Azo and Verrith fanning ahead, Zuri herself at her back, Tellurith catches breath in a gasp. But the other Head leans on her stick and greets confederate and heat with equal disinterest.

Like her, Tellurith is wearing the summer uniform of wide white muslin trousers, tiny gold-thread silk top and open white muslin robe. Let the enemy have armor, swords, bows. She does not intend to compromise her trust in her troublecrew or her Ruand's dignity. Nor to let this outland dangle suppose her fearful if she raises a sweat.

A narrowing of eyes is all the greeting Zhee vouchsafes. Her troublecrew are twitchy enough for three. Tellurith feels Zuri's scowl. Composure is compulsory; for the honor of Amberlight.

It is Dhasdein's request that the negotiators be the heads of Hafas and Telluir House. Mother forbid, shudders Tellurith, that I have to suffer such another fuss,. when even Maeran's accusations of treachery and desertion hold less malice than fear. It is Averion's wary generalship that ordains they shall in no way reveal ingress, egress or even ladder height of the new dyke wall. Instead, they are to take an ancient and pitiful rowing boat round the head of the canal to the meeting place.

Which, as Averion points out, allows a thrifty blend of their own transport in case of flight, and a hefty rower-load of troublecrew in case of fight. "I'm well aware, and they may be too, that we're hazarding half the brain of our defense."

To which Tellurith's sole, flattered reply is that the safeguards are ample. Two high officers to stand as hostages. And the safeconduct under a pledge Dhasdein soldiers have been found to honor more often than break. The general's personal word.

Assandar. She tries it on her tongue to the oars' creak. A scribble at the document foot that the envoy has to decipher, the mark of a seal. A desert hawk. No noble Dhasdein family badge. Possibly a personal emblem, maybe awarded by the emperor. Some stolid career soldier, some ambitious noble scion, some pampered Imperial favorite?

His tactics, she considers, hardly suggest the latter two. A veteran commander, then. She wonders what he knows of her—what Alkhes has told him of her—and her stomach rolls over as if she is preparing to approach the face. The boat-nose turns. Mud and reeds and stone-protected river edge are bisected by a vivid, staring stripe.

Carpet, a long hall-runner such as are used in noble Dhasdein houses, stretched to the water's edge.

Zhee's lips twitch. Tellurith lifts her eyes and blinks, dazzled by more than sky.

The pavilion almost occupies the wide bridge-head square. Double thickness white linen, twin-peaked, wide-eaved, with outrageous tasseled emerald and purple side-ropes, and more outrageous emerald and purple pennons cavorting overhead like lazy exotic flames. A great many shiny metal lobsters seem to be crowded inside, but midway their mass opens on a muted gleam of crimson and white. The double-cloth spread of a proper negotiators' table. With the backs of tall chairs showing on the nearer side.

Respectful minions attend their landing, to a flourish from hidden trumpets. Not a national fanfare. Something anonymous. Tellurith has to control a grin. Entering the tent, they find the crowd diminished, space for their troublecrews at either side, the armor almost out of evidence. Taking position by her chair, Zhee stands and waits.

The trumpets ring again. Not the fanfare of a Dhasdein general either. An invisible but brazen-voiced herald proclaims, "The High Commander of the Worshipful Coalition, Her Excellence's Zenadar," a Verrain military viceroy, "His Excellence's Lieutenant, His Imperial Majesty's General, Assandar."

The male military divide. The sun beyond blinds her on a blaze of scarlet and polished iron.

The military cloak flares behind him like a forest fire. The embossed and burnished breast-plate is mirror-brilliant above the immaculate dark-red officer's kilt, the sword-hilt glitters to each pace. But the red-crested helmet is under an arm. Baring the crow's-wing fall of that black, outland hair.

Zhee too must know, must recognize, cannot fail to recognize that lithe, supple, troublecrew's stride. Must recall that face whose every feature is graven on Tellurith's memory, sharp nose, sharp jaw, fine-cut mouth. Ink and ebony eyes.

Zhee's response is one slightly quicker breath. Struggling for equal aplomb, Tellurith already feels the difference. Face, hair, walk, yes. But not merely Alkhes.

Assandar.

It is in every nuance of carriage and gesture. Decision. Power. Authority. The wit, the danger of the killer and mercenary. But beyond that, the weight of rank. Dhasdein's general.

"Ladies," the appointed steward of the meeting, an anonymity ushering from the table end. "Please sit down."

Zhee does not move.

"I am not a lady," she says, when all the eyes are fixed on her. "I am Hafas House-head. I am a Voice of Amberlight."

And amid the lackey's consternation his general intervenes with unhurried swiftness and the merest blank look to imply suppressed drollery, "Ruands. Please sit down."

Tellurith is glad of an acceptable offer. More glad of the chair. The sight of him has been a body blow. The familiar slight Iskan burr, with its soft inimitable undernote, is a dagger in the side.

"Ruands, you have honored our presence for one purpose." And all Alkhes too is the way, once seated, he gets straight to the meat. "To hear terms of peace, which I ask that you put before the Thirteen."

No negotiator has ever said it so easily, so like a native. Tellurith offers a thanksgiving that Maeran is not here.

Zhee inclines her head. "Amberlight," that rustling old voice is still perfectly empty, "will hear your terms."

Terms? thinks Tellurith, as attention becomes shock, becomes disbelief, becomes outrage. Mother's blood, is this mockery, an insult, or a jest?

Effrontery enough to demand that Amberlight recompense the besiegers for their dead, their expense and their time. Insult enough to require that the price of statuettes be fixed by "the Coalition." Outrage to propose that Amberlight admit outsiders to its council. Beyond forgiveness to ordain that the city become a vassal of "the Coalition," administered, like the merest Dhasdein colony, by a governor.

But to demand that the working of "so-called pearl-rock" be opened to anyone, in or out of Amberlight. And that it be administered by officials of the governor.

That they abolish every House . . .

Tellurith hardly hears the end. A red rage has blotted the detail out of everything. She clenches hands in her trousers, digging fingernails into her thigh. She is too far gone even to attend the crucial details: the reader's tone, his body language, whether he dares—dreams—of meeting her eye.

The voice-noise ends. Black and red and shining metal swim somewhere beyond her ken. Through it come the measured cadences of Zhee's reply.

"You demand of Amberlight . . ."

Word-perfect, she recites back the terms.

By their end Tellurith's eyes have cleared. Vision enough to see across the table. To the blank, respectful stance of standing subordinates. At his leader's elbow, the waiting scribe. And the quiet posture, eyes courteously fixed on Zhee's face, lack of expression a perfect armor, of the man in the general's chair.

"Man," yes. Not, to be sure, Alkhes.

Who would know these terms are entirely impossible. Who, given Assandar's authority, would never see them voiced.

Unless he never meant them to be used.

Cruel, final jest?

As she takes breath Zhee speaks again.

"Here, now, are the terms of Amberlight."

That the besiegers withdraw at once. That the city be recompensed for its Navy, its loss of trade, its time and trouble and disturbed dependents, let alone its dead. That "the Coalition" expect no further use of any qherrique until the instigator of the assassination attempt on a Head of Telluir House, "at a House-head's funeral," be uncovered, and sent to Amberlight for the Thirteen to decide his punishment.

"Whatever his rank—or his position—may be."

Choking down the bubble of mad laughter, Tellurith cries inwardly, Two can play at insult—bravo, Zhee!

And without pause, Zhee is levering herself out of her chair. "When you have an answer," offering the enemy no title, in itself a profound insult, "you may send us word."

He rises in turn. Inclines his head. Impervious to affront, maintaining respect for age? Blight and blast it, Tellurith thinks, maddened by bewilderment as a bull by flies, what is he *doing*?

"Ruand, if I might have a word, before you go?"

The black eyes have swung. Are looking straight at her.

Zhee checks. Do you, asks the backward glance, want help?

No sign of censure. No sign of doubt. Her greatest accolade, Tellurith thinks, as she makes the troublecrew sign for, No; and tries to keep her heart out of her gullet as she answers, "If my colleague can rest—in the shade."

Assandar cocks his head. Invisible orders, bustle of departing aides. From somewhere a madly incongruous parasol, offers of cool tea, Zhee's diminishing voice.

Before her, black eyes. Steady as sword-points in the thin, taut, familiar, unfamiliar face.

"Tel . . . urith."

The waver in her perception matches the wobble of that voice. Assandar—Alkhes? Looking at her so weirdly, so hungrily, movement just checked before he reaches out both hands. Black circles under the lash-line that are Alkhes resurrected, a set of the mouth that is all Assandar. Before the doubling can disorient her Tellurith asks, "What did you want to say?"

This time the lack of title brings a quirk, so predictable, so demolishing, in a corner of the mouth. The eyes, still devouring her, say something else.

"I wanted to know you were all right."

Tellurith feels herself swell like a goaded porcupine. Just before the rage bursts, words explode into her mouth.

"Just tell me, why?"

More incredible, the little shiver that runs through him, Alkhes to his fingertips. Before he lets his breath out. And murmurs, "Somehow, I knew you'd say that."

Still staring across the table. As if, impossibly, ridiculously, he wanted to be closer. Then, collecting himself. "Which—Why—do you want first?"

So many priorities. Only one matters now.

"When did you first remember—everything?"

"When I—"

He stops. The eyes widen, all Alkhes.

"Tel, I give you my—"

Another stop.

"No." A deep breath. Arduously, he begins again. "You may not believe this. If you don't, there's nothing I can do, no—oath—I can swear to change your mind. But it is the truth. I only remembered—everything—that last night."

Amberlight, her House, her people rely on her. Staring across that three feet of white and crimson cloth, Tellurith can only implore the Mother to let her be sure. To look into those eyes, those almost beseeching eyes, so at odds with his military grandeur, and know if it is the truth.

When she does not speak, he turns his hands out. Takes a deep breath. And bows his head.

Her throat is dry. It comes flatly, instinctive, involuntary recourse to the commerce in which they have never lied.

"Where did you come from—first?"

The head comes up. Alkhes, the light in the eyes, but the assurance is Assandar.

"I was born"—the tiny glint says, I know what you ask, and I will give it you full measure, overflowing—"in Verrain. My family is from Shirran. My father was a hire-guard for the caravans. Then we went to Dhasdein. I joined the Imperial army when I was fifteen."

Dhasdein, and not Dhasdein. Verrain, and not Verrain.

"And when you came to Amberlight?"

The eyes meet hers steadily. "I was sent by the Coalition—Cataract, Verrain, Dhasdein."

The third—the final?—coalition. An irony, to be proven right by your worst terror affirmed.

Those eyes are a duelist's with blade poised. He could almost be back across her dining table. Except this time the only constraint on his answers is his own choice.

A gamble to follow other gambles. Yet here, now, perhaps, there is just enough mutual leverage, in her moral high ground, in his military superiority, to ensure the truth.

"And did you have a contact—inside Amberlight?"

The eyes flare like a black corona. "You mean a *House*?"

Testament enough. Before the head-shake, understanding now, from past experience, from burnt-in knowledge of the Thirteen's tie-webs, grim, but not with disbelief.

"No, Tel. Inside Amberlight—I never had any contact at all."

Greater irony, that in the pit of nightmare, there can be relief. Carefully, Tellurith eases her shoulders. Lets that shift signal a change of topic, before she speaks.

"And this time?"

Now there is wariness. An answer in itself.

"I asked for the command."

Very softly, Tellurith says, "Oh?"

The eyes flash. Sun on turned steel. And as suddenly there is all Alkhes' killer ice in the corners of the mouth.

"Come out here."

Four swift strides from among his subordinates. Round the side of the tent. Into full sun. Full view of Amberlight.

He has swung round. More than challenge in the stare.

She takes the four steps after him.

"I know what you're damn well thinking, and you're wrong. I did not do this for revenge. Not on you. Not on Amberlight."

"Then what?"

And more suddenly the eyes soften. He half reaches out. They are closer now, no table between them. It is a patent effort to withdraw his hands.

"Damn it, Tel—I did it for you, that's why."

"For *me*?"

"That's what I wanted to say. I'll make you an offer. Safe conduct. Clear passage through the lines. For all of Telluir House."

It is too astounding for riposte. Tellurith can only stare.

He takes a step closer. Now it is definitely a struggle with his hands.

"Tel, gods damn it, I didn't *want* to go. I knew what you'd think—what you'd feel—I know I can't make you believe me, but I never deceived you, not like that. What we had—what we were—that was *real*."

Surest balm. Sweetest consolation. The ulcer salved at last. It was no deceit in the deepest truth. If they have played at intelligencers' commerce, they have been honest in the trading of the heart.

"I knew what it would do to you—in the House—with the Thirteen—gods' eyes, I sweated all the way down river, every time I thought of what that bitch Maeran might—" he shudders, and actually shuts his eyes. "Even knowing what Zuri would think of me . . ."

The eyes open. "You may not believe it—but it *hurt*."

As much as to break those unremembered bonds of secrecy. Because these bonds of trust and faith were equally binding. And to a man who respects his word, in breaking, equal pain.

Her hands ache to reach out, to take him as she did for love or comfort in her arms. But they are on a quayside before the assembled eyes of his army. Not to mention Amberlight.

"Then in the Mother's name—*why*?"

"Because I *had* to! Because I'd made promises and contracts—I couldn't have stayed and been who I am—or been someone else, if it was a lie!"

The sun is beating on her head, her shoulders, a downpouring relentless fire. Sweat rolls down her back. And in that unforgiving furnace she feels her muscles relax. Testing, accepting the truth.

Silently, she sees him sigh. You understand. You do understand.

"Tel . . ."

I want to touch you, the eyes say. I want you here between my hands, to hold you and feel your physical reality as much—no doubt about it—as you want me.

And only a siege-wall, and a city, and two or three nations, and eighteen inches of empty air, lie between.

Tellurith gathers herself up. Finding the old tactics for the old commerce, which has only now begun to matter again.

Says very softly, "Then why?"

"Why what?" A genuine frown.

"Why are you offering—these terms?"

The flick of the eyes is a sword engaged.

"It's a siege, Tel. I've seen sieges before. I care about you. I want you out of there."

More softly, Tellurith says, "So why these terms?"

The eyes fix. The body goes still.

"You know they'll never take them. Not in a million years."

Silence.

"And you won't take ours."

Something turns in the blackness like a flicker of steel. "Blast it, Tel, I thought you were the trader? Of course we won't take yours, any more than you'll take ours! Did you ever take first offer when you buy?"

Her heart thumps. Almost, it sings.

Almost.

"You expect us to bargain?"

"If Hafas House-head don't expect to bargain, I've never seen a better double-finger in my life." The River gesture for obscenity. She very nearly hiccups on the laugh. "God's eyes, Tel!"

Bargain. Not lunacy, revenge, final insult. They expect to offer leeway. "And you want me to argue . . ."

"If they'll listen, yes!"

Bait. Dizzying possibility, heart-stopping temptation. Life. Hope.

"But still—you wanted us out."

The shoulders collapse. Inside the shell of military magnificence is a tired, strained, desperately worried man.

"I told you, Tel—I care about you."

The mouth tightens. "And you know—I know—what could happen . . . if they won't play."

Their eyes meet. She has never seen those eyes look like that, never felt so fiercely how he wants to touch her, to reach out, merely to touch. Or felt such a matching desire.

"Tel, just do it, will you? I can protect the whole House. Send you wherever you want to go. Money. Transport. Anything. I can do it. Just let me get them out."

Doubt flares, a black and sickening flare, saying, screaming, If this is not revenge or insult there is still some other deadlier, undisclosed trap. Something he has side-stepped, something he will not disclose. Even to you.

She opens her mouth. And the qherrique, or Amberlight, or someone retorts, And is there nothing you have kept from him?

She shuts her mouth.

"I'll speak to the Thirteen." Voice lifted now, formal enunciation. A perfect pretext to detain me, she thinks, what damnable wits that can set three goals in one: see me alone. Make the House its offer. Seem to make clear that these terms are only a starting point. "I'll do my best to see that they—consider your terms."

The eyes flare. His hands jump, a half-reach that cannot be controlled.

"But Amberlight is my city." Quieter now, for his ears alone. "Whatever terms we make, we make for us all."

Distress, consternation. Alkhes' black anger sparked with the imperial affront of Assandar. And then a wry, more than ironic smile.

"How did I know you'd say that?" He asks it with pure resignation. Inclines a head, Assandar's permission. And goes on with Alkhes' unstoppable presumption, "I'll see you to the boat."

VII

"**W**ell, 'Rith . . . after all, it's nothing we didn't expect."
Sunset on Amberlight, the long parched day fading, reluctantly, from a suffused dusty-rose sky. A prickle of early lights below them. And beyond that the noose, the fiery necklace of enemy fires.

Nothing unexpected, no. Soundlessly, Tellurith sighs. Seeing that other sunset on the Arcis council-chamber, in transit from ruddy sun to pale qherrique glow. Hearing the interminable, predictable, futile uproar, Sevitha and Eutharie bleating about Amberlight tradition and the honor of the House, Damas and Falla fulminating amid Denara and Liony's, "I told you so's." Ti'e's silence. Averion, chin on hand, thinking furiously. Maeran's glare.

And the more than inevitable outburst when she herself says, "We should consider these terms."

Before the three-day word war that leaves Tellurith and her backers, Averion, Ti'e, Jura, and press-ganged Ciruil of Terraqa, deadlocked with Maeran's supporters who will consider no terms at all.

Until Zhee's first words fall like ice-drops into the quiet.

"We should hear Telluir."

A measure of Zhee's unacknowledged leadership, that Maeran herself only gasps.

"We can afford to cancel recompense—except for the Navy ships. We can afford to—consider—changed negotiations over price. We can afford to promise consideration of a Council with foreign representatives."

A pause.

"We do not, naturally, consider vassalship. Or abolition of any House. Or failure to produce the assassin's source."

Terms on the qherrique need not be discussed.

Maeran draws an enormous breath. "But, Ruand—"

Zhee lifts one crabbed, imperative hand. "While arguing, we can also find out—why we are offered these terms."

* * * *

How much, Tellurith wonders again, does Zhee guess? Even accept? Behind that lizard's impassivity, impossible to tell. Except it is Zhee who decrees negotiations shall be carried forward by Telluir House.

Freezing Maeran's protests with, "Are you personally acquainted with the general?"

Do I alone, she wonders, seeing those black eyes lift across the table, recognize the burning anxiety, the starvation, behind that commander's face?

Can I alone decipher the tiny shifts of hope, affirmation, unsurprised exasperation as I speak?

Or the tap of a knuckle on the table rim, unconscious habit of thought that is not, and yet so heart-shakingly is Alkhes?

Before he sits back and says, expressionless, "If we cancelled compensation—on what grounds does Amberlight exclude its ships?"

* * * *

As well, Tellurith considers, that she is a House-head, proofed against endless negotiations and word-wars from birth. Because Assandar is an opponent who presses her to the wall on every point, with equal wits, and uncanny anticipation, and perhaps greater endurance than hers.

Then when that first session has left her feeling like a squashed pomegranate, says coolly, "I shall escort the Ruand to her boat." Leaving her to wonder, Which of us most wants to get the other alone?

In the preamble to evening their steps clack across the deserted stones. Amberlight's unofficial market-place, once. Awnings, stalls, small animal pens, swept clean. Briefly, Tellurith mourns. Turning to see aides and troublecrew a decorous ten paces behind. Before she asks, "Why are you bothering with all this?"

"Tel-l-l . . ."

The hiss is long-drawn exasperation. Disbelief.

"You don't need a siege." What disadvantage to point out what he must already know? "You could take us any day."

"Haven't you been listening? Can't you imagine the price? Do you think, in a sack, I could keep this lot," wave of an arm to the squalid Cataract bivouacs, strewn piecemeal about the siege-wall, "under control? Gods damn it, Tel!"

"You know perfectly well we will never take those terms."

"You're talking, aren't you?"

"But for what?"

They reach the carpet's end, swing, part the troublecrew. It is another three strides before he speaks again.

"Don't you know?"

Her eyes go sideways of themselves. It is all she can do not to tear off the burnished breastplate, kilt, officer's cloak. To reach the slight resilient body underneath, the flesh and blood that is all and only Alkhes.

Like him, she is out of breath. "You didn't care before about—price."

"What?"

"At the first assault."

"Like you, I tow a cart-load of nincompoops." Irony. With a hurtful bite. "In particular, the Dhasdein brigadiers. So five hundred men—people—had to die—to prove I spoke the truth."

"About the light-guns?"

Twist of the lips. Ducked head.

"Pity the lesson couldn't have been first-hand."

A disconcerting revision of view. Grown terrifying. That no more than she does he have absolute control or command. That he has to manage an unruly crew of doubtful allies and pushing subordinates. That . . .

"Should we be talking like this?"

Quick glance, doubled irony. Sudden open grin.

"Oh, they're as sure I'll bewitch you as the Thirteen are that you can off-side me."

A punch in the heart. Not the anticipation, or the insult, but the smile. That says, And I'll let them think it. For nothing more than this.

"Alkhes . . ."

"Damn, clythx, I never meant to hurt you—oh, damn, damn—" under his breath now, humor utterly gone. "Damn, if we could just—"

"No. No." Torment that it must all be public. That they must not stop walking, must not speak openly, touch. Mercy, she thinks, as the knife turns. Because if I laid hands on him I would not let go.

"Tel, just forget the damn talks—" he has swung round as if he cannot stop himself. "Stay here, I can look after you—Amberlight doesn't matter—gods' eyes, every time I think about what could happen in there I go crazy, clythx, please . . ."

The pain burns like fire. Her whole body cries to turn to him, to throw away House and rank and Amberlight, to cross that eighteen inches of impossibility and shout, Yes!

And what will his unruly wolves say?

What will Iatha and Zuri say?

She clenches her fists. Feels the nails, with vague astonishment, go through the skin, and recalls, in some strange corner of her mind, blood on white table-cloth, a black, bowed head.

"Alkhes." Where is her breath? "I can't."

"Damn it, Tel . . ."

"I can't leave my House."

Iatha. Hanni. Shia. Caitha. Ahio. Zuri. Verrith and Azo.

The names, the presences rise between them. She can see the roll-call in his face.

Before he bends his head. Says, faint with more than wits' exhaustion, "I'll see you to the boat."

* * * *

"It's not like," Iatha, valiantly casual, "we didn't know."

That the Thirteen, agrees Tellurith, leaning on the balustrade now, staring out into the slow, slow onset of night, would never accept those terms. That they could not accept those terms. That under them, Amberlight would die.

That under those terms, whatever I may know about the internal corruption, about the old form of the city, matters not at all.

"So that is your City's final word?"

Zhee to back her, that time. Tellurith demanded it. She needs more than troublecrew to withstand the eyes, named and known and doubly dangerous now, at their general's back. The Dhasdein brigadiers, big, beefy, confident men whose scowls have darkened by the day. The sullen, black-burnt Verrain cavalry captains, who have had to forage for this extended blockade. The infinite menace of the Cataract officers, whose blank eyes say, We are doing a job. However it is done, we will be paid.

"Amberlight will agree to cancel compensation claims, even for the Navy ships, to match with yours. We will negotiate a new way to fix prices. We will consider, once the siege is over, admission to City councils of a foreign representative. We will waive identification and punishment of the assassin's master. But to ask that we renounce independent rule, or change our Craft-laws, or alter our living ways, is to destroy Amberlight."

"You would sooner see your city sacked? Your people dead?"

"We would sooner die."

It resounds into the silence. In Zhee's remote, silvery tones, the timbre of ultimate truth.

* * * *

"**Y**ou knew it would go this way from the start."

"I thought you backed me in this! You listened when I told you what they do with the things! You refused Verrain! I thought you understood—I thought you wanted it stopped!"

"Not by destroying my city! My life!"

"Tel—gods damn it—" he swings from the tent wall. His own tent, aides and allies and servants expelled, all camouflage shed. "I thought you knew—I thought you agreed—that it's bad?"

"What?"

"God's eyes!" A stamp and snatch at his hair that is all Assandar. "The pearl-rock—what's done with it, what it's doing—to Cataract, to Dhasdein. What it's doing inside the City. River Quarter. The Houses. The imbalance of wealth—of power."

"Is it so good anywhere else?"

"Never *mind* anywhere else! Anywhere else doesn't turn its men into catamites—doesn't kill a woman's child!"

Tellurith feels her face go white.

"You must have felt it, Tel. What he—your husband's like. A pampered stud-horse. And if he gets sons it destroys you both. What it's doing to you all! Damn it, there are bad customs elsewhere, but not so bad as that!"

There are no words she can speak.

"And all for some ingrown goddamned historical—*prejudice*! Just because the tradition says men can't work qherrique!"

The heart dies in her chest.

"You must understand, Tel. You must see it. You see and feel and know everything else, you cried for those poor idiots in River Quarter, you understood me when I was—can't you understand this?"

The eyes, the voice, the outheld hands are tearing the heart out of her. Yes, she wants to cry, to scream, I understand, I know, it should all be changed, I want to give you what you want, yes, yes!

But I can't.

The light is dying, momently. Outside, and in his eyes. Over her heartbeat, she almost hears him breathe. Before he drops his hands.

And she says, so quietly it rasps in her throat, "You meant this all along."

"Tel—"

"You knew we would never take those terms." Not *would not*, her tongue longs to scream. *Can't.* "You always intended—to bring us down."

His lips part. And close. Is there pain to match that, she wonders, in my eyes?

His shoulders lift. And droop. Then he sets his teeth and lifts his chin. Assandar.

"I hoped they'd do it peacefully. It wasn't just for show. If you knew how much I've grudged this time—how impatient Quizir's getting." The Dhasdein brigadier. "How much riskier it is when you make troops delay . . ."

He stops again. Final courage, meets her eyes.

"I suppose I made up my own mind—a long time ago. While I was still—Alkhes. In a way—it wasn't intentional, but in a way—it's why I came to Amberlight. To know."

In the pause, she hears the outer world, the rumble of male voices, the rumor of a great camp. The sounds of war. And death.

"But, yes. If that's the only way to stop it—then, yes."

Her eyes sting. She draws a great breath, as if commanding her muscles for a last cut at the face.

"If that's how it must be—you know the rest."

The eyes cling to hers, blacker than velvet, blacker than sentient, suffering night. The garb, the stance, the face is Assandar. The eyes are Alkhes. As is the voice that whispers, "I know the rest."

* * * *

"**N**o," says Tellurith, remotely, watching the light die. "It's nothing we didn't know."

* * * *

Any more than they doubt the form of the opening shots. Averion's projection needs no confirming sight of the Dhasdein brigadiers. The Thirteen have the night to prepare. To have troublecrew from Hezamin and Jerish mass out the gun-crews on stand-by at the Dead Dyke wall, turn-and-turn-about since the Navy was lost, day and night. To have others from Hafas and Terraqa down at the quays, posted before dawn in the warehouses that Averion's plans have seen converted, long since.

All of them with the big new guns for which Telluir and Keranshah and Hafas and Diaman have been cutting slabs the last four months.

Charged, aligned, set up in cover, with ranges worked out, and fields of fire, and savagely overlapping traverses, all along the waterfront, right across Dead Dyke wall. So when the regiments mass at daybreak, when the trumpets peal and Cataract's irregulars surge forward, howling, beside the immaculately squared Dhasdein front, when the cheering surge hurls its ladders across Dead Dyke, they are ready. For the canal-bank glacis to reach optimum crowding. To become the most terrible of killing fields.

"Just try to drink this. Please, Ruand."

Tellurith's stomach rolls. The taste of vomit gags her mouth.

"Been heaving all rotted afternoon." Low, furious undertone, somewhere behind the gun emplacement, its crew fallen out and eating now. As silent, as appalled as all the rest. Everybody but lookouts carefully, rigorously avoiding a glance over the wall. Onto the glacis where, in mid-afternoon, the enemy sued for truce.

To remove their wounded. And their dead.

Quizir, Tellurith thinks remotely, should be patient now.

A flicker of scarlet above them in the night. Relay signalers transferring a message via Arcis summit from Main Quay. Yet another thing Averion has insisted on. Communications, clear, fast, day and night.

A wind breathes and her stomach turns over uncontrollably, the wrenched muscles screaming as it heaves. At the vile charred meat and excrement smell of which nothing can cleanse the field.

A wash of movement in the firelight. Voices. A hand on her shoulder, a light, unfamiliar grasp. Hunkered uncharacteristically beside her, Averion.

Who takes the basin from Caitha. And presently, coaxes water down her neck. And then cajoles her away, silent and tender as a lost mother, to an angle of the wall. Staring back on Amberlight.

And says at last, very softly, "When it came to it . . . we had to pay the price."

We. Planner, killer, strategist. And still human enough to see the killer's price as the worse.

Who presently puts an arm about her, and says more softly, "Telluir, we need to ask you—what will they do now?"

Staring up into the moon's dark, Tellurith balances forces in her mind. Quizir and his colleague will want to try again. Dinda's troops, whose armorless spearmen took the losses' brunt, will probably have had enough. Assandar?

Will doubtless have the ascendancy now, having let his dissenters rush upon disaster yet again. Wants to hurry. Does not seem to mind spending, but will not waste his men. Will he go for escalation, spread those numbers extravagantly across the quayfronts, a river-borne assault?

Exposing troops for the river's width, pinned in their boats? After what today's repulse has told him of this fire-power? Send men to their deaths against those odds?

Not Assandar.

"Then will he wait?"

With a start Tellurith realizes she has been thinking aloud. Feels her face burn, heart thump with the shock of a near-miss. If she had said anything else . . .

But wait?

"Assandar," it comes out so coolly, "will do something different."

Averion's body relaxes beside her, draping on the wall. Curious, she thinks, to find a wildcat in the fastidious, aloof Head of Keranshah. A catamount, a killer, a soldier. To know the truth of her, after all these years.

"If I was fighting light-guns . . . and knew I would be fighting light-guns . . . I'd work out long-distance weaponry . . ."

"Bows?"

A soft laugh. On her shoulder, an absent pat. "Nice, Telluir. But no. I think I'd go far longer."

Catapults.

* * * *

No surprise, then, when five days' lull brings the sight of approaching sails. Running downRiver with the summer wind behind them, three narrow Cataract river-craft, loaded deep. Unloading, upstream of Dead Dyke, the special components for those massive timber frames that the siege forces have labored to raise. And the specialist crews to man Dinda's big city catapults.

"Of course, he had it pre-arranged, like the Dhasdein ships. And of course, they won't throw stones."

Averion draped, elaborately boneless, on the gun-site fire-wall. Safely, their work-crews calculate, out of throwers' range.

Beside her, Ti'e says, "We send criers into River Quarter. Tell them, soak their roofs."

Averion cocks an approving brow. Tellurith looks across the crowded animal pens, the makeshift shelters behind Dead Dyke, and groans. "What's the limit of their range?"

Ferally, Averion grins. "Tomorrow, they'll find out."

When at sunrise next morning, the battery of work mirrors behind Dead Dyke wall catch the light calculated, focused and fired from its guns. And the single huge amplified beam tracks across the river. To rest, gentle as a finger, upon a catapult.

As the tiny surrounding figures jump, spin, dance, inaudibly curse and shriek and run, distantly waving fists, Averion breaks into a soft, genuine laugh.

"Ants in someone's pants?"

* * * *

"**P**robably," good dining chairs dragged onto the balcony, to flank a table bearing a carafe of wine, Averion's elegant summer sandals cocked up on the balustrade, "they'll work at night."

"Unless the Dhasdeiners overrule him. For an all-out assault."

"They won't overrule him. Not unless he wants."

Tellurith stares. Such absolute certainty, in that tone, in the cool, coffee-brown eyes that stare out over the balustrade.

The eyes turn sideways. "I know you know him. But—in a way—I've come to know him too."

"So—now—you think he'll wait?"

Averion considers. "Patience isn't a Cataract virtue. I don't see it pleasing Verrain. If he waits too long—his troops could just ooze away."

And we would be safe.

Tellurith's throat is still tight with hope when Averion goes on.

"It depends if he really wants—what he wants."

Tellurith's eyes blur. She hears her voice say curtly, "He does."

Averion sips her wine. Sets down the cup. Remarks plaintively, "I really was hoping you wouldn't say that, Tellurith."

"So," brusqueness to cover her distress, "if you really wanted, in his place, what would you do?"

Averion sighs and puckers her eyelids. "If I had Dinda's engineers—and a river—I think I'd go for hydraulics. Big shield walls. And moveable catapults."

* * * *

It all takes time, Tellurith tells herself, squinting against the glitter of distant water in the sun. Time to dig the diversion ditch, time to set up the hydraulic screws, to build the solid flooring disc, let alone seat the catapult. Time for Verrain cavalry to grow impatient, and upRiver tribesmen to leak away.

And reinforcements to march in from Dhasdein.

And more City supplies to be consumed.

And boat-crews to labor sweating in the airless secrecy of a warehouse on a dozen light rowing craft. And guerilla volunteers, River Quarter ruffians, gang-tribes, to train under Averion's carefully prescribed conditions, night after night.

So when their best guess makes the catapults near ready, three boats slip across to raise mayhem and murder with a light-gun on the waterfront sentry posts. While four more, black-painted, the black-clad crew with carefully blackened faces, race for the catapult sites.

"Exquisite!"

Averion in the wash of crimson torch-light, acclaiming as for some great wine's bouquet. Swirled by a frieze of rascals, dancing, cavorting, laughing, screaming at the top of unpent lungs. Behind them, across the river, three sullen low stars of fire.

"Got the three of them! And never a scratch!"

* * * *

"**O**f course, they won't let us do it again."

I wish, Tellurith thinks as her heart again somersaults, that you wouldn't unleash your worst forecasts in that calmly casual voice.

Averion nods confirmation. "They'll pack the sites five-deep every night."

"Couldn't we afford—"

"We couldn't do it at any price."

"Oh."

Averion's eyes slit. "I wish," she murmurs, "I knew what else he has lined up."

"Why should he have anything—"

"Come, Tellurith. He knows from that range he might as well shoot peas at us."

Amberlight glitters hazily in the morning light. A high, harsh cloudless late summer day. A veil across the city. Dust. Open fires, a fog of cooking smoke. Averion taps her stick, one, three, one, three, mirror signalers' Stand-by code, against the warehouse wall.

"If worst comes to worst—it might be worth his while to make that full assault."

Tellurith's mouth dries. Averion looks round sharply. The faint frown is understanding, all but tenderness. It is the voice of envisioned destiny that goes on, quite quietly, "Come on, 'Rith. We always knew it might."

* * * *

But an offer to return prisoners they do not expect.

"Ten from the early raids—gangs, River Quarter men." Behind the Dead Dyke gun emplacement Averion's troublecrew Second counts on her hands. Averion squats on the pit-floor, fine muslin trousers trailing like the gunners' in the dirt, squinting under a disreputable Korite straw hat. The last anyone will do is laugh.

"That hardly seems worth the rations . . ." She eyes her Second's face and stops.

"The other fifteen are Navy. Wounded. One Second. Two gunners. Twelve hands."

Across the dyke the black and white truce flag flutters in a simmer of early haze. Tellurith feels all their hearts yearn. Navy folk. Women. Fighters. Redeemed, honored, their own kind.

And gunners. Skilled gunners. A weapon beyond price.

Averion hardly pauses before she says, "We'll take the lot."

Scarcely noticed, in the fêting and cosseting and bestowing of diamond ear-studs, when River Quarter sends delegates to ask access to the river, at least once a day.

Since the water that windmills pump to Arcis cistern up the north-side pipeline, and which rejoins the River through Uphill and business quarter plumbing, is hardly available in River Quarter. And the extra demand is choking the wells. And with the enemy idle, there can surely be no harm in opening the barricades that seal every street access to the quays.

Not just once a day.

Especially when the privilege is cancelled a week later as marchings about, gathering of boats and parade noises presage the general assault.

"No way will he try the whole perimeter. Far too expensive for him, much too helpful to us." Averion in general council. Cynosure of twelve anxious, wholly attentive pairs of eyes. "He'll use spearheads. The real problem is who outguesses who on where."

In the silence, Zhee's question seems very loud.

"Guess?"

"I know him. He knows me. He can choose a target—and try to convince me otherwise. Quite subtle. But subtle is not the word for Assandar. What if he knows I'll disbelieve him, and takes the first one after all? And if he takes the double-bluff, can I?"

"Sweet Mother, it could go for ever," groans Liony.

"What targets," presses Maeran, "will he want?"

Averion stares out into the pure morning sky.

"He could go for the Dyke—for land access. He is going to try a river crossing somewhere—unless that's a bluff. If he took Main Quay, he could split our defense."

"What would you do?" asks Tellurith.

The glinting chocolate eyes turn. There is time to think, Mother. She's enjoying herself.

"I'd go for something more—devious. Nuisance attack at Dead Dyke. Tie up Cataract. Rotted if I'd let them in the main assault."

"And the main attack?"

Averion smiles without amusement. "Iron Valley, for the citadel road? Pipe Spur, to cut the water supply? Main Quay, for a major bridgehead? Any one's a good choice."

"All we can do," she says coolly into the clamor, "is have every signaler and look-out and gun-crew on stand-by. To keep our communications open. And our minds."

And at Damas' bellow of, "Minds?"—"To keep our minds open, yes. To expect anything. We're fighting Assandar."

* * * *

Black night on Amberlight. The new moon has already set. A sword-play of lightning far to the north. Down at the Telluir quay command-post, Tellurith fights for composure. To be still. Not to flail the dark and shriek, Get me back to my balcony, up the men's tower, on High or Dragon Spur or Arcis itself, anything for sight!

Struggling reason re-asserts itself: Averion will be on Arcis. Eyrie of command. Racing up the road which runs by Keranshah's wall, in response to those signals that have shot you to the quay-side, and the signalers to their posts, and every available hand, light-gun, bow, sword, sleeve-sling to their battle-sites.

Since torches and uproar have signaled Cataract gathering to the attack.

All splendidly predictable, there is time to think, while the signals stitch the sky. Diversion attack on Dead Dyke. Now, where are the boats?

Aeons of struggling for calm, for military composure, while the messengers scuttle, and her troublecrew's stillness tightens round her, and the faint light of signal lamps, of charged light-guns, of power-panels on the wedge of vehicles next the command post, flickers through the dark. Until a runner scurries from the warehouse, gasping, "Boats out! Boats launched! Heading for us!"

The signals fly. Wilder ones fly back. The assault is general. Every quay from Gate to North.

Work-mother, help the Iuras and Prathax gun-crews, prays Tellurith, on the north side, with no experience, and no cool head to order them. Work-mother, help us.

She slips out her old cutter and wakes the charge.

"Give them till mid-stream," she can hear the gun-leader just inside the warehouse saying. Cool as a House-head before the mother-face.

Darkness stretching, endless, unbearable tension. I must run, scream, tear something, hit—

"Fire."

Longdrawn stinging hiss. Brilliant-beam of white.

Silhouetted prows spring out of the black. A glitter as helmets duck. Confusion of oars. Spearheads jerk and shatter light and vanish as the beam sweeps majestically past.

"Traverse."

Hisss. Over the barricade shows a lightning-flash of tangled oars, collided boats, thrashing metal, waving arms.

And, crisp as a cutter-slash inside the warehouse, "Off."

Darkness. Through it, the gun-leader, icy as ever. "It's a long time until light."

Let it not be too long, Tellurith prays, hands jittering on the cutter haft. Not enough to drain the qherrique. She can almost hear the spendthrift uproar down at the Dyke. How high will Cataract pay?

Far higher, she comforts herself, than hired tribesmen who are pledging their own lives.

We have the guns. All we have to do is hold and wait.

Then the night explodes behind her on flying rocks and bludgeons and a screaming onslaught amid rivers of torchlit flame.

* * * *

Averion's strategic brilliance is all that keeps a shambles from becoming a rout. Her insistence on communications, on alternative plans, her persistent vision of the quay-guns as mere forward defense. For which there must be immaculately organized systems of retreat.

So even under the impact of the entirely unpredicted, when River Quarter rises to savage its oppressors and fling the gates open to the liberators beyond the barricades, Telluir and Diaman and Keranshah and Hafas and Hezamin and even Jerish get half their guns out. Get many of their gun-crews to the vehicles. Get a good number of those vehicles up through the fire, the rocks, the ambushes, along the raging streets to Hill-foot road. Where, in obedience to the signals that have never ceased to regulate their action, the gun-crews, under cover of troublecrew skirmishers, set up temporary firing-posts.

So if the enemy wins the quays with hardly a casualty, River Quarter pays dearly for the assault.

But not dearly enough.

"Zanza lost all but three guns. Most of the gun-crews. Prathax has run clear to the House. North Quays are lost. Terraqa, Iuras and Winsat had to concede Dead Dyke. They botched the retreat."

Dead Dyke gone. Numbed by the blood and uproar and massacre, by the sensation of a cutter-beam slicing human flesh, by the cumulative body-blows of guns, vehicles, people, district, city lost, the thought of Cataract tribesmen in among the Kora refugees hardly touches Tellurith. But the signaler, ice-cool as Averion herself, is going on.

"Hill-foot is untenable. The enemy is currently massing on the Arcis road. Another force is at work on the pipeline. Terraqa gunners and troublecrew will attack them, assisted by any force available from Hezamin. Keranshah and Vannish will defend Arcis road. Telluir House, if Hafas, Jerish, and Khuss will work with you, establish a perimeter between High and Dragon Spur, using clan houses for cover. Diaman will put gun-sites on Iron Spur to harass the enemy on both sides."

If Amberlight's perimeter has fallen, Averion has not.

* * * *

At last the prayed, longed-for, abused creeping light. Colorless illumination of false dawn. Tumult and heart-stopping uproar deny it, the lunatics pillaging their own folk in River Quarter, the groans of wounded around Telluir's forward post. The nerve-shattering, bloody hubbub, along the southern spur-side, of a disciplined, heavy military assault. Again and again the white lance of Hafas' guns above them, occasionally turned onto the skirmishes that swirl out of the business quarter onto their own guns. Far more often firing westward, where, the signals tell them, between Iron Spur and Canal Spur Diaman and Vannish and Keranshah are carrying the brunt of the organized assault.

Time to consider that: the enemy has discarded the rest of Amberlight, open for the taking, to throw his forces up the citadel road. Time to pray, and drink cold coffee, and try to deal with nightmare. Defenses breached. Amberlight betrayed. The city opened like a dropped melon, no hope of concerted resistance or district defense. Amberlight does not have the military might, let alone the numbers, to reverse this.

Time to think, and curse, and come near hate in wanting vengeance, for a cutter's apprentice who dies with her cheek on her House-head's knee, with her last breath murmuring about a partner on the *Wasp*. To help tie up Zuri, spouting blood from a slashed thigh. To literally burn a raider off Azo, in time to save her more than a rip across the throat. To physically hurl Iatha from a gun-crew and scream, "Get home! Prepare the House!"

Because it can be only a matter of time before they are fighting behind their own walls.

And some time in there, amid the red lost memories' curtains, to wonder if the Coalition general co-ordinates his troops from behind the battle like Averion.

Or if, somewhere out in that pitch-black morning river, Amberlight's guns have already had his life.

VIII

Broad day on Amberlight, storm-haze brooding in a milky northern sky. Stained by the pillows of sullen smoke from burning shacks, street-blocks, tenements in River Quarter, the black swords that stand above blown light-guns, burnt-out vehicles, that smolder in debris-strewn streets. Wreckage of buildings and humanity beneath.

Under Telluir House the flood-mark swirls up through the business quarter, smashed windows, burnt-out offices, fallen beams and stones. Stopping short at the verge of Hill-foot road.

Above it, the old Amberlight lies weirdly intact: the walled demesnes, the flowering gardens and modest towers of Uphill clan and client houses. The whirling mill-vanes, the high block shapes of Khuss and Telluir and Jerish and Hafas House.

Above that, the citadel gnaws the skyline, still defiantly, vitally flying the crossed thunderbolt standard of Amberlight.

And between lie the gleaming moat-walls of the qherrique.

Remember it all, Tellurith warns herself, remember now, for very soon it will be gone. As it is already gone beyond Dragon Spur, where the tide has washed clear up to Zanza and Hezamin, relayed messages from Jura telling of her House walls battered by the riot. From Zanza, since first light, "no report."

And northward between Citadel and Pipe Spurs, the valley commanded by Prathax and Terraqa? Or the long hill-face down to Canal Spur, under Iuras and Winsat?

Worse still, the southern hill-side, where there has just come an awful, ominous pause in the battle tumult. So she wonders leadenly, Has the road fallen? Have they taken Vannish? And Diaman?

And above all, Keranshah?

There is a flutter behind her. A mirror flicker. A hoarse sound from the signaler.

"From Arcis—the enemy wants a truce!"

* * * *

"The whore's get slipped his agitators in with our Navy wounded; that's why the exchange, no question. And I'll lay odds they used the River to trade messages when we so kindly opened it."

"And River Quarter rose."

Zuri's report draws no orthodox fulminations on lower-class treachery from Damas today. From Averion, soot and blood-smeared, only a steely look.

"I expected everything from the sod but that."

Her party has slid down the hillside from the Arcis gate. She has no intention of meeting the envoys—"Let him go on wondering who I am. He's already guessed too much." When she looks out on the combs of bright Dhasdein helmets beginning to penetrate River Quarter, the taut look becomes a glower.

"How dare he put *our* city back in order?" Then she cuts the rest off and folds her lips.

"See what he wants."

The general, word comes back, will speak in person with Voices of the Thirteen. Preferably Telluir and Hafas House.

"Oh, he knows the politics!" Averion bites off the laugh. Gives Tellurith's arm a little push. "Go on, 'Rith."

The center of Hill-foot road feels far too vulnerable, to more than the rumor of distant riot. When the shadow of a carrion bird slides over, Tellurith has ado not to duck. She slits eyes at the military blaze, so unlike their own muslin robes, their vulnerable straw hats. Showing damage in its own way.

"Tel . . . Tellurith."

Doffing the helmet, that leaves a soot-mask over brow and cheek. A pulled look about the mouth, eyes big with ghosts. That persist beyond the soundless, anomalous exhalation of relief.

And then, more formally, "Ruands."

Before he begins to spell out their defeat.

"Your city's perimeter has fallen. Order is being restored in the Lower Quarter. Cataract's troops have withdrawn beyond Dead Dyke. The refugees there will be removed to holding quarters, and we have confiscated their supplies."

The eyes hold hers, steady, yet with an undertone of grief.

"Prathax House has surrendered. Iuras, Winsat, and Terraqa are currently under tight investment by my troops. Hezamin is besieged by River Quarter people. I regret that they have sacked Zanza House." The eyelids crease. Distress? Pain? "Any survivors will be put in our physicians' care."

Liony of Zanza. A face, a presence, life's known quantity across a council table. Shot, stabbed, mutilated, raped?

Quietly, Tellurith says, "And Vannish? Keranshah?"

A pause. A sigh.

"Ruands, up to this point we have avoided a sack. We can still avoid it. The rest of the city can be spared. I don't even ask that you surrender. Just that you come to terms."

It is Zhee's voice that asks, "What terms?"

"The terms previously offered. In addition, after the—negotiations are completed, Amberlight resumes its freedom. As a sovereign state."

Oh, Tellurith thinks, her heart riving. What is crueler than a generous enemy?

"But," Zhee, more remote than ever, "the other terms stand."

Inside the military panoply, she feels him straighten. Upright, implacable, as a sword unsheathed.

"The other terms—must—stand."

Another endless hiatus. Then Zhee turns slowly on her stick.

"Grant us two hours' armistice. We must put this to our clans and clients. To the entire House."

* * * *

"**S**'hurre, this is now the House's—this is now the choice before us all. Will we destroy our Houses, and let outsiders at the qherrique? Or will we resist the invader, until we are overthrown? Until we die?"

Tellurith looks down over the faces of House and client and clan-folk gathered on the perimeter. Iatha and the Craft-heads will be passing the word uphill, in the signal-sites, the lookouts and work-wings of the House. As it will be passing in Khuss and Hafas, and, relayed on through Arcis, among Diaman, Vannish, Keranshah. And perhaps, to Winsat, Iuras and Terraqa.

In the quiet she adds, loud and clearly, "Whoever wishes to go does so in freedom. The decision is for each alone."

Tellurith offers them half a glass to think. When she asks, "How do you vote?" there is a longer pause. Before the movement, slow, inexorable as the partitioning of a watershed; with reluctance, and grim determination, and shame, and regret, and grief.

Most of the client and clan women will go.

The House-folk, to a woman, will stay.

"I'll die," says a panel-shaper face to face with her House-head, "before I see my daughter raped."

"I'll die before my husband's killed!" Behind her, a furious shout.

"In Zanza," another cry, "they raped them first!"

"Called them catamites—eunuchs—bashed them, outside Prathax, while the officers stood and watched!"

The whole crowd snarls. A babble of lurid stories about the women's own fate. And then Ahio, thrusting up before them, shaper in hand, diamond stud and scar vivid in the morning light.

"Telluir's my House, and Amberlight's my city, and qherrique's my life! You'll see me dead before I let some dangling outland bastard ruin that!"

In fifteen, twenty minutes, the other votes come in. Most clients and clan folk will go. House-folk, almost unanimously, refuse.

"Now," Averion, red-eyed and tight-lipped amid a hugging crowd of signalers, "get them some terms."

* * * *

"We require guarantee of safe-conduct for all departing folk; that they be detained if necessary, but treated honorably, and not harmed."

Assandar inclines his head. Behind him, there is a flurry of pen-strokes from the scribe.

"Both women and men."

Some expression crosses his face. There is a bite in the voice.

"None of my troops will lay hands on any—any more—prisoners. Woman or man. I have dealt with those who did."

Decency, and compassion, and clemency. Why, her heart mourns, must I have an honorable enemy?

"The Thirteen thank you for your offer. For the rest of the House-folk, I say this:

"'Amberlight is our city, and qherrique is our life; before we let some outland invader destroy that, we will be dead'."

Let my lungs work, she wishes. Let me go on breathing, however it may hurt.

And pain, too, in that face before her, its soot-darkened features going slowly, unmistakably, grey. Before he bows his head. And faintly, so faintly, she hears his whisper.

"Oh, Tel . . ."

* * * *

A refinement of torture, then, that with nerves strung to die they are allowed to withdraw on the Houses, now the only defensible perimeter, to chew nerves and fingers for the rest of the day. While Dhasdein patrols subdue River Quarter, and troops occupy the intact Uphill streets, whence the prisoners have been duly escorted. And they wait to hear the noise of battle resume behind the spurs, and dwell on their last farewells.

A fast one, in the end, for which Tellurith now gives paradoxical thanks. A fistful of cameos, incised memory. Damas turning from the parley group, iron-and-tawny brows, square jaw: curt, leaving-council nod. From Ti'e, a grave, silent courtesy. Inscrutable to the end. Averion, a grasp of the arm. A general's grin. A quick, casual, "Thanks, 'Rith. Good luck." A last glimpse of the high-nosed profile, then the slim back under the disreputable hat receding, and Tellurith mourning: why did we know each other just in time to part?

Leaving Zhee: hunched on her stick, still inscrutable as a two-legged lizard. A last glimpse, under the thin whitened hair, of the folded mouth, the wrinkle-armored face. Before she says softly, "In the Work-mother's hand"—prayer, decree, invocation? gives Tellurith the cutter's salute, and turns away.

Idle noon has stretched into evening when a signal from Arcis laces the dusk.

"Conserve water. Pipeline will be cut."

"The bastard!" snarls Iatha, hurtling to order every bucket, dish, jar in the over-crowded House filled, and someone to lever the stone-blocks from the ancient courtyard well. With the pipeline cut it is only a matter of time till Arcis' cistern goes dry.

"When," she fumes, on her Head's balustrade in the grimy, gloomy, lurid yellow sunset, "are they going to start on us?"

Tellurith shakes her head. Round the hill, the signals tell her, it has already started: attacks pressed on Terraqa, Iuras, Winsat, the latter two stormed, Terraqa set afire. What befell the Heads Arcis does not know. But all too clearly they have seen the casualties as House-folk, in the final pinch, defend wings, rooms, men's towers with their lives.

"But they haven't touched Vannish or Keranshah. Are we too tough for him? What's the sod trying to do?"

* * * *

Midnight informs them. Moon's dark, lightning's realm, riven by a furious outburst on the zenith sky. Flares, torches, light-guns, trumpets, war-cries, shouts, screams, pandemonium unleashed.

A surprise attack on Arcis itself.

"Got up the pipe-crew's work track, took the wall with scaling ladders." The report comes through Hafas House. "Keranshah House-head and folk escaped by the road. Acceptable casualties."

Acceptable loss of life, Tellurith thinks savagely, for the loss of communications, co-ordination, high ground and psychic vantage? And with Arcis in his hands, what will occur to Assandar?

The answer to that appears three interminable days later, when the citadel wall grows, slowly as a cancer, a new silhouette.

The head of a catapult.

* * * *

"**K**eep all unnecessary traffic from the courtyard. Clear the men's rooms on the uphill side. Watch the garden gate from the Craft wings." Tellurith has studied fire-paths and range calculations and the scope of a high-based battery with Averion. "Yes, we'll have to pass signals through the attics. Yes, the well-traffic is wide open. Yes, Yath, his troops can storm the garden under covering fire, and we can't do a thing. Do you think it's different anywhere else?"

Work-mother help, she prays, the fighters in Vannish and Diaman and Keranshah.

There are ripostes. Light-gun batteries from Khuss and Hafas posted on the ends of High and Dragon Spur can harass the gunners, if not damage the three catapults, and signalers can pass word as far as Khuss, where Falla is proving an unexpectedly fiery commander, using House guns to rake the troops in Uphill both sides of Dragon Spur. As Telluir and Jerish do in their valley, leaving the catapults to Diaman and Hafas.

"Whoreson genius," rages Iatha, squinting out the main courtyard door, past the cover of the men's tower, up to that ominous linear framework on the citadel's rim. "He can cover his troops and knock holes in our defense and we can't get at him. And we're in perfect range. We can't get away."

The ultimate pincer, Tellurith thinks. Too tired, too wrung now, for rage. Take Arcis, and the rest is only a matter of time.

Protracted, agonizing time. With six Houses and half Amberlight taken, with impregnable advantage in land and supplies and time, the enemy delays to haggle with each resisting House. Only after a day's fruitless argument, says the signal from Diaman, does he finally close the pincers on Vannish.

"They offered safe conduct if Vannish would surrender, return of the Kora holdings if they would open their mine." The signaler's eye glints. "The House-head told them to burn in Dhasdein's hell."

But it is Vannish that burns.

* * * *

"**F**ire-bombs." Zuri's profile, worn, sleepless, immobile as rock, staring from an attic window into the black and copper-smeared southern sky. "You can throw them with a catapult."

Onto roofs and into windows raked by catapult bolts and stones to repel the fire-fighters. Women, men, children. A House's population, trapped in a burning house.

"Troops have attacked the garden with battering rams."

A charnel, a holocaust, fighters and the helpless caught between the charge of steel and fire.

"Troops have penetrated the House."

No need to spell out the rest, the chaos of fighting through the power and shaper shops, hand-to-hand, the destruction, the massacre.

Clear over High and Iron Spur, flaring across the sky, runs one brief searingly white flash.

* * * *

"**D**iaman says the top of the tower blew off. The fighting in the main House stopped almost at once. The Head must have taken the last light-guns up there. And blown them all."

Destroying herself, and her doughtiest fighters, and their menfolk. Preserving, beyond violation, the core of the House.

"Diaman says the enemy has tried to parley with Keranshah."

Tellurith almost laughs.

"Diaman says Keranshah will talk."

Tellurith snorts. Re-visioning that cool, recalcitrant profile under the straw hat, the ice and fire in those general's eyes. "I'd give a tooth to know what's in her mind."

"Keranshah signals they have been offered truce terms, including safe conduct for the other Houses and return of Kora holdings as well as sovereignty, once the negotiations are done."

"At this rate," Iatha, too furiously amused for good taste, "we've only to bargain at a House a clause, and Telluir can keep the qherrique."

At which Tellurith surprises herself by shattering a wine-glass on the wall.

* * * *

"**'R**ith . . . I'm sorry."

It takes a mental eternity to turn from the stars, paled now by a cool, so cool and pure climbing moon, and say with some semblance of composure, "So am I. I didn't intend that."

Silence. A heavily drawn breath.

"But . . ."

But do you think it just possible that it will happen? That with you in the balance Assandar will leave Telluir till last, and if he raises the stakes at each House, one, at least, will keep our life?

As well as our lives?

Tellurith answers through her teeth, so as not to scream: *I will not take my life at such a ransom. I will not live in a world bought with Averion's blood.*

"Did Keranshah reply?"

"Demanded the night for the Houses to consider."

"Didn't ask for safe conduct to discuss it?"

"It was refused."

Too clever to give rein to cleverness. Tellurith grits her teeth.

* * * *

Pale dawn over Amberlight, signals lacing a copper-stained, smoke-smeared, storm-sullen sky.

"Keranshah wishes to know the opinion of Hafas House."

"Hafas sends, No surrender, without protection of the qher-rique."

Tellurith feels a stoppage in her heart.

"Jerish sends, Concur."

"Khuss sends, We have already voted. Is the emperor's pig so short in the memory he has to ask again?"

"Rith?"

It has stopped. It has all stopped, Zuri and Iatha beside her, the signalers crouched, ready to send. All the eyes fixed on her. Waiting for her to dispose of their lives.

She stares into each face in turn. Turns to Iatha. And asks, "What was the vote in the House?"

Iatha thrusts her jaw out. "The same as before. Tell 'em, No!"

As House-head, Tellurith has condemned wrong-doers. A Freight-head who cheated, a shaper who stole. Three children whose faces she never saw. Not women who have lived and fought with her. Not Averion, and Zhee, and Ti'e. Not all the folk of her own House.

The words stick. The signaler is waiting. Tellurith gulps.

"What was the vote—from Keranshah?"

The signal flickers, red motes arcing across the dirty sky. Forever passes before the reply.

"Keranshah votes, No."

* * * *

"**M**ay the Mother look with love on Keranshah."

The faces blur in the pure qherrique light, filmed by Tellurith's tears. Not so obscured as to hide the other tears, and the fierce pride, bayed, triumphant, the strengthening of fury and resolution in the hands on every lifted glass.

Keranshah's wake.

"And may the Mother," Zuri, rising for the toast after Iatha's, "warm Herself at their fire."

No chance the Mother will have missed it. No tame last-ditch defeat for Keranshah. Tellurith swallows dutifully. Tasting nothing. Eyes still blurry, ears still ringing, to the shattering detonation, the fireball that soars above the mountain into that violently expanding mushroom, the pall of pearl-shot dust.

No need, either, for anyone to explain in other Houses, where the defenders stare, open-mouthed, stunned rather in awe than grief. Averion has not frittered away her night's space. Nor has she bothered to defend an indefensible demesne.

"The enemy has signaled Diaman: Keranshah folk, including some men, have surrendered and been taken under guard. None, repeat none, have been harmed. The enemy regrets that the House and Craft-heads with their men and many of their folk have not been found."

"They blew the face."

Tellurith hears herself say it, forehead against the attic window-frame, ears still singing in that unnatural ensuing quiet. Feeling Charras and Ahio nod behind her. Knowing it in her bones, her cutter's ear, beyond any doubt.

"They went up there in the dark last night. Sent out the ones who wanted. And then—they woke the qherrique."

The oldest name comes back to her. Sky-light. Mother's Fire.

The tiny sparks that leap at Her will when silk is rubbed on that other substance that shares the City's name.

The power imaged in the carven thunderbolts.

* * * *

"**D**iaman signals: The enemy offers truce, safe conduct for all who surrender, return of Kora holdings, sovereignty for Amberlight."

Tellurith bites her lip.

"Telluir signals: Respect for the remaining Houses?"

A long, long delay. And finally, almost reluctantly, Hafas' signal flickers.

"The enemy regretfully declines."

Tellurith bites her lips again. Wonders, suddenly: What would Averion do?

Not, at least, sit idly while the enemy eats Amberlight, piece by piece.

"Telluir house signals Diaman and Hafas: If you fire at Arcis and troops in Uphill, our troublecrew will try a raid."

"Hafas signals: On what?"

"Telluir signals: To kill or capture their general."

* * * *

Forgive me, Alkhes, she thinks. Fingers steady, eyes dry, as she tries the power-panel for the light-gun that will go on Zuri's hip. We can't sit and watch our city burn. We don't have the numbers to recapture Arcis or re-take the rest. We have no option for flight. You know, and I know, that you are not only the brains of this assault, but its heart. You know, and I know, that you will offer infinite mercies. That you will suffer with every one of us who dies.

And that until you have the qherrique, and the Houses destroyed, and Amberlight's evil excised, whoever dies, nothing will make you stop.

It has taken every effort up to imprisonment to exclude Azo and Verrith. Appeals to Zuri's rank, her irreplaceable value, bring the merest grunt. She knows, Tellurith thinks, as I do, that her greater value is to go. On what may be our very last chance.

They say their goodbyes at the courtyard door. Before Zuri and her trio slip out and over the garden wall, faces and clothes blacked, bedecked with every weapon from light-guns to garottes, under cover of the bombardment that opens now, in response to Telluir House's signal flash, white lances reaching out from High and Dragon Spur. To uproar in the streets, to the piercing scream from the citadel of the enemy's Alarm.

Under its cover Tellurith embraces Zuri, quick and awkwardly. Not something she has ever done before. Not something either of them has expected, Zuri's body rock-solid and hair-triggered in shock as Alkhes' would be in her arms. But quite certainly, she knows she will not let another friend go as lightly as Averion.

And both of them know it is unlikely they will meet again.

* * * *

So less a shock than astoundment then, to be haled to the street door by a furiously profane Iatha in the broadening dawn. To peer through the window-slit on a flag of truce, and a detachment of

Dhasdein troopers, as resentful as they are terrified, by their body language; and in their midst, arms bound, face an eloquence of mute infuriation, Zuri herself.

Less astounded than her House-head when the officer in command announces, "We are returning this prisoner," and the squad, about-facing, tramps away.

Hauled inside, unbound, stayed with coffee and comforted with breakfast cakes, it is still half an hour before her rage lets Zuri speak. But her first words raise consternation enough.

"They can read our signals. They were waiting for me."

And only when messengers have flown to send final wild messages to Hafas and Jerish, and the tumult has subsided to its normal fraught anxiety, can Zuri get out the rest.

"We never even got across the perimeter. We were in Quicksilver when they picked us up."

Central street of Telluir's valley, named for the speed of its gutters in rain. Barely a bow-shot from the House.

"They surrounded us. A pox-blasted detachment of them. He—the general—was there himself."

Zuri literally grinds her teeth.

"They squeezed us in the tortoise, with those gangrened shields. 'Zuri,' he said to me. 'I know you. And you know me'."

Tellurith, not knowing, stares.

"They had us packed like statuettes. Couldn't raise a hand. Couldn't use a gun. Couldn't—even—kick."

Tellurith watches Azo's eyes bulge. Telluir troublecrew, renowned no less for address than for street-killer speed and fighting skills, immobilized, captured, without a scratch.

"'Zuri,' he says. 'We read the signals.' So then I knew."

She lifts her eyes, at last, to Tellurith's. "And he offered me amnesty, to come back. If we surrendered. And I knew—we couldn't get him. And I knew—we had to have that word."

She lowers her head again, neck-muscles swelling, biting out each word.

"And he—knew—I—knew."

As Tellurith knows, now. And says it, resignedly.

"Was there a message for me?"

Under brows, Zuri stares at her. Then shakes her head, No.

And in cover of the table, hidden from everyone else, makes the troublecrew hand-sign. Yes.

Tellurith's heart-beat plunges like a galloping horse. Madness, elation, fright. Horror, as she knows what she must do.

"Give it," she says to Zuri, "here."

So Zuri, after another long stare that reads more than her Head's face, slides a hand inside her black shirt, gropes into the breast-band, extricates a folded, crumpled, sweaty square.

As Tellurith undoes it her fingers, she notices, barely shake.

Tel—

Time to thank the Mother that he has not used an endearment, at least.

For the gods' love, don't go on with this. There's no way you can hold us off. You know that. You know we know. You have my word that you and anyone who surrenders with you will be safe. If you want, you can put your Houses together after we've left. Just dissolve them officially. Just let us have the qherrique. You can administer it, if that's what you want. Once we've broken this stupid taboo you can do anything you like. Just don't force us to any more of this. I swear to you, it's turned the men's stomachs. They're sick at the thought of killing any more women, of having to sack another House. Have some pity. For what's left of your city, if not for us.

And at the bottom, a double signature. The general's scribble. And a stark, single *A*.

* * * *

Time trickles into timelessness, as in that other decision he asked of her. Time to see the faces round her, pity, shame, embarrassment. Pain. Love. Time to see the ruins, and the shattered remnants of Amberlight. To hear, too clearly, Iatha's jesting words. To yearn for life and hope with all her mortal body, which passionately desires an end to terror, an escape from death. Time to see, limned as clear as in fleshly vision, the writer's face. The pain, the pleading, in those black eyes: Don't make me do this. To them, to you, to all of us.

Time to ask the final arbitration where she has always asked.

And sure, inexplicable as in that moonlight over Exchange Square, the qherrique answers, No.

There is time for shock, and disbelief. To ask again, and have the answer twice as clear. To see her feelings mirrored on each watching face. To shut her eyes, and beg the Mother for explanation as well as strength. To open her eyes, into Zuri's stare.

At which, as at a spoken question, Zuri nods. And says quite quietly, "Nearly everything we'd want."

Tellurith shuts her hand upon the small, scribbled square. When she speaks, her words sound very remote.

"Iatha, get Hanni for me. Tell her to write a message to the general. Tell him, the Head of Telluir House thanks him for his concern, and feels for his feelings—" and if there is a twist in that, so much the worse "—but with the greatest regret, neither she nor her fellow House-heads can meet his terms."

* * * *

For whatever reason, it goes very quickly after that. In the small hours of next morning, the remnants of Amberlight come under general assault.

Not merely the Houses, invested by storm-troops under a hail of catapult bolts. Troops out of Arcis also charge down the spurs to overwhelm the gun-sites of Diaman and Hafas and Khuss.

And behind them army engineers disable the windmills along each crest.

When the qherrique light falters and pales in Telluir House there are cries of alarm from women who have never flinched before. Flying down the stairs to her central command post, Tellurith feels the failing of her House's heart before she hears Ahio cursing like a volcano in front of her.

"Whoreson outland donkey-spawn's tapped the power-sink!"

The windmills fill the gap between the qherrique's daily light absorption and the night-time drain of the House. Without the windmills, the qherrique cannot match the drain.

Tellurith shouts it into a gloom that is more than physical.

"Turn down the lights!"

So it is in a dawn twilight, amid the thunder of assault upon each spur, that they prepare for the end of Telluir House. And amid the silently embracing women, marriage and love partners, old lovers, present friends, all saying goodbye forever, as their Head takes flight to the Power-shop lookout she is spun round by a voice asking, "Tellurith?"

A male voice.

He—they—are in the door. Silhouetted against the courtyard light. All too fair targets to the catapult gunners who can sweep the court. She screams and leaps, galvanized to the snatch.

"Get in here!"

Others yank in the rest. The hall resounds to women's infuriation, that only equal fear and love could see released.

"What in the Mother's name are you doing—here—like that!"

From somewhere Sarth has found troublecrew trousers and shirt, camouflage-green and black. Behind him, Azo's husband Herar nurses in one hand an iron window bar, in the other, a long stone block. Behind that, dressed and armed for this lunatic, heart-breaking battle, are the other men from Telluir's tower.

"You can't do this!"

Hands dug in Sarth's arms, shaking him as so many women are doing to their men, shaken by the warmth and muscle and too well remembered maleness of him, all too precious now that it is in such peril, that it so madly imperils itself. "Go back! Stay safe!"

"My dear, it's hardly safe anywhere in Amberlight, is it? Let alone if we go back—"

"The Mother blast—!"

You at least, she wants to scream, I want to know you remain undamaged to the end. You at least I do not want to see reviled and mocked and maybe violated because of what we made your life.

Tellurith bites her lip. Grips harder on his arms. With an Amberlight man's response, he suffers her grasp.

"Tell me," she hisses, "do you want to get out?"

Those perfectly groomed eyebrows rise. Weirdest moment of a beyond weird morning, to see Sarth outside the tower without a veil.

"No, Tellurith," says her husband with his full precise elegance. "We do not want to get 'out.' Whatever you made of us, we belong to Amberlight. We are here to—ah—fight."

* * * *

By the time she completes the lunatic diversion of posting men as auxiliary lookouts, back-up fighters, fetch-and-carry crew, the enemy has taken the spurs. Almost at their elbow, the din of full assault has closed around Falla's valiant Khuss.

Sickening, all too sickening at such close quarters, to sit and watch. The catapult fire to pin the defenders, the battering rams to break the doors, the catapult loads employed now with merciless accuracy to smash holes in walls, house, tower. The scaling ladders that send massed troops over the garden wall for the decisive assault.

The hideous, hideous tumult in the House.

* * * *

And before it dies away the fresh crescendo, as up on High Spur the pincers close upon Hafas.

Like Averion, it seems, Zhee has made her own plans. The catapults have hardly breached a wall when up from the shattered men's tower jerks a flag of truce.

And in the lull, so clear Telluir House can hear the cry of, "Call the general!" pass down the enemy ranks, the hill speaks.

Not Averion's splendid detonation. This is a steady, almost somnolent roar.

And then a garish white and clay-yellow dust-cloud that bellies skyward as the rock face caves in, with Zhee's own ponderous impassivity, upon the mine of Hafas House.

* * * *

Afternoon receding, presaging sunset, over Amberlight. Veiled in the dust of destruction, the smoke of death and battle and the great spiral of circling carrion birds, like a shrouded corpse.

A storm sweeps over the ridges of the Kora to the west and north. High into the pure distant sky the grey skirts of rain raise their mighty silver and grey-blotted, lightning-brilliant thunderhead. Under it is a sudden quiet.

And once more, outside Telluir House a flag of truce.

"The general will speak to the Head of Telluir House."

Do I go? Do I stay? Do I suspect treachery? Do I spit in his face?

Tellurith stares wildly about. So wholly, so hopelessly her own mind has been set upon death that this seems hallucination. What in the Mother's name, she cries, can he treat for now?

In panic she turns about. Snatching, with all other anchors gone, for Zuri, for Iatha's face. Crying silently, What now?

Their faces look back at her. Driven, exhausted, blank. In the end, she is the House-head. Only one place remains to ask.

Do I, she demands, go out?

And the qherrique, inarguable, lunatic, answers, Yes.

Tellurith lifts both shoulders in a shrug. Says, "In the Workmother's hand." And to the understanding in Iatha's face, "Open the door."

Small point, now, in precautions and guards. Tellurith takes her tattered straw hat. Makes a futile brush at her filthy trousers, three days worn. Nods to Zuri. Who lets back the great door, on its double chain. And she is on the porch.

Three wide granite steps rise from the street to the vine-draped porch of the central facade in Telluir House. She is vaguely aware of massed and blazing armor beyond, highlit against the wrong, raw blast of vacant smoke that used to be Khuss House. Of broken trees and mangled vinery, the outer decorations of a great Uphill demesne. Mostly, then wholly, of the knot of men waiting by the steps.

Guards. Scriber. Assandar.

The helmet is off. The sooty, grimy, haggard face looks worse than any behind her. A man ridden by nightmare. A man—bizarrely her mind reverses it—not dealing, but under sentence of death.

"Tellurith?"

The whisper is hoarse. The eyes speak far louder. Despair, torment. A last, fading sight of a promised land.

She takes a step closer. And suddenly he moves out from among the guards, the gesture almost hurling them back, his head offered, bare, unwarded, to the honor of their truce and the decency of Telluir House.

"Tel, will you stop now—please?"

Even the night she condemned him to the tower, he did not sound like that.

"The whole city's smashed. Vannish is gone. The fools are gone. So are your friends. We've had to clear them out up there, room by room. Women, Tel, for the gods' love. Not soldiers. Not even men. For god's sake, isn't it enough?"

Not Assandar and the Voice of Amberlight, she thinks with some disconnected still-analyzing part. This is human to human. Creature to creature. Tellurith. Alkhes.

"I'll hold by all the terms. Safe conduct. Return of the Kora. Sovereignty. Restoration of the Houses, if you want."

So long as you stop, the eyes say. So long as you stop.

When she does not answer, he lifts a hand, as if he would, still, reach out to her. And then, too slowly, lets it fall.

His voice is silent. But the eyes speak, as they spoke once over a gag in the Telluir infirmary. Don't do this, they say. Don't do this to me, Tel. Please.

She draws in her breath. Mother, she prays, give me strength. To say, No, not only for my folk, and my city, and myself.

But for him as well.

"Telluir House . . ."

It speaks to her, in one long lightning flash. The names, the faces. Zuri. Azo. Verrith. Hanni. Caitha. Shia. Ahio. Charras.

Herar.

Sarth.

The breath goes down and catches. The street swims, the armor swims. All that is clear is a pair of black, hopeless eyes.

And the qherrique.

Saying, Yes.

Tellurith finishes the breath. It comes out husky, from somewhere beyond herself.

"Telluir House . . . do we have safe conduct, if they lay down
their arms?"

IX

Full moon over Amberlight, consummated, perfect, a remote orb of qherrique riding the deferential sky. Shaping the ruins, tracing that blasted skyline as indifferently as if Amberlight were still entire. Watching it from her blanket, Tellurith wonders, Do I dream?

Did I dream that surrender? The shattered looks, the numb faces, defenders filing out, so locked in the trance of death that they were beyond reaction. Not relief, not chagrin, not humiliation or reproach. Not even fear.

Certainly it was a dream, that petty chaos of weapon-search, confiscation, gathering of personal "prisoners' needs." Of course, something registered, by now they are used to this. Swirling us down to Hill-foot, over the dyke. A dozen pontoon bridges, troops and materiel surging to and fro. What part of her remembered that?

* * * *

No doubt which part remembers the prison pen. It is burnt deep into heart and mind. Gatehouse, palisade. And within, one of the enormous siege-wall excavations, an ant-heap of uprooted humanity amid a grassless, treeless mass of makeshift shelters and ramshackle kitchen-hearths, a mosaic of temporary authorities cluttered round House and Craft. Which greets Telluir House with all the disbelief, frantic joy, chagrin, abuse and heart-stabbing reproach a surrendered Head could ask.

Clan-folk of Vannish who scream, "Traitor! Murderer!" and strike Tellurith in the face with clods of earth. Lightly injured Keranshah gun-crews who shriek, "Betrayer! We died—our Head died for you!" Witch keenings from remnants of Diaman and Hezamin. Screams of joy beyond ecstasy, embraces and sobbing delight from Telluir clan-folk finding House-crew, past hope, alive.

Sour, sour silence from the folk of Jerish, filing in behind.

More chaos as the prison officers try to explain rations, latrine sites, issue of spoilt or unused army tents. So many tents, she remembers ironically, that only the hardiest need sleep under the sky.

Fogged over then, by shock. Discarded now, like a loathed suit of clothes, compulsorily worn a handful of times.

Compulsory as that meeting when she left the gate. Going to confront her new, mad world, some part of her mind still wanting to wonder, Where is he? Suppressing grimly the more frantic questions, Did he send me here, has he abandoned me, was it all, all of it, after all, only a show, made for the one ultimate prize? Retorting with grim fury, Shut up, you're with your people, did you want silk cushions in the general's tent?

Forgotten as from the crowd before her steps Damas of Jerish.

And Eutharie of Prathax, and Ciruil of Terraqa.

And Damas says, with deep-burnt, resentment's courtesy, "Do you have an explanation for this?"

Some sense must have remained to her, she thinks, shifting on the blanket, its heavy mottled-russet wool so incongruous on naked dirt. It belongs in the spacious bedroom of a Head in Telluir House. But like it, her transplanted wits worked. Well enough to retort, "Do you want an answer here?"

Removal from enemy earshot, ludicrous dispute over a new site, does give her time to marshal sense. So when Eutharie rounds on her, squatted on the blankets of her wall-less shelter floor, squawking, "You'd better have an explanation! Telluir House surrender, after everyone else fights to the death!" She can rap back, "At least Telluir House surrendered *after* they fought!"

Which gags Eutharie in a crimson twitching heap.

Ciruil's look, the hurt, the bewilderment, stabs her to the heart. Deeper than Damas' somber, "I followed your lead, Telluir. But I do want an answer. Now."

No chance to fall down here and let the woman weep, tear her hair, beat her breast for lost House, lost Houses, lost pride, lost city, lost life. Probably, irrevocably, trust and lover lost.

"Jerish—Damas—we couldn't win. What was the use?"

What was the use for Hafas, and Vannish, and Keranshah? And they died for it. The answer is in the thrust of Damas' lip.

"You didn't have to follow me. If it mattered that much—you could have fought!"

The lip retracts.

"It was your choice!"

No eye-contact now, shoulders hunched.

"So why did you give in?"

And when she waits, when they all wait, skeleton Crafts and troublecrew gathered in a pale echo of council, Damas twists again. And mutters it, into the mud-tracked wool at her knees.

"I didn't—I had to . . ." Then, jerking her head up, red in the face. "Mother blast you, Telluir, it was the House!"

Their eyes hold. Saying, reading, the same thing. When it came to the pinch, who could force their folk into death?

Very quietly Tellurith says, "It was the same for me."

And Ciruil cries, "If the Houses came first now—why couldn't they come first then? Why did we have to fight at all?"

The hurt, the grief, the bewilderment are too much. Tellurith is on her feet, lashing out at them. At everything.

"Because we were trying to save our city and our lives! Because we had no choice! Because our folk backed us—and mine still don't know why I didn't let them die!"

"Then why," Damas slashes, "didn't you?"

"Because I'm House-head—and the qherrique told me, No!"

Then she sits down, breathing heavily, feeling the hysterics build like the pressure of a storm, feeling an utter fool, feeling the battery of their stares.

"Well, don't you feel it? You were both cutters—you have the ear! Don't you feel it, when you make decisions? Isn't it more than you—more than the House? Don't you *know*?"

And from their pole-axed looks, understands they do—but that they have never dreamt another shared it, or where it must have come from, until now.

It is Ciruil, all but in tears, who asks the ultimate question. "But if it told you to fight—and then told you to give in—*why*?"

* * * *

Why, why, why? Let it go, she tells herself, gritting teeth yet again over the endlessly, futilely debated question. Insane, unfathomable. And finally, disastrous. The impossible, inscrutable will of Amberlight. Of the Mother? Of the qherrique.

Far less of a dream that third morning, when trumpets ring beyond the palisade, and the more agile prisoners, squinting from a foothold against the stakes, cry with outrage of a triumphal procession. Of trumpets, and notables, and a blaze of military grandeur from an honor guard for the tyrant of Cataract.

"The whores! The cow-shickers!" An hour later, Iatha is still beside herself. "Not enough to smash our House and tear our city apart, they have to bring that turd-eater to crap on the wreck!"

* * * *

The harshest moment, perhaps, in the enemy repair of Amber-light's ruin. Worse than word of Kora refugees dispatched to their farms. *"We'll let you know,* they said," foams one climber who managed to bespeak a passing family, *"who you're working for now!"*

Easier to watch the Verrain cameleers and cavalry strike camp, not long after Dinda arrives. Easier still, in vindictive vengefulness, to tally Dinda's shrunken forces, evidently not to be swollen by fresh levies. "The whoreson dangle rushed here just for the thrill!" Ahio snarls. Anything but easy to watch Dhasdein troops move across the bridges, shifting quarters into Amberlight.

"May they find pleasure," Damas spits, "in my House!"

Trying to control the light. And the heat. And the cooking ranges, and everything else reliant on qherrique, hence deaf to the pleas of men. It is some solace, Tellurith thinks, watching the stolid, armored ranks tramp past, that we have left so many gaps. Almost as much as to imagine their difficulties in the maze of an intact House.

It is next day the summons comes for her.

* * * *

Two young aides, respectful, immaculate, unmistakably general's staff. Requesting, with impregnable courtesy, that they be accompanied by the Head of Telluir House. And no, her House-steward, and her troublecrew, even her secretary will not be required.

Tellurith gathers up an outer robe as ravaged now as Amberlight. With a spurt of defiant memory, dons her current and most raffish Korite hat.

Back over the bridge, their own stone bridge, this time. Along Hill-foot, clear again, full of military traffic. Past Canal Spur, under the wreckage of Keranshah. Up to the Citadel?

No. Tellurith's heart sinks, as they trek under Vannish's charred ruin. Oh, no.

All too surely, yes, past High Spur's marred skyline, gun-site remains, windmills dangling broken vanes. Past Hafas' wreck. To the agonizingly intact, familiar shape of Telluir House.

Military bustle in the hall, the great doors standing wide. No, she thinks, while alternating rage and panic sear her. He would not—he could not make it in my own rooms?

Staircase, ushering hands. A dormer window, open on the empty tower.

A desk, scribers, military command paraphernalia, cumbrous as rule of a House. The room is dim, fusty, daylight boosted by oil lamps. Subordinates and scribers scurry. The door shuts.

He comes to her across the Verrain rug where she once wriggled her stockinged toes. Quick, unaltered troublecrew stride. Military splendor shed. The washed-grey under-tunic, the Cataract boots, could almost be pure Alkhes. The earthquake within her, blind need to bawl and curse and tear his eyes out, frantic urge to snatch and squeeze his breath out, is almost beyond control.

He stops in arms' reach. Perhaps those black eyes read hers. Certainly, there is tumult in that long-drawn breath.

And the sense, even now—or the sensitivity—not to touch.

"I—thought you'd want to be with your folk."

Oblique explanation? Apology for his absence, for the prison pen? Foresight of how the prisoners would have read her absence?

Or omission of deeper, more heartfelt words, the only mercy a wounded conqueror can offer in such a defeat?

If he'd said, Thank god you're all right, she realizes, or, horror of horrors, tried to touch me, I would have spat in his face.

"What are your plans," amazing, her voice's quiet, "for us?"

"Uh." Less a pause than a grunt. Shoving a hand, a gesture purely Assandar, up through that wing of hair. A grin whose pain is pain to her.

"How did I know you'd pick the one—I have no plans. They depend on you."

In the maelstrom of her emotions, the madness to strike, the frenzy to embrace, it is a rock of refuge to be crossing wits.

"On me, Amberlight? Or me, Telluir? Or me, Tellurith?"

"Probably all three."

"All—" blessed refuge, exertion of the mind.

"You want me to do something. As Telluir House-head. That will hold for Amberlight."

When his wits out-paced me, she wonders, did I look like that?

"You—I—yes."

Tellurith waits.

His hands move. Jerk. Converting a wide gesture out of something that too nearly became an embrace. "Damn it, you can have clean clothes at least—a bath—something to eat . . ."

Pain for the memory of an immaculate House-head, for the offer of her own amenities, turning charity to coals of fire. A courtesy too exquisite to resist.

"Am I," she asks with interest, "to owe the clothes on my back?"

The flush burns clear to his hair. What cuts her is the wince.

"That was unnecessary." She looks round, a House-head retrieving the meeting along with herself. In place of Iatha's lounging cushion, takes a scriber's stool. "Perhaps you should just tell me what you want."

Is it Alkhes' or Assandar's magnanimity that concedes the initiative without affront? He follows her to the desk. Paces up the rug. In the roughened stride she reads distress as well as unease.

"I told you I wanted to stop the trade in qherrique."

Tellurith lets her silence say, And you have.

"Even when I was making terms about its change."

Silently, she says, Go on.

He swings about at the rug's heart.

"But I'm only the Coalition's general. Not the government. Even of Dhasdein."

It is all very clear. A simplicity. Destiny itself.

"They want," she says, "to take over the qherrique."

Those eyes answer, Yes.

In the garden a pair of saeveryrs flit, flirting scraps of black and white. Outside, everything looks exactly the same.

"Then what, precisely, do you want from me?"

He rubs two fingers between his brows.

"I can't stop this. No one can." Her bitter silence retorts, You did not have to start it, and he glares.

"You couldn't stop it either—not against the Thirteen!"

"At least we still had Amberlight!"

It comes more savagely than she meant. Worse than her penitence is the way he does not fight back.

"What is it," she says more gently, "you want me to do?"

He lifts his head, his eyes, his shoulders. Settles himself, as if to defend the indefensible.

"If I can't stop it, I can try to control it. So . . . we mine qherrique. A guild, a council, some authority. Including those who did it before."

Now those eyes meet hers, solid black.

"Not Houses, Tel. Not that sort of monopoly, ever again. Not that sort of—warping—people. I'll give you Amberlight, I'll give you control of the—council or whatever it is—but not that."

Tellurith waits. That there is more, she already knows.

"And . . . no monopoly, on working the qherrique."

This time there is no pain. Only an assent, a resignation to the weight of destiny, that settles over Tellurith's mind.

Quietly she says, "No."

The eyes flare. Blacker than coal, deeper than living night.

"You may do what your masters want, or not. You may choose to mine the qherrique as you like. But I will see my House, and the folk of the other Houses, and all of us prisoners dead, before we agree to this."

"Tel, for the gods' sake—"

"No."

"You can keep Amberlight. You can keep the qherrique—"

"Not like that."

Silence. Deeper distress. Annealing over, into wounded quiet. That will not accept defeat.

"All right. The terms stand. Safe conduct, wherever you choose. Even to stay in Amberlight. For all the prisoners. If I get what I want, there'll be a break-up of Kora holdings, but only the timber-fief goes back to Cataract. Anyone who wants can draw lots for land from the rest. Personal gear goes with you. As soon as the government negotiations are done."

Tellurith waits, holding his eyes.

He sighs, driving that hand back through his hair. "Oh, Tel, if I know you so well . . ."

Then how well do you know me?

"The mine adits are nearly all down. Keranshah—you know, of course. Hafas. The others are in a mess."

He pauses, watching her eyes.

"Telluir's is clear."

It is very, very quiet in the small fusty room. The heart of the problem. The heart of two human beings. Of Telluir House. Of Amberlight.

"We haven't tried to use the guns. We know it blows up, once it's been shaped. But the raw stuff . . . If you won't help us work it, let me show them it can be worked. By men."

Tellurith does not feel the stool go flying. "You're out of your mind!"

"No, Tel." The eyes are steadier now than leveled steel. "It will accept men. It will answer them. That night you let me touch it. It answered me."

She does not know what her face says. All control, all composure is lost in the prickle of rising hair, the ice that scales her spine.

"It won't work—!"

Oh, Tel, the eyes say. Fight me, defy me, wound me. But don't demean yourself. Don't lie.

"Why not?"

Tellurith takes a great swallow of air, and it sticks like porridge in her throat.

As the qherrique orders, *Don't speak.*

"It's just prejudice, Tel. Just class and—and—tradition and— if we have to mine it, at least let's get rid of this."

Tellurith's hair crawls. And the qherrique orders, *Quiet.*

"You don't have to believe me. You don't even have to watch. All I want," very softly, "is your assent. To let us in the mine."

Tellurith gapes. Gasps, feeling the mad laughter rise, foul as vomit, in her throat. "You think what *I* say—! Oh, Mother—!"

"It's Telluir's mine. You're Telluir House."

With a huge effort she forces laughter and nausea away. It comes out, wonderfully, almost steady-voiced.

"You don't know—you can't know—what you're doing. You're out of your wits. My—our—the House's assent has nothing—nothing! to do with it!" Hysteria rises again, a screaming tide. "Alkhes, for the Mother's sake—don't go on with this!"

"Tel—"

"Please!"

She stares, appalled, speechless, into appalled, bewildered black eyes.

"Tel, could you just—"

"There's nothing to explain!"

She can see the eyes shift. From pain and bewilderment to pity, to compassion. Poor woman, the strain has been too much. To that steely resolution, smooth as velvet, impossible to move.

It seems forever that she stares at him, across a city, an empire, eighteen inches of rug. Before she feels her lungs empty. And the voice of the qherrique, of destiny, says, *Enough.*

"Alkhes." But there is one last effort, one last thing she can do. "If you're determined . . . For my sake . . . If ever I meant anything to you . . ."

The face twists, the eyes wince.

"Then for the Mother's love . . . don't do it yourself."

The pain turns to startlement. But he has grace enough to let her go, when she reaches the door, yanks it open, sending her escorts half up the passage wall as she cries, "I'm going back!"

* * * *

The preparations take another two days. Within her shell of closed mind, numbed feelings, Tellurith hears the others talk, the buzz on that third morning; a sullen late summer morning, full of boding storm. And a great gathering of soldiery toward Main Quay, a procession of military notables, drums and trumpets blaring, scarlet-hackled rivers flowing along Hill-foot. Brigadiers, Dhasdein and Cataract officers. The tyrant of Cataract.

I wonder where they quartered him, she thinks, as fraternizers spin word back from the gate: There is to be some major spectacle, some ritual, a symbolic claiming, before the assembled armies' audience, of Amberlight.

And of course, the general will take a central role.

In the depth of their makeshift camp it grows eerily, peculiarly quiet. Tellurith sits in the torn army tent, the only woman in the enclave, perhaps, who is not looking toward Amberlight.

"What is it, Tellurith?"

Long ago he would speak to her like that. So concernedly, so tenderly. When she came to him in the tower, galled, as now, by some trouble she could not right.

Except the shared troubles they could not share.

She turns about. The topaz eyes hold hers so earnestly, all their glittering malice gone. Lost with the house-veil, the cosmetics, the lovelocks. Shirt and trousers now, hair tied, like any Craftless woman's, in a tail.

"Oh, Sarth—"

But after all, what can she explain?

"They're going to do something," she has to swallow, "up there."

The eyes gauge her. Then he flows from a hunkered squat to settle at her side. A shoulder barricading them from Amberlight.

And at once she must turn about. "They—" But what do explanations matter? "Just stay with me."

* * * *

The environs are silent now. Expectation has quieted even the detainees. Amberlight looms above them, shattered Houses, captive citadel, flying no flag of any nation, marred suburbs below.

And between, the great luminous bulwarks of the qherrique.

The pause elongates. Silence has thickened like mist. Even in the camp, tension grips.

And then every set of eardrums reverberates, blasted, pulverized by the crash. The world-shaking blast, the huge pearl-shot fireball spouting above Canal and Iron Spurs, shooting high over Arcis, the dust-cloud mushrooming out to blot carrion crows from the shaken sky. A staccato torrent of lesser explosions, an undifferentiated crackle and blast of after-shocks. And suddenly Tellurith grabs her husband and flings them both flat, bellowing in a House-head's roar, "Get down! *Shut your eyes!*"

But they pierce closed eyelids as their impacts batter upon stunned, cringing ears. Flash after flash, enormous, blinding, huger than any rogue mine or workshop flare, firebolt after firebolt, white incandescence shearing the murk. Flame after flame. Crash after ear-splitting crash.

Some of the first impacts strike the siege-wall. Tellurith feels the impact through nerve and skin and bone. Hears, faintly, as the earth quakes, the drowned, abbreviated screams.

Dead Dyke wall blows outward as if a giant kicked it in the guts. All around them the earth shudders to other impacts, and between blows, now, comes the purr of fire.

Tellurith gets her head up. Peers, blinded eyes shrinking, toward Amberlight.

There is no sky, no city, only the immense white-shot pearl-glistered pall of dust, torn ever and again by fresh lightning bolts. The skyline is gone. She sees it go, Iron Spur dissolving like a watered cake. She sees Arcis' walls sink in the middle and slide majestically, an imploded landslide, into the earth. Sobbing, praying, she watches the death, the final death of Amberlight.

And in the dust-pall, the writhing clouds form for one moment the lineaments of a face. Wispy white hair's aureole about folded skin that limns the shape of eyes. Wrinkle-graven cheeks, lipless, infolded mouth.

A face that speaks to her, cryptic, inexplicable. For what reason, from what source?

That tells her, as the city dies behind it: *Daughter, be blessed.*

* * * *

Then she is flat as a trampled worm amid the wreckage of Telluir's shanty camp, with Zuri's iron arm hauling her upward and Zuri bawling in her ear, "Ruand! Ruand, come on!"

Perforce Tellurith comes upright, staggering, gasping, "What?"

Zuri spins her round. Points, all but aims her eyes. A section of pit wall has collapsed. Palisade stakes have cascaded onto the landslide's ramp. Beyond it is writhing smoke, a red leaping fringe wide as a fire-front in the sapless summer Kora: burning tents.

"They won't look for hours! They'll be running like singed dogs!" Zuri's bawl, Zuri's hand propels her forward. Troublecrew, Iatha beyond her, looking, staring. Starting, with hardly a snatch at possessions, to run.

"But what," Tellurith screams, "for?"

She has never seen Zuri so nearly burst.

"Desis! When they caught us! Brought here—she saw the light-gun dump!"

"What?"

Zuri fairly screams.

"The light-guns! The cutters and shapers! Not the vehicles, couldn't shift them! But they stockpiled the rest—out here! Out of," a banshee's delight climbs all but beyond hearing, "harm's way!"

Then Tellurith understands. And like so many others in the wave going cross-camp behind her, grabs her husband and runs.

* * * *

Guards at the pen, guards at the dump? If any remained, the stampede would have gone clean over them. It flattens the intervening tent-rows, its sheer mass levels the palisade. Into the compound it streams, and the roar that rises then mutes the fire. Tellurith hears her own scream lost among it, as her hands close, greedier than a lover's, on a cutter grip. Life, mastery, power.

Qherrique.

The surge throws a face into hers. Familiarly scarlet, roaring. "Telluir! Come on, Telluir!"

She goes at first, run on a wrenching arm. Swung about to face the siege-camp's chaos, leveled tents, tumbled supply heaps, a cauldron of swirled smoke and rampaging fire. And the great dust-tomb of Amberlight beyond.

Tellurith stops with a jerk. Bawls, as the check spins Damas back round to her, "Where?"

Damas' mouthings are lost in the roar. The gesture is clear. There. Home. Amberlight.

Tellurith opens mouth to yell and charge.

And stops.

There is a shell of silence amid the screams, the jubilation, the snoring of the fire. There is a plummeting emptiness, a dizzy strangeness, under her heart. A presence whose presence was never recognized until it is lost.

The qherrique is gone.

Against the dust-pall images flow through her. A broken eggshell, dry. A corpse of thistle-bush, plaything of the winds. A snakeskin, sloughed. Rain on a broken house.

She shakes her head, pierced as at the moment of hearing her mother's death. Torn open. Bereft.

Damas hauls and howls. Tellurith does not hear.

"'Rith? 'Rith?" Familiar hand and voice, home, safety. But not the voice she needs.

"Ruand?"

Tellurith holds her belly, a woman wounded in a woman's core. She will crack like a melon from the loss.

"Zuri—!"—"What is it?"—"The Ruand—"—"Oh, Mother, is she hurt?"—"Did they hit her?"—"What happened—"—"Oh, not the Ruand, no!"

Not that voice, no, not a mother's voice. But in need of a mother's voice. The voices of the House. A House-head's child.

The breath she gulps travels like a lead-stone down her throat. Her ribs seem to burst. And as she chokes, Damas, taking motion for assent, hauls her arm, shouting, "Come on!"

And Tellurith answers, "No."

Her very quiet enforces quiet. In a sudden hurricane eye of silence, the women round them stare.

"Telluir!" She has never seen Damas so near apoplexy either. "It's the best chance we'll ever have! That's our city! We can throw them out—take it back!"

"No."

Damas erupts. When she collapses, spluttering, Tellurith speaks. Clearly now, to those beyond her folk.

"That is not my city. That is a corpse. Why should we bother to take it back? What made it is not there. The qherrique is gone."

There is a plunging pause so deep the camp around them seems to disappear. Into it one voice rises. The keening, wordless note that opens an Amberlight wake.

"I am not going back." She speaks across it. Dry-eyed, womb closed now. She can almost feel the sealing wound. Why go back, after all? For a smashed city, a dead House, a corrupt trade and a foul, cruel custom?

For a lover who is dead?

Ahio materializes before her. Eyes slit, the shaper clutched like legend's treasure in her paw. A new shape, a new world forming in her eyes.

"Ruand?" Dazzled now. Too like the expression in another pair of eyes, cutting the last thread that has girdled up her heart. "Ruand—where?"

Tellurith turns about.

Space, distance, vacancy, lost in sheaves of smoke. Not the hill of Amberlight with its fabulous pearl-moats. Never again. Never again the glow in those black eyes, the sheen of qherrique marbling a night-lit wall.

But through the brume, the horizon takes an upthrust, shaggy, familiar shape.

She lifts her arm. The cutter-beam is familiar tension in her wrist.

"There."

Mutely, Telluir House-folk stare.

"The Iskans," Tellurith speaks to carry across the assembly, "are where Telluir began." Ancient tradition, older than Amberlight's first name. "The Iskans are still ours. They have a stone quarry. There's always a market for marble. And I was trained," she shifts her hand, the cutter slits the air, "in cutting stone."

* * * *

Of course it was not that simple, Tellurith thinks dreamily, face upturned to the sailing moon. How much quarrelling arguing tangle afterward between those who wanted to stay and those determined to go? How much maddening, fiddling detail, amassing carts and packs and riding beasts, plundering the plunderers for gear and necessities and supplies? How many days leeway before the shattered remnants of Dhasdein's army could regain courage and plod back out of Amberlight?

We had that one day, she tallies, when we sent them yelping in across the bridge.

There were the Cataract reserves. We shot them down.

Mother, but I was glad.

Telluir had most of its gear settled by the second morning. Zuri and Iatha. Once launched, a human avalanche.

Who decided what we could and couldn't take?

I think I did, sometimes.

And next day, when the dust fell down again, we were ready. To see off Damas, and Ciruil, and that fool Eutharie, still squeaking about rebuilt Houses and the honor of Amberlight.

Idiots.

I hope the Dhasdein rag-tag ate them raw.

Not to think, now, about Dhasdein.

Mother be thanked, their command—their command structure was broken. So nobody had the control, or the time, or the initiative, to chase after us. Because Mother knows, we're strung like a traveling fairground along this road.

And there has been one full day traveling. Five days from—

Before tonight.

A fortnight, maybe, to the Iskans, with this crowd. Slap that mosquito. Lucky the Sahandan is dry, there's somewhere to camp. The Korites seem willing to feed us. We have almost a month left of autumn. Time to settle in, before the snow.

There is an enormous hole beneath her thoughts. A waiting, ravening vacuum. She cannot look that way. If she thinks about— what she cannot think—the vacuum will rip her soul away. And she will never come back.

Tellurith turns on the blanket and stares away to the shadow of the Iskan summits, an irregularly penciled horizon fading into the threshold of the sky.

A step crunches. Warmth settles beside her. A blanket folds about her. A deep, soft voice asks, "Are you cold?"

Pulling up his blanket, she answers, "Not now."

* * * *

In the daytime, the journey trivia are blessed, blessed occupation, nagging, overfilling the mind. So it holds very little except a need not to shriek aloud if the one-time panel-shaper working this bullock-cart does not admit she can get her beasts across the washout onto this bridge before evening, when Zuri comes pelting, a bundle of rocks astride a Korite pony, down the long, motley, patiently or impatiently halted line.

"Ruand! Traffic back there!"

Tellurith's heart stops. No, she wants to scream, blinded by images of Dhasdein infantry, the mounted poison wasps of Verrain. Not when it was all so good, so easy—no!

But her mouth gets out, "How many? What? Who?"

"So far," Zuri has yanked her beast about, staring back where a light-gun serves as signal flash, "a rider. Only one."

"A scout?"

Zuri employs her light-gun. There is a hiatus. A flicker of answer. Like her House-head, Zuri frowns.

"They think not."

Korite? Straggler? Decoy? She wants to bundle the whole straggling vulnerable line under her coat skirts, to hurl lightnings and trumpet, Let us alone!

Aloud she says, "Kasra, straighten that thing out. Now. Zuri, double me back there."

At the rear, two orphaned apprentices with a hand-cart, they find Desis the former raider staring hawkishly from the fork of a plains hellien. A pair of horses below her. And with them, Verrith and Azo.

Who greet her outcry with a beady stare, and Zuri with, "Saw her leave."

Azo hefting a light-gun, Verrith stolidly stringing a bow.

Desis is still staring down the road.

"I think—it's only one rider." A pause. "And I think . . . not a Korite. Doesn't ride right."

"One of ours?"

An interminable pause.

"I think—I'm almost certain—it's a man."

Azo jerks like a puppet. Verrith goes bluish white. Zuri's eyes bulge. She swallows. Mutters something that can only be prayer.

Tellurith does not jump, pale, feel her heart climb out through her eardrums. She has seen mines fall before.

Nobody at the face, when they did whatever they did to it, had a chance of getting out.

She says, "Signal, Halt column. Close up. Stand by."

* * * *

It seems forever, there on the wheel-runnelled dusty road amid the stubbly, dried-quag paddies on the brown-pied plain, its edges shivering gently in hot afternoon air. Away to the north, far beyond Amberlight, the horizon is dwarfed by the anvil-head of another storm. Its silver and blue-shadowed cloud-sheets rise through three levels, like a mountain, before its summit strata gleam in the zenith light.

And under its magnificence comes that tiny, crawling shape.

Still nothing touches Tellurith. Not when she understands Azo and Verrith are near incoherent, that Zuri may actually have begun to pray. Not even when she hears Desis mutter, "You ever see him on a horse?" And Zuri, clipped to brusqueness, "No."

The rider dips in a hollow. Climbs again. A black horse, she sees now, incurious. It is as if, since that other morning, nothing can touch her. As if she is in a shell where no feeling can reach.

And the rider, under a straw hat disreputable enough for Averion, has—his?—right arm in a sling.

Zuri has, indubitably, begun to pray.

"Let him get in range." Is that really her voice? "Then tell him to halt."

Four hundred yards. Three hundred. In the quiet, broken only by the burring whisper of late cicadas, they can hear the horse.

Then Desis' hail. "You there! Stop!"

The horse checks immediately. No panic, so far as she can see, no guilt. Merely alacrity. And considerable control.

"Get down!"

Readily, if clumsily, she is obeyed.

Desis looks at her Head. Who, in her shell of torpor, wonders what is wrong with them. Is that excitement in Azo's face?

Zuri pulls her pony back. Leans down to grip her shoulder. Says in that soft metal-rasp, "Want me to finish it?"

"Finish," says Tellurith blankly, "what?"

"I could do it for you. One shot."

Verrith makes a low, small noise. Azo's answer grates.

"He wouldn't even suffer. Not enough."

Tellurith's jaw drops. She gapes at her troublecrew. Realizing that flush, that glitter, that shortened breath is not excitement, not hope's fulfilled ecstasy. It is the arousal, almost beyond control, of hate.

Because they think they know who it is. And they want to kill him. For her sake. Because they are sure that she, even more brutally than Amberlight, has been betrayed.

"No!"

It is out before she thinks. Not reason, simply that they must not murder an innocent.

Because this man cannot be anything else.

"He's alone. Injured. Go down and get him. Search him if you want. Then bring him here."

Tellurith has never seen her troublecrew's Head go so near mutiny in her life. But then Zuri slams the pony forward, the others on her heels.

They reach, surround, crowd the waiting traveler. Tellurith opens her mouth to shout, "Cut that out!" But Zuri, apparently, has telepathy. The jostling pony is reined back. Zuri leaps off.

They propel the rider clear of his beast. Azo grabs his good arm. Zuri, with the refined viciousness of hostile troublecrew, pulls the other from the sling. By the wrist.

Tellurith sees the victim sway. Even at that distance, can make out the greyness of his face.

But he holds his good arm clear. Lets Azo pat down his sides, and Verrith, none too decently, slap his trouser-thighs. And Zuri, suspicious beyond cruelty, feel up and down that arm.

Which is splinted, and bandaged heavily as well.

Broken, somewhere below the elbow. Three times, under Zuri's ministrations, she sees its owner flinch.

Then they are moving. The arm re-slung, Zuri's grip above the elbow, Azo clenching his other wrist. Verrith brings the beasts.

Two hundred yards. Fifty yards. And now, at last, she can make out features, under the shade of the hat.

Black, black beard stubble on the long sharp jaw, around the fine-cut mouth. Black, black eyes, through the bruise that tars half the side of his face. Haggard, gaunt, hag-ridden. Nightmare's apogee looks back at her, from that black stare.

They reach her. They have halted. Reeling before the impossible, she says the only words she can find.

"What in the Mother's name are you doing here?"

* * * *

There is another hiatus, all time, no time, before he speaks.

"I took them—into the mine."

Hoarse with exhaustion. With mistreatment? With far worse than that?

"Dinda. His officers. Quizir. The rest of—the high command."

The brows knit. The eyes look somewhere far beyond her. "Especially," the eyes clench, the onset of pain, "my staff."

He stops and looks, as if exhausted, at Tellurith.

Who says, hearing it echo as from another's throat, "But how—in the Mother's name, how are you here?"

He makes to move his good arm. Discovers Azo, and is still.

"When we saw the—the qherrique—Dinda pulled rank." He forgets and makes to move again. "He wanted—to make the cut."

For a moment Tellurith shuts her eyes. Feels her whole body scream as at a physical rape. Men, a multitude of men, in the mine, in the qherrique's heart. Not during Alkho, unable to menstruate. Not knowing even how to ask consent.

Let alone having a light-beam to take the slab.

"I did ask!" Sharp now, with memory. With despair. "I did ask! And I swear to you, it answered me."

Tellurith's eyes fly open in sheer disbelief.

"It answered—" her hair stands up. "Did you touch—did you put your hand on it?"

Baffled, he stares.

"No, I—Dinda interrupted. But it did answer. It started to glow . . ."

Glow. She has ado not to put a hand over her mouth. She feels physically sick. "Then how in the Mother's name—"

"When he got hold of the chisel," Tellurith does clap the hand to her mouth, "I started feeling—I can't explain—like cramps in the gut. I said something about an announcement—Dinda thought I was vexed. That smirk . . . I started off down the passage—" suddenly his face is wet with sweat. "It kept saying, *Go, hurry, run, run*—! I ran like a hare. I could see the entrance door—"

Azo has let go of him. The women are all staring. It is not every day one meets the survivor of a holocaust face to face.

"The blast threw me—clean out the adit." He draws a careful, shaky breath. "It wrapped me round a pine—" Gingerly, he touches his right side. "I've got three broken ribs."

"Then," quite gently, "the hill came down."

The hill came down. On his armored body, thanks be, on his helmeted head. Though how he was not incinerated when the qherrique discharged, when the entire mother-face became a light-gun that ripped its setting apart . . .

"You are lucky," Tellurith hears herself say, "to be alive."

The grimace is not mirth.

"But what," far more vehemently, "are you doing here?"

He eases his arm in the sling, his forehead creased, his whole face tense. Summons the dregs of reserve from more than physical exhaustion. And goes on.

"I was knocked cold—till sometime that night. I crawled down the hill . . . The first men I met ran like lunatics. They thought," a humorless twist of the mouth, "I was a ghost."

So, Tellurith wants to say, did I.

"The army . . . the city—it was a shambles. I tied this in somebody's cloak. Then I worked all night."

Mother aid, Tellurith wants to cry. With probable concussion, and three broken ribs as well.

"By the time we cleared the city, they said you'd gone." He straightens the tiniest fraction, and for a moment those black eyes hold black humor's ghost. "I think I was grateful for that."

Having, she does not have to be told, afflictions enough.

"But—*what* are you doing here?"

He turns his head aside. She has time to notice that clay color, before he says huskily, "Can I—" and without waiting Azo's permission takes a sidestep to get his arm over the horse's neck.

"Blight and blast—" Tellurith comes belatedly to her wits. "Zuri, call for Caitha. Alkhes—sit!"

And she has said the name. And it has been no more than a reflex, an unconsidered normality. Not even a dagger in her mouth.

"No, I can stand—" Fending Azo off, more than determinedly. Needing, she realizes, to tell her this. And to tell it on his feet.

"Dinda—had the Cataract troops up nearest the mine. There wasn't much left. Dhasdein—lost most of a brigade. I promoted a fair sort of a captain. Then I sent them home."

Tellurith feels her jaw sag. The siege, the garrison, the conqueror conquered. Amberlight released.

He sways a little. But his eyes never move.

"I wrote a letter for—Antastes. I said there was, unfortunately, no chance to change the trade. The—qherrique—was gone. I recommended he set the Cataract border south of the timber-fief. That there'd hardly be trouble up there for some time. But it would be worth his while—to let people re-settle Amberlight."

Our city, rebuilt, reclaimed.

"As a sovereign state."

We could have all we lost.

No, thinks Tellurith. Never. Our Amberlight is gone.

He is still watching her. That skewed black stare is full of suppressed pain.

"It could be a river-city. There's plenty of trade."

And too much history, and too many memories.

"I didn't tell Antastes—but without the qherrique, the colonies will keep him too busy to meddle beyond Verrain. And Verrain'll never get the Oases, either. And—perhaps—after a while, they'll stop taking colonies. Because there'll be no more need."

And the balance will settle, Tellurith thinks, between nations, including Amberlight, in a world that may see war and rivalry; but with nothing distorted, nothing unnatural.

As there was with the qherrique.

"Then I told Antastes—I was unhappy with my handling of the campaign—and I resigned."

The horse shakes its neck and rolls its eyes longingly at the lanky roadside grass. He catches his breath, and Azo, with a suddenly very different expression, shoves a shoulder in his armpit and hauls his arm over her back. He tries to pull away, once.

What, wonders Tellurith, am I, are we doing? Standing here like a folk enspelled, with a man among us out on his feet.

"*Where* is Caitha?" And before she has thought, it seems natural to add, "Zuri, signal to Iatha: Move."

Some change has come over Desis', Verrith's, even Zuri's face. She waves to Desis, Signal. Without looking away.

But it is Tellurith who wants to say, You could have gone anywhere. You are a top-price, top-flight mercenary. How can you be . . . She finishes it aloud. "But still—what are you doing *here*?"

He pulls himself upright over Azo's arm. The eyes flare, for a moment, with their old deadly fire.

"I came for one thing, Tellurith. To ask you—why?"

Echo of all those other duels. Time replaying dizzily, so she can only repeat yet again, "Why what?"

On his good arm, an imperious twitch. Azo demurs, but yields. He catches his horse's bridle, takes a step. They are all but face to face.

"You showed me how to wake it. It did wake! It answered me . . . And then it blew, the whole hill blew. Just explain, Tellurith—what happened? Why?"

The restraint is gone, now. There is no ban to forbid her. Only an emptiness located physically behind her breastbone, where the qherrique's presence will never be again.

"Because," she yells, "I told you! Men *can't* work qherrique!"

He is too stunned to do more than gape.

"You thought it was just prejudice—We learnt it the hard way, seven hundred years ago! A woman found the seed-bed, and it was so pretty she touched, and it woke. But when the men tried it burnt them, in the end it struck one dead. Out of the face, it bites women sometimes, but men it won't tolerate at all. And at the mother-face—You nincompoop, the only cutter who can touch that is a woman. With a light-blade! In her month's dark! At the dark of the moon!"

"And," she bawls into his astounded stare, "not always then!"

The final secret. The real secret, the thing at the heart of Amberlight that House girls learn in their infant clothes. That in seven hundred years, has never been betrayed.

"But—" The eyes are glazed. Then he swallows. Get his jaw up. Tears the good hand back through his filthy hair.

"But—why—why didn't you *tell* me? Why—at the end, for the gods' love—Tel, why didn't you *say*?"

She takes a deep breath. Feeling the shards of history, ritual, custom, ingrained secrecy crack away from her. Because even this does not matter any more.

"Because if they'd known—if they'd really known—the River would have destroyed us outright. Because they've tried and tried to take over the qherrique—but if they ever succeeded, all your Outland societies would find they had turned into Amberlight. Because the women would rise, just as ours did, into the places of power."

Now his eyes are well and truly glazed.

"And can you see women allowed to rule Cataract? Or Dhasdein?"

She stares back into that mute, midnight stare and watches him understand. At last.

"No. Never." She says it for him. "And once they understood that . . . What they couldn't have by any road—they would have destroyed."

As his lips moves mutely, she goes on. A perverse pleasure, in telling it all.

"But if they thought they could use the qherrique, they'd just keep on trying. And when we beat them, they'd remember for a while, before they tried again. So long as we could win—"

And we took good care always to win. I told you that. She sees the memory, resurrected in that stare.

"It's what I never told you. We couldn't accept your terms—no matter how we wanted." His eyes speak back to her how desperately that wanting revives in her own. "Because to have men try to work the qherrique—was the one thing we *couldn't* give."

Down the road, to a lowing of cattle and squeak of axles and various shouts, the column begins to move.

He shudders and clenches his eyes shut as if to bring the vision clear, before he speaks.

"But—" it is a whisper, "it did let me—It did answer. It did speak—to me."

"You were in tune with me, I was House-head. Of course it let you touch it! Of course—"

She stops dead.

"It *spoke* to you? You heard it? Later? You asked something? And it understood?"

"I asked in the House. Put my hand on it and asked: Shall I try to cut? Should I break the taboo? And it said, Yes."

Tellurith opens her mouth to scream, Liar, Hallucinator, Imbecile. And shuts it on a gulp. As her mind reels, staggers broadside, to a possibility beyond any imagining.

They are all staring. Zuri and Azo look ready, now, to sustain her.

"Did you," she can just whisper, "ask it—at the face?"

The glare is conscious, defiant. "Yes!"

Tellurith holds her head. While through her bludgeoned mind runs Ciruil's question: Why tell you to fight, and then give in? Why, her own wits howl, tell him to cut, and then bring down the hill?

And still get him out?

What reason, what impossible unreason, could make sense of that?

Daughter, be blessed.

When I, protest her staggering wits, had brought destruction, brought him, the agent of that destruction, into Amberlight. Had given him the knowledge, and the access, to cause that fall—to bring about its end. To smash, wholly and forever, the qherrique.

Daughter, be blessed.

When it told me he mattered, on Exchange Square, that first night.

When it assented, after I refused the contract for Verrain.

When it accepted his touch. When, just possibly, it healed his memory. When, if this is true, it did what has never been done before. When a man heard it speak. To him.

Daughter, be blessed.

"Ruand, are you all right?"

She is laughing, wildly, crazily, holding her head before its top flies off and blows away.

It spoke to him, it spoke to me. Two conflicting messages, two conflicting aims. Joined at one irreversible end. Whatever it said to us, it had its own reasons, its own purpose. And it didn't have to make sense to us.

Because it meant to remove the qherrique, forever, from human abuse, and human distortion. To do what we could not. To destroy Amberlight.

And by its ruin, that I truly brought there, save itself.

Daughter, be blessed.

I thought it was Zhee. A last vision of a Head who was my mother in all but flesh. But was it only Zhee?

Or was it Someone, greater than the very qherrique?

Tellurith lifts her hands to heaven as the women of Amberlight do to pray: Mother, if I did Your work, now may I indeed be blessed.

* * * *

Then she looks back to her ragged, dirty, battered outlander, swaying, bewildered and pain-bedeviled, on his feet.

"It—spoke—to me. It told me to save you—that first night. It told me not to tell you—who could cut it. It told you—to cut."

He is goggling, beyond speech.

"Because," says Tellurith gently, "it wanted what you wanted. No more trade. No more abuse. No more," somehow, it is easier to say than she expected, "Amberlight."

Daughter, be blessed. Why, she wonders, could She not have said that to him?

And understands, the last flare of vision, that she has indeed been blessed.

"Mother blast it, where is Caitha, Zuri, get him on that horse . . ."

The column's motion has almost reached them. Blindly, he shrugs Zuri away. Before them, the orphans heave up their handcart. Behind them Verrith's charges shuffle, willing to be off.

"So now," she says. And feels the blessing rise, slow and sweet and sure as the moon's vanguard luminance. Washing away loss, and rancor, and the memory of destruction, and all obstacles between them. Even grief. "So now, what are you doing here?"

The black horse takes a forward step. Another, unrebuked. His owner matches him. A wobbly, absent stride, his eyes never leaving her, his good arm through the reins.

"'It' wanted. 'It' said. Tel, does it—did it—think?"

Tellurith ponders, and as always, reaches the same conclusion. An answer that is no answer, not a closed door but infinite openness.

"Think. Feel. Talk. I don't think—our words apply."

He picks his way, breathing with an injured man's care, amid the wet-time ruts.

"Then it's probably stupid to ask—was it alive? Was it a rock, a vegetable, a—anything."

Except qherrique.

"Probably, yes."

Now the frown comes. "But it could move minds. I thought I decided for myself. But we did what it wanted. Even when we didn't understand. We—our people, your people, died for it. You have to wonder. Were we ever more than puppets? Did we—have any choice?"

Tellurith ponders that in good earnest. "I never felt—as a shaper, as a cutter, as a House-head—that you did what it *wanted*—so much as it offered you—if you listened—advice."

"And if you didn't listen?"

Denara, faced with qherrique's abuse, averting her eyes. Eutharie, squeaking about the honor of the House. The obduracy, in contention, of Vannish.

The entrapment by her own defense schemes of Ti'e, Jura, Zhee, Averion. Was the plan futile as others' denial, just part of the ultimate aim?

Without it, we would all have died.

That answer comes from her heart, as sure as ever from the qherrique.

"I think you could refuse to hear. And it would let you. I think it had its own," survival? "good as the final aim. But—I never thought I was a puppet. I—"

No puppetmaster would have known gratitude. Would have given me those last words.

"I think the contact went both ways."

The touch of the cutter grip, the statuette's glow. The warmth, the tangible assent, of the mother-face. The rapport, the ineffable contact, for whose loss women died. That face in the dust-cloud. If it was not human, it was more than rock, more than plant, more than beast.

And less than god, having to die for its release.

When she looks aside it is a shock to find him blinking too. A greater shock when he speaks softly, looking down at his good hand twisted in the reins.

"The night I touched it—I'll never forget."

A rapport, a meeting of impossibles, that no one can describe. That no one will ever repeat.

"And when it spoke—I know I never had much to do with it—but to feel that . . . to feel it like that. Just once . . . "

Sharing the memory of that more than human moment, the black eyes are glossed, like hers, with tears.

Tellurith swallows hard. And then, somewhere within her, another voice speaks.

Enough, daughter. She can see the face in the dust-cloud, acerbic as Zhee in the flesh. *Mourn, remember, never forget. And now, get on with your life.*

"So now, again—what *are* you doing here?"

* * * *

The column is stretching out, more than half its length across the bridge. He stares ahead of them. Tension in his face, his gait now. Almost, he has begun to limp.

Tellurith pulls her hat down. Silently, keeps pace.

It is his patience that breaks first.

"Where are you going?"

"To the Iskans." The words come easily, flowing, bright as assent from the mother-face. If the qherrique never speaks to me again, I know that this, this is right. "After all, the one thing that always sells is marble. And the one thing we do understand is working stone."

He claps a hand to his ribs and chokes. It is a moment before she understand it is the consequence of mirth.

"God's . . . eyes!"

Gradually, the mirth ebbs. The column is picking up speed. The horses lengthen stride. Frowning, he keeps pace.

In the end, she cannot play it out. Time enough for that, when he was coerced to her bed. This choice, so much greater, must be free.

"Are you coming with us?"—"I can work in stone."

They say it together. Check together, and stare.

Then the black eyes widen, incredulous. Softening, glowing, deeper than the River-depths. Waking, a sheen on velvet, to the marveling, marvelous smile.

Before he says huskily, "Tel," and she steps forward, taking him carefully, delicately, lovingly, in her arms.

* * * *

"You'll have," he says, when he finally lets go, "to strap my ribs."

"I've brought Caitha." Smugly, she smiles.

"And get used to my outland ways."

"Hmm." Far down the column her eye catches, her heart lurches, at the sight of a tall, bronze-brown head. "You may have to get used to a few outland ways yourself."

It is wonderful how the grey has thawed out of his face. But it gathers wariness now.

"Oh?"

"We won't have a men's tower. But I think," she clasps hands behind her back, lifting eyes skyward demurely, innocently, "that we have to look after the ones we let out."

This time he turns his head and stares.

"You—I thought only the *men* married more than once?"

Those indestructible wits. She cannot help it. Spontaneously, Tellurith laughs.

"I don't see why I can't have two husbands—if one of them has other wives."

"God's teeth . . ."

He lets it die away. The black eyes roll at her, hot less with rage than mirth.

"So, can you handle being married to Sarth?"

A long pause. A very deep breath.

"I can handle being married to *you*. I can handle you being married to—but I will *not*, damn it, not for any godforsaken outlander, be married to *Sarth!*"

He has to hold his ribs before they sober. She does hold him, however carefully, first by the arm, then around the waist. How many times, in fear and deadly anguish, have I wanted to walk like this?

The troublecrew are beaming fatuously as a new daughter's aunts. The orphans keep stealing backward looks. When the horses overtake them, Tellurith cannot help a grin and lordly wave.

"Hassa, Daman—this is my new husband. Just married today."

The girls essay a smile. The more forward, Hassa, slides a look at Zuri, august troublecrew. Mysteriously encouraged, ventures, "And—ah—what do we call you?"

For another moment their eyes meet. Then he looks back to Hassa, and answers, smiling.

"My name's Alkhes."

Printed in Great Britain
by Amazon

41659044R00118